THE MECHANICS' INSTITUTE REVIEW
ISSUE 13 AUTUMN 2016

G000016670

The first Mechanics' Institute in London was founded in 1823 by George Birkbeck. "Mechanics" then meant skilled artisans, and the purpose of the Institute was to instruct them in the principles behind their craft. The Institute became Birkbeck College, part of London University, in 1920 but still maintains one foot in the academy and one in the outside world.

The
Mechanics'
Institute
REVIEW

The Mechanics' Institute Review
Issue 13 Autumn 2016

The Mechanics' Institute Review is published by MA Creative
Writing, Department of English and Humanities, School of
Arts, Birkbeck, Malet Street, Bloomsbury, London WC1E 7HX

ISBN 978-0-9575833-6-8

Project Director: Julia Bell

Editorial Team: Grace Blackwood, Michael Button, Madeline
Cross, Basil Lawrence, Vanessa Onwuemezi, Jamie West and
James Wise

The Editorial Team would like to thank Julia Bell,
Sue Tyley and Tamara Pollock for making this project
possible.

For further copies or information, please contact
Katherine McCurdy, MA Creative Writing, Department of
English and Humanities, School of Arts, Birkbeck, Malet
Street, Bloomsbury, London, WC1E 7HX. Tel: 020 3073 8372.
Email: k.mccurdy@bbk.ac.uk

Website: http://mironline.org/

Printed and bound by Berforts Limited, 17 Burgess Road,
Hastings, East Sussex TN35 4NR

Cover design and typesetting by Raffaele Teo

The Mechanics' Institute Review is typeset in Book Antiqua

TABLE OF CONTENTS

Introduction
TOBY LITT

In 1998, a documentary was released about Radiohead and how and what it was to be a member of the biggest band in the world, and to be on a World Tour. The title was *Meeting People Is Easy*.

In 1980, a documentary was released about *The Shining*, Stanley Kubrick's movie about exactly what it feels like to be a writer, and in one scene of this the actor Jack Nicholson observed, "The average celebrity meets, in one year, ten times the amount of people that the average person meets in his entire life."

I like that: "the average celebrity". Jack's funny.

Major bands play nightly to audiences in stadiums, and even concert halls, made up of many more than the entire number of people who will ever read a reasonably successful first novel. Big movies, though often based on books and short stories and comics, are now routinely financed to the level of quarter of a billion dollars – and are expected to recoup that, through ticket sales and merchandising, within a year.

Bands and movies meet, and need to meet, a lot of people. They seem to find it easier than novels and short stories. A covers band can still fill the pub on a Friday. Student films can get thousands of hits on YouTube. It's not that there aren't plenty of small bands and ignored movies, just that it's very easy for writers to feel overawed by kinds of success that aren't available to them.

1

Or that, when these successes do occasionally occur, writers shy away. Salman Rushdie strolled onstage to stand alongside U2; he was wise enough not to try being their support act. J. K. Rowling could have played Madison Square Garden, if she'd wanted. The Royal Albert Hall was enough.

For most writers, meeting people – by which I mean readers – is hard.

No one really gets my stuff, you'll hear them say. Because getting, and being got, is the important part of meeting.

For celebrities, such as Radiohead or Jack Nicholson, the idea of meeting is debased. It means nothing for them to be told, again, I think you are wonderful, I love your work, your thingy-X got me through just such a hard time in my life, and I just want to say thank you, sob, thank you. The nice ones try to keep meeting meaningful, to begin with, but eventually the relentless repetition exhausts them – as it would you, however nice you are. Even if you are as nice as Radiohead. Better for the famous only to meet the also-already-famous, the more-likely-to-be-blasé, the unfazed. That means there's less chance of sobs and crass flirting, mad-eyed attempts to connect and hyperventilation.

Auden wrote, in his poem "This Loved One", that "'Good day, good luck'/Is no real meeting".

Really meeting people, in terms of encounter, of coming together (sometimes – yes – in bed, sometimes intellectually) is not easy. It's one of life's most difficult accomplishments.

How many people have I really met? One in a bakery, when I was four years old. One in a tutorial room in Oxford. One outside a fish restaurant. One in a pole-dancing club in Croatia. One last week, in Montreal.

No, I don't think I've really *met* more than ten people in my life. Writers, though – writers I really meet all the time. That's why I need them so much. That's why I'm addicted to them.

I have really met, and know I have really met, John Keats, Virginia Woolf, Marianne Moore, David Foster Wallace, and perhaps a thousand more.

Some writers are such powerful intensities of presentness that you meet them in a single sentence (Simone Weil, Karl Kraus) or you meet them before you've ever even met them (Franz Kafka,

Emily Brontë). You sense them afar off, like a house burning in the next-but-one street. You hear of them, and know your heart should take warning.

Gerard Manley Hopkins I met in a highly critical description of him, from an essay title – it said he "makes of language a muscle-bound monstrosity". Discuss. I wrote my first sincere imitation of Hopkins before I'd read a word Hopkins wrote. The influence would have been obvious to anyone.

For real meeting to occur, with writers, an introduction is often necessary. As readers, we cascade down through time: C loved B who was influenced by A who got their idea of what writing (meaning life) was from Z. Or the book is placed in our hands, by hands we love. "This is for you."

But introductions, however tremulous, guarantee nothing. Anthologies are often where readers meet writers. And the Introductions (capital I) of anthologies, in trying to force real meetings, can overegg. I could say what I've been building up to: "Reader, meet [insert name of any of the writers between the covers of this anthology]. They're wonderful. You're going to love them." It's still chancy. Whatever I say, you're quickly going to make up your own mind. You've done it before. You pick up so much from the very first.

You glimpse them in their names, their titles; estimate them from where they occur in the running order (the editors wouldn't start with a duffer or end with a flub); you look at page numbers and suss the long and the short.

You almost meet them after the page turn – you're almost there in the millisecond scan you make of their first page, taking in paragraph breaks, capital letters, dialogue or no dialogue, polysyllabics or streaky I, I, I. Just the shape of it.

You're an experienced sizer-upper; it's the head-to-toe-to-head, hair-shoes-hair glance in the gay bar.

Get you, darling – and now I'm going to have you.

But *really* you meet them in that first sentence – then comes the mumbled or omitted or zinging or heart-vaporising "Hello"; then comes that handshake of the eyes – or maybe they'll kiss you, and that'll be it?

The promiscuous, contrary to reputation, really meet more

people – it's just that they insist on parting from them.

Meeting writers is easy because writers are easy; they're loose; anyone can have them. They are the most known (not the best known) people in the world. For millennia, they have been trying to find someone to spend the night with, someone to hear them confess but also, ever since they began scribbling, they have been giving themselves away.

Each writer is, potentially, the average celebrity.

Isn't Jack funny? Aren't Radiohead nice?

Here, person, are twenty-three writers for you to meet.

Easily.

I hope you get on famously.

Warm Feeling

LAUREN MILLER

Peter knew he would marry Mandy Turner the day he burnt her house down. That same morning he was removed from school for the very last time. He had strolled up the drive, keying any car that looked half decent, then relieved himself on the tyres of the headmaster's Audi. Now he was expelled and would have the summer days all to himself. His mother would be out in the Latest One's Land Rover, and he wouldn't have to explain a thing, at least not for another day or so. He slung his blazer over one shoulder, walked through the school gate and showed the world the warm, carefree feeling he had about the day ahead.

He paraded through the village, passing his sun-baked neighbours along the road, their eyebrows raised. He robbed a couple of honesty boxes: a marrow, some tomatoes and a box of Mandy Turner's eggs from the farm. With arms burdened, he still managed to rat-a-tat at the post office window, and gave the ancient clerk a wink and the fright of her life. He dragged his knuckles along the old stone walls and turned in at the narrow gate to his cottage, the last out of the village. He faltered with his awkward load and placed the items on the ground. The key was under the doormat, so he had to move the sweating milk bottles to retrieve it; he didn't bother to take them inside. As he stood up, his ears thundered, and a dizziness held him that made the garden flicker with the movement of insects and plants. Their colours melted for a moment, then all was still. He felt the morning had really taken it out of him.

Inside the house was cool and dark. Peter unbuttoned his shirt anyway and let it fall off his shoulders to the floor. He left it there, and sniffed the deep, acrid smell of his armpits. Gathering up the marrow, tomatoes and eggs from the doorstep he carried them to the kitchen and dropped them on the counter. He turned on the cold tap, letting it run until the water was freezing, then stuck his head underneath; tilting his face he drank, and tasted his own sweat. He combed his hair back with his fingers and the kettle provided a good reflection while he pouted like Mick Jagger. One of his mother's half-smoked cigarettes lay in the green glass ashtray next to the bread bin, lipstick wrinkles around the filter, the deep-coral shade she'd only started to wear since the Latest One. Peter thought it made her look whorish, and confirmed the reputation she had in the village. He rolled the cigarette between his fingers, then moved it up to his mouth.

"Pete?"

He chucked the cigarette into the ashtray.

"Petey? You back there?"

Saul's footsteps boomed through the house. Peter flattened his hair, his brother's voice making him timid despite the fact Peter was the elder by fourteen months. Saul leaned into the doorway, grasped the doorframe above his head with both hands.

"Found you."

Saul's biceps strained against the cheap fabric of his school shirt. Peter glanced down at his shirtless self, the slight and fragile jut of his hips.

Saul swept his wavy hair from his eyes and called back to the front door.

"He's in here, Mands."

Mandy Turner, her eyes full of light Peter couldn't ignore, slid into the crook of Saul's arm and Peter wished he'd kept his shirt on. Saul was the freak of their gene pool: a rugby-built body and an unwavering popularity that dumbfounded Peter constantly. No ancestor of theirs could ever have heralded someone as spectacular as Saul, not a bit jittery like their mother and, even better, no trace of their father.

Saul went on. "Heard about you and Mr McCulloch's car."

"Everyone has!" Mandy added. "Did you really slash his tyres?"

Saul pinched her waist. "No. He pissed in the petrol tank. You pissed in the petrol tank, yeah Pete?"

Peter noticed Mandy had changed her hair.

"I pissed *on* the tyres," Peter replied and leaned his clammy back against the cold kitchen worktop.

"So that's it?" Mandy asked. "They've expelled you?"

Peter ignored her question. "What're you doing here?" he asked Saul.

"Lunch." Saul winked at him.

"I see you've got some of my eggs." Mandy's voice broke in as if she were looking for something to say. "Suppose you won't be needing these."

She took her school bag off her shoulder and retrieved a brown shoebox, placing it on the counter. Saul rolled his eyes as she slid off the lid to reveal a dozen pale eggs nestled on a bed of hay.

"Just some spare. Thought your mum might want them."

They were cleaner, paler than the outcasts Peter had grabbed from the honesty box. She'd taken her time to select them. But Peter already knew this because he had watched her, as he did most afternoons. From his usual place behind the hedge that encircled her farmhouse, he'd watched her roll them around in her hands and check the colouring in the bright sunshine. He'd wondered who she could be choosing so specifically for. Now, as he stood before the shoebox, his cheeks blushed, his lips curled into a smile that was barely perceptible. Because in some ways, she'd chosen them for him.

"Nice one, Mands." Saul leered sarcastically behind her shoulder. "They look like a good batch."

"Tell your mum she can keep the box when they've gone," she said to Peter. "We've got enough."

She smoothed her hand over the eggs. A tiny feather rested on top of them, too perfectly placed to be an accident.

Saul checked his watch and whispered something in Mandy's ear that turned her face a deep pink as she slid the lid back on.

"Just going to do some revision, Petey. Won't be long." Saul led Mandy out of the kitchen and they clambered up the stairs to his bedroom.

Saul spent nearly all of his lunch hours shagging Mandy Turner. Or that's what Peter assumed they were doing. But he couldn't be certain, since he had no experience of his own. Disgust and hot anger fought for space inside him. Because he loved Mandy Turner. And he knew that pretty soon Saul would put on the Lindisfarne record Peter'd stolen and given to him for a birthday present. Then the floorboards would hammer like the keys of a piano.

He clattered around the kitchen, trying to block out the sound of the bed springs upstairs. He touched the lid of the shoebox where Mandy's fingertips had been, lifted it, and blew the little white feather to the floor. The music started and he grabbed a box of matches from the top of the cooker, turned on the gas. The blue flame lit quickly. *Sweet baby, send me, bee-bop baby, bend me.* Peter snatched a pan from the sink, still coated in the grease from yesterday's meal, and set it down on the hob above the flame. He cracked one of Mandy Turner's eggs into it; the whites bubbled immediately. *You look so good, make me wish you would hold your dress up high.* He watched the whites curl, half captivated, half repulsed. The bedframe shifted against the floor overhead. Peter collected up the pieces of shell and was about to throw them in the bin when he noticed a small heart drawn in blue pen on one of the shards. He turned the eggs over in the box. Each was tattooed with the letter M and a small heart. Some were marked with an X for a kiss, some with an S for Saul. The egg was almost done and sizzled in the pan. He turned off the gas, prodded the membrane, watched the yellow ooze out. A thudding rhythm came from the ceiling, insistent and unrelenting. Peter didn't feel much like eating. He wanted to ram his fist into the nest of eggs Mandy Turner had brought, leave the mess for someone else to clear up. He imagined Mandy's new hairstyle bouncing around her shoulders and breasts, Saul's massive arms keeping her propped up on top of him while they screwed to the tune of Peter's birthday gift. He threw the shells in the bin, picked up the box of matches and ran out of the house.

Tyres had ridged the parched earth of the track that led up to the farmhouse. All around the sun glared off the dusty fields and Peter raised a hand to shield his eyes as he scanned for Mandy's father. Since his wife had died, Mr Turner worked all the hours God gave him. He could always be found nurturing the land in his tractor, so long as there was enough diesel in the tank and homemade wine in his haversack. It didn't take long for Peter to find him, cutting slowly across the top field as he sprayed a billow of fertiliser over crops that had been dead since May. The farmhouse would be deserted.

As he approached, Peter could hear the chickens clucking away happily in their small wire pen in the garden. The farmhouse's thick thatch roof hung low over uncurtained windows. Pressed against the dirty glass were piles of furniture and old trunks of Mandy's mother's clothes. The house was dim, bathed in shadow, but the garden trapped the sun, which in turn did its worst for the sprawl of untamed vegetable patch and rose beds. Like the house it was unkept – except for the chicken coop. Mandy tended to it daily, freshening up the powder-blue paint whenever it began to dull and regularly sweeping the ground of feathers and pellets. Peter would watch her careful movements; she was so proud of the bloody chickens and so eager to dish out eggs to everyone. He remembered an Easter when she'd brought a chicken to school, a big glossy bantam with a yellow bonnet she'd made strapped around its head. But the noise of the thing proved too much for the teachers to bear, and she was instructed to take it home halfway through the day. Peter had seen the tears slide down her face as she put the chicken back inside its cage, the yellow bonnet still tied under its chin. Peter had followed her home that afternoon with a fanfare of chicken noises and impressions as her face turned red and her head hung low. Mandy talked about her chickens less these days, but she still took good care of them, fed them from her weird apron after school, hurling great, golden handfuls of stuff into the air, giggled as they pecked at her feet, scolded them when they flew too near her face.

It would take Mandy's father about five minutes to drive the tractor back from the field. The engine spluttered too loudly to miss. Peter squeezed through a thinned section of hedge and his feet sank into the potato patch. Soil crept into his shoes. He grappled with overgrown broad bean vines and dead tomato plants, and was soon close enough to see the chickens' shiny copper backs jerking about in the sun. He felt nervous of the shifty, greedy creatures; never still, never satisfied. They'd respond to Mandy's voice with a clamour of wings and squawks, but they were silent as Peter grew closer, and shuffled into a brood at the shady end of their pen. In the shadow they were a mass of grey feathers and beady eyes. Peter felt them catch every one of his movements as he unlatched the wire gate and stepped inside.

Across the dusty ground Peter closed in on them. Then the brood split, half heading to the other corners, the other half juddering up a wooden ramp into the coop. Once inside they didn't dare venture out again. Peter batted at the others with the flat of his hand so they skipped into the air, some landing heavily down on their side. But eventually they were all contained within the coop, even the last few stragglers almost too stupid to bother with. He locked them away and licked his lips. He was satisfied with his hard work.

Peter reached through one of the small round windows carved into the sides of the coop and snatched a tuft of straw. Sometimes Mandy would sing to her chickens through the same little windows. The straw didn't catch from the match flame straightaway, it only smoked a bit, so he grabbed another handful. The chickens grew louder and thudded about the henhouse as if they were bashing their heads against the walls. The hot day pressed down on the roof above them. Peter sniffed and tried to block them out. He lit another match, cupped his hands, and this time a small flame took to the blades of straw. It burned, small and weak, but it burned. He slid the taper back inside the window and didn't want to spend another minute with the sound of the birds. But as he turned his back and edged away, he was certain he heard them hush, stunned by the light of the fire or the smell of the smoke. He waited by the hedge. The tractor rumbled on in the top field; the birds were silent in their dark hotbed. The chicken coop looked unchanged, apart from the spiral of white smoke that spun out from one of the windows.

When he got home Peter was pleased to find that the house was quiet. He could go about his day undisturbed, just as he had planned. It hadn't been completely spoilt. But the heat and his work had made his head throb, and dirt caked the cracks of his hands. He wanted a bath. He slipped off his trousers and underwear while the water ran, coughing, into the avocado bathtub. He climbed in before it was full and got to work on his filthy nails with a brush and soap. Soon the tank drained and the flow of water stopped. Peter sat in the still bath, the clean water now grey, white billows of steam floating above his head and out through the door. He lay back, pinched his nose with his fingers and submerged his head. He stared up through the haze of the water, listening to his body slide against the tub, the trapped air rattle in the pipes below. He tried to hold his breath longer but panic struck him and he broke through the surface. Water cascaded off his head and rained down into the bath. As the sound petered out, he heard a creak, a step in the corridor. Before he had time to do anything, Mandy Turner appeared at the bathroom door. She wiped her eyes. Peter covered his crotch with his hands.

"Sorry. I'm such a mess," she said.

Peter's mouth searched for words. He wanted to shrink down into himself.

"It's just . . ." Mandy's voice was shrill. "Saul's finished with me."

Another torrent of tears spewed from her eyes. She covered her face. Peter wondered if he had enough time to stand up and slam the bathroom door on her.

"I'll be gone in a minute," she said. After a loud sniff she carried on. "It's just . . ."

Mandy's chin trembled and she ran from the door to Saul's room across the corridor. "He can go fuck himself," Peter heard her shout as she threw herself onto the bed with the same strain on the springs.

Peter stood up, climbed slowly out of the bath and reached for a towel, nearly slipping over on the wet tiles. Once he'd wrapped himself in the towel he peered across the corridor. Mandy's shoulders shook while she bawled, flat out on Saul's bed. Peter stared for a moment then remembered himself, pulled the bathroom door shut and locked it. He slumped to the floor to catch his breath, which was difficult in the steam-filled room. He was trapped. He listened for some sound of her movement. The tap dripped. He waited, pulled the plug out of the bath. The water gurgled away down the drain and the room was quiet again. He was certain she must have gone; lunch hour had finished ages ago. He had nothing left to do. He unlocked the door slowly, inched his head through the crack. Saul's door was half closed; it was difficult to see inside. He stepped across the corridor and pushed the door open ever so slowly. It creaked and made him jump, just as Mandy Turner sat bolt upright on Saul's bed, eyes startled and red raw. They cried out in unison. Mandy grabbed her chest.

"I thought you were Saul," she said. "You scared me."

Mandy stood up from the bed and brushed her hands over her school skirt. Her shirt was untucked and hung down over her waistband. The parting in her hair had shifted to the side. Peter couldn't move.

Mandy sniffed snot up her nose. "Your brother's a prick," she said and wiped her face on her sleeve.

"I know," Peter said.

She stared at him. He saw a glint in her eye, as if she'd just had an epiphany. It made him uncomfortable, that stare of hers. She walked towards him.

"What's all that dirt on your face?" she said and got closer to examine the smudges left from the dirty bath water.

"Just dirt," he replied.

Mandy Turner raised her hand and wiped at the scum with the pads of her fingertips. Peter's eyes were locked to hers. He wanted to turn away, run back into the bathroom and hide. But he knew then, with the heat of her touch, that he couldn't help it, and that he would marry Mandy Turner. She kept on smoothing his skin with her fingers, until his eyes closed and his head slumped forward in complete submission. Mandy stepped back.

"Why are you always watching me?" she asked. There was a hardness in her damp messy face.

Like a stupid animal terrified into its own trap, Peter fled to the bathroom.

Leant over the sink, he stared at himself in the mirror. A thick ring of scum still circled his face. It looked as if he were wearing a mask of his own features. There was a knock at the door.

"Come out, Peter."

Mandy's clothes swished against the other side of the door as she went on.

"I don't mind it. I don't mind you watching me."

He scrubbed hard around the outline of his face with the corner of his towel.

"I got fed up with those fucking chickens ages ago."

The heat had painted a red rash across his shoulders and chest. A pulse in his neck jumped up and down. He heard the floorboards creak as Mandy walked away. Then music. The Lindisfarne record. He could have sworn he heard her singing. But he couldn't be sure. Because the next thing he heard was a whine, a wail that grew louder and seemed to be coming from outside the house; a siren.

"There's a fire engine, just gone down the road."

Peter didn't say anything; was still.

The sound of another siren grew louder in his ears. He looked back at himself in the mirror. The dirt around his face had barely shifted. He heard Mandy walk away down the corridor, pause for a second, then thunder down the stairs and out the front door.

The Girl Who Turned into a Jug

MELODY RAZAK

I t was an early afternoon in May when the old fisherman and his young son took their blue wooden boat out to the Bosphorus. They had heard, through a series of whispers, that fat spring mackerel were jumping straight out of the sea and into fishermen's nets. To mark these good tidings (Praise be to Allah!), Mother had promised to bake them a pie. They rowed their boat to the middle of the sea. The city around them waned to a dreamy mist of pointed turrets and minarets. If the young son closed one eye and squinted, he could just about make out the pale dome of the Blue Mosque to his left and the tall tapering tower of the Topkapi Palace to his right.

"Baba," he asked, "have you ever been inside the Palace?"

"No, my son," his father replied, "I have not. But I have heard, from Old Ali the Baker of Marvellous Bread, that the walls of the Palace are lined top to bottom with cerulean tiles from the West and that Sultan Suleiman, The Beneficent, will only eat or drink from vessels that have been made in Chin."

"Chin?" asked the small boy in wonder. He had never heard of such a place.

"Yes, my son. The potters in Chin are renowned for their craft. They train for years under strict supervision before they are allowed to sell a single pot or jug or plate."

"Oh! Is Chin very far away?"

"It is as far away as the time it would take us to walk from one birthday to the next."

"Oh!" said the little boy again. "That is very far."

"Yes, my son. I have heard said that the Chin Masters cast with a liquid clay that is as pure and as soft as cream."

"Cream?" The boy tried his hardest to imagine something that pure and soft, but he could think of nothing now except the promise of his mother's pie.

"Baba? Where are all the fish?" he asked, with a placatory pat to his belly.

Their net continued to float empty. The sea and sky were barren.

"Baba," he said, "are we always to be hungry? Are the fish all dead?"

"No, little one, they're not dead. They're merely asleep. Let's count to three, and see if we can't wake them. One, two, three. Inshallah!" The fisherman threw his net into the water for one final time.

A full minute passed, and then another. By the third there was a sudden pull downwards and the net sank, heavy and full. The little boy clapped his hands and jiggled with joy (he could taste the pie). He helped his father haul the catch into their boat. The net contained a hessian sack and a single skinny sardine with a large glass eye. The boy looked at the sardine with disgust. The sack was tied with a length of frayed rope and was full of odd-shaped lumps and bumps. The fisherman laid the sack on the floor of his boat and used an old gutting knife to slice it open. Father and son peered in. Inside the sack were two arms, two legs, a body and a head. It was a severed girl, yet as delicate and as lissom as could be. Where there should have been a bit of bone, or a bit of gore, at the end of each limb, there was just a mottled surface of seamlessly healed skin and a trace of seaweed. The hair on her head was like a skein of gilded silk: fair beneath the slight green of decay. The boy spat on his fingers and rubbed her cheek to reveal a faint rosy glow. Her skin was much colder and harder than he had expected and it made him shiver. It was not like skin at all, but rather like the surface of a very fine cup. More curious even than that was the way she smelt: neither of the sea nor of rotten flesh but instead of midsummer roses and sugar.

* * * * *

Six months earlier at the Topkapi Palace, pandemonium was purring and ready to pounce. It was the eve of the Sultan's birthday (thirty glorious years, no less), and Begum, his mother, or Queen B as she was known in the inner sanctum, was flapping her wings in a most uncharacteristic way. Alalai, knock-kneed and moon-faced, hidden in the harem for ten years and groomed especially for this day, was nowhere to be found. Where she should've been asleep, curled up in a ball, there was just the faintest whiff of attar of roses and a smudge of icing sugar.

"Where is that bloody girl?" Begum raged, pacing across the chamber. "Wait till I see her! Alalai! Come out. Come out. Wherever you are. This is no time to disappear. Alalai! I would throw her in the Bosphorus, if she wasn't such a catch."

She stopped suddenly, caught mid rant, and froze. From the corner of her eye, owl-like, she could glean the slightest tremor of someone veiled behind the curtain.

"I can see you, Zainab!" she called. "You may as well come out now. There's no hiding with a belly like yours."

"All right, Queen B?" came the silky voice of Zainab from behind the curtain as she pushed the tapestry to one side and stepped forwards. "Why all the fuss?" She used her foot to inch a water jug out of her way and back into the folds of curtain. "Ouch," she then said, rubbing her stomach and wincing. "This little beast of an heir is really giving me what for."

"Kicks like his father did. He'll gut you open on his way out. Mark my words. You'll need stitches from your quim to your throat. What's that behind you?"

"That? Bit of old crockery. Mama B, if I didn't know any better, I would think you were trying to scare me. You should be kinder to me, you know. I am carrying something that is precious to us all – your grandson. When this baby comes out, everything will change."

"Nothing will change. My son will soon tire of you when you're baggy. When you have a mewling brat clamped to your teat. I have girls a-plenty jostling to take your place. And if you give birth to a girl, when you have promised us an heir, I will personally have your head."

"My head would look good on a platter. If I give birth to a girl it's all yours. You can put a peach in my mouth for all I care." She twirled a strand of her hair around a finger.

Begum knew that Zainab didn't give two hoots about all those other girls, who were childish and inexperienced. They were mere fodder to be chewed on at leisure and then spat out. Virgins were two a penny and everyone knew that. Alalai, however, waif-like and pale with her rope of yellow hair, was a different matter altogether.

"I'm guessing now," said Begum, "that you're up to no good. What business have you to be skulking about like this, hiding behind curtains and what not, just when you're about to pop? Alalai has vanished and my blood is on the boil."

"So I see."

"Have you seen her?"

"No. Not a whisper. I was just passing through on my way to the kitchen, looking for Turkish delight. My sweet tooth is aching for the stuff. Can't seem to get enough of it. I've been told I am to have whatever I wish. The Sultan himself says that I am a very, very important wife."

Begum glowered at this, her temper like embers stoked and teased to light. There was no question about it – she adored her son. But his bad taste in wives and his particular bedtime habits were quite frankly starting to get on her nerves. Girls were running riot in every corner whilst the Empire was going to pot.

At midnight Alalai was still missing. Begum was nursing a headache in the hamam and four young girls were administering to her every need. She simply couldn't work out where on earth the girl had disappeared to. The Black Eunuch had been guarding her chambers day and night. No one had been seen to enter and no one had left. If it wasn't for the fact that it was the Sultan's birthday celebrations in just a few hours, she would have turned the Palace inside out. She muttered and swore to herself as she mulled things over. The girls pummelled her shoulders and legs, punching and kneading her body with their quick little fists. They lathered soap into her hair and rubbed essence of jasmine oil into all of her deep creases. None of this helped to soothe her; she became even more fractious and out of sorts.

Elsewhere in the Palace, Zainab, who was also wide-awake, lay idly across her quilted cot. The bed had been plumped up and filled with goose down to support her ever increasing weight. She stretched and yawned and stroked her belly with a self-satisfied and circular motion. She then threw, with precise aim, cubes of crystallised sugar into her glass of mint-filled tea. A small child was brushing her hair and another was playing with her painted toes.

"It's late. Leave me," she said to them both with a wave of her hand. "Go on. Shoo." And the children scampered like lambs, gambolling into the far corners of the large chamber.

"So," said Zainab, crossing her arms above her balloon-like swelling and biting her lip. She directed her glance to the water jug that had been placed on the low table in front of her. "You really do make a remarkably fine vessel. Somehow you have managed to be even more charming in porcelain than I ever could have imagined. It's almost as if you are enchanting me, when it was actually I who bought the spell and fed it to you."

The jug sat motionless and taciturn.

"I did it for your own good, you know. The Sultan would've devoured you in a single mouthful, crunched on your bones, sucked on your heart and licked his lips."

A thin ghost of a crack appeared just above the jug's gilded rim. It looked to Zainab as though Alalai, knock-kneed and moon-faced girl no more, was trying to speak, but all her words were stuck, amorphous in porcelain.

"I almost wish now that you could speak," said Zainab, staring transfixed at the jug. "What are you thinking about, if anything at all? Are there words forming inside your mind? I wonder if you would like to see yourself? I expect you would." She picked up the jug and walked heavily across to an enormous mirror.

"As you can see, you are really rather exquisite. Can you still see? The Mistress of Potions promised me that you would not lose all of your wits, just some. Where would the fun be otherwise? The Masters of Clay in Chin could not have fashioned you any better than this."

Alalai stared in the mirror. But a filmy varnish of glaze frosted her sight and the now unfamiliar world looked as if it had just been dipped into milk. She could not see herself. She could not feel or smell herself. The only thing she could sense was that whilst her

19

mind was fading, her essence was gathering luminosity. What she saw in the mirror was a water jug and not a girl at all. Her bewildered senses could not understand that this was her. The jug she saw was the colour of pearl in some parts and a darker eggshell in others. Thin strands of raku glaze splintered in gold fissures across its surface, and if china could blush, then it blushed a pale crimson of buried blood. It had a spherical middle that was fulsome and round and an elegant tapering neck. Wrapped around the base was a silver band with the whisper of a prayer etched in fine calligraphy. Moonlight shining through a latticed window peppered the jug with dappled geometric gold. It was as if every element in the room had conspired to make the jug ever more lovely and lifelike. Alalai tried to speak but she could not find her mouth or her tongue. They simply weren't there. What she could feel, and it really was the strangest thing, was that a drop or two of menstrual blood had frozen just above where the innermost top of her thigh would have been. The fetid blood was caught in a fleck for evermore beneath the glaze. It caused a slight tickle but she had no fingers with which to scratch it.

By this point Zainab was starting to feel very unhinged, for here she was, conversing with a jug that had not a single syllable to offer in return.

"Oh dear," she said, sighing. "What happened to you when you changed? Is your mind still in one piece or are you terribly confused? If you'd only had your wits about you in the first place, you would never have accepted a sweet from me. From me! Did you ever guess that I could be so malicious? Perhaps I should put you in the dining room for the Sultan to use in the morning: an exceptional birthday treat? Granted not quite what he was expecting, but still . . . I am sure the water that flows from your lip could be nothing but sweet. And yet here I am, not wanting to part from you. How curious is that, that the parting makes me feel anxious? This spell is not as straightforward as I had first imagined. Tomorrow first thing, I will speak to the Mistress of Potions."

She clapped her hands twice and four young girls, the same who had been massaging Begum, appeared in the room. They looked at Zainab with sly and sideways glances.

"What?"

"We have heard," they began, for they spoke as a whole, each one in complete harmony with the others, "that Moon Face has vanished! Is this true? Where has she gone?"

"How should I know? Help me get ready for bed. I am far too fat to move. What else have you heard?"

"We heard Begum tell the Black Eunuch to keep an eye . . . on you! She thinks you are up to no good!"

"Does she now?"

"Yes she does, she really really does! She also said" – and then they dropped their voices and crept in closer – "that she will have you murdered if you give birth to a girl! Murdered!"

"You don't really think I'm scared of that old bag, do you?"

"Oh! But she could if she wanted. She's more powerful than the Sultan. She told him to start the war and he did. She told him to drain the sea of all its fish, that hungry people were quiet people, so he did. She has private counsel with the Vizier. In a secret room! Every day! We have seen her. We hear everything." They twittered noisily as they danced around her, nibbling her arms and blowing raspberries on her belly and gently tugging at her hair.

"Fiddlesticks. You're all naughty little things for gossiping so. No one is more powerful than the Sultan and certainly not his mother. And no one can drain the sea. It is bigger than all of us. It's more than half the world, you know. Now help me take this off."

The girls undressed her, chattering incessantly, and then reswaddled her in bedtime silks. She was quick, despite their entreaties to kiss her and sing her to sleep, to shoo them away at the first opportunity.

She sat back down across her cot and stared once again, unblinkingly, at the jug. She was grudgingly memorising every contour, every line and reflection, drinking it in like a tonic. Was this love – *love*, already? For Allah's sake, surely not?

Under Zainab's gaze what little remained of Alalai began to dissolve like a cube of sugar in a saucer of tepid water. The milky film that kept her suppressed within the jug began to thicken like starch. She could no longer see, nor could she hear, but what she did have was the lasting memory of taste. When everything else about her was waning, the remnants of Turkish delight lingered on with an overwhelming and delicious depth.

Zainab, self-absorbed and completely unaware that the younger girl was thus fading, continued to prattle on.

"Why on earth am I so drawn to you? I didn't like you when you were a girl. I despised you, in fact, and now – now you're just an object. Do you feel cold, Alalai, in your china grave?"

The jug moved but so slightly that it was barely discernible.

"Did you just move? Is that possible? Oh dear God, what exactly is going on here? My skin is on fire." Zainab touched her cheeks with her open palms and her breath came shallow and unsure. "I feel as if I'm burning *up*. This is too much."

She eased herself to her feet and moved across to the jug. She picked it up, cradling it in her arms with an unusual tenderness. Settling slowly down she sat, cross-legged, and opened her gown. She pressed the jug to her distended stomach and then to her breasts and neck. The cool of the ceramic brought immediate respite to her blistering skin. She brushed her mouth and cheeks across its fullness in a peculiar and clumsy embrace, more awkward in this strange lovemaking (could she even call it that?) than she had ever been before. Zainab had never been so enamoured with an object, not in her entire life. She hesitated to think that words like love or even desire were appropriate, but how else could she explain it, that the cool touch of the porcelain was the only thing she wanted? The baby somersaulted and kicked, eager now to come out.

The Black Eunuch was standing concealed behind her. He surveyed the scene with a great deal of interest. He couldn't quite work out what was going on, but he watched her, as per instruction, until she fell asleep. There was something odd about that jug and it made him think of something, or even someone.

The Black Eunuch spent most of his nights flitting bat-like, in and out of the shadows of the Palace. He had been inside the most private of chambers and seen the most unmentionable acts, but this, this peculiar tenderness, confounded him. When, later, he reported back to Begum, he was as scrupulous in his descriptions as possible and lucid to a tee. Begum, whom he knew was expecting, at the very least, the thread to some kind of scandal, from which she could then draw a number of suitably nefarious conclusions, was left speechless.

"What do you mean? With a jug? Are you absolutely sure?"

"My Queen, there was something uncanny about that jug. It was uncommon. I have never seen one of its kind in the length or breadth of the Palace, and yet it seemed to breathe with a familiar consciousness that I could feel pulsing through my own veins. I would wager gold that some sort of enchantment is at play. You may need to speak to the Mistress of Potions. She usually has a hand in any mischief of this kind. As for Alalai, I have had no sight of the girl."

"I will choose another girl. Allah only knows there are plenty of them. What she may lack in fair features, she will absolutely make up for in her submissive nature. She will have to do for the time being. As for Zainab, I will deal with her as soon as it is light. You are dismissed."

Begum woke up at dawn. She considered the Black Eunuch's words carefully. What with one girl misplaced and the other out of her wits, things were not looking as auspicious for the Sultan's birthday as she would have liked. She was determined to put an end to all this nonsense personally and to do so before her son woke up. The slap of her bare feet across the tiles could be heard resounding from corridor to corridor as she made her way to Zainab's chamber. She barged in without knocking.

"Wake up." She clapped her hands, one two, in the sleepy girl's face.

"Queen B? Is it morning already? Am I late for something?"

"No, my dear, you are not. Wake up anyway. I have heard some ghastly rumours *and they involve you.*"

Zainab rubbed her eyes with embellished lethargy and yawned, opening her mouth in an enormous O. As the girl stretched, Begum looked over her shoulder and gave a sudden start. In front of the window, on a low table bathed in the gossamer dawn, was a water jug. It was the most extraordinarily lovely thing that Begum had ever seen and she was quite taken by it – mesmerised, in fact.

"Where in Allah's name did you get this jug?"

"Oh, that old thing?" answered Zainab with what seemed deliberate insouciance. "I just borrowed it from the kitchen."

"The kitchen, you say?"

"Exactly." She bent over and cradled her stomach.

"Why would the kitchen be allowed such a prize, I wonder? This jug has been crafted in Chin and only the Sultan may drink from a porcelain vessel. I shall take it to him with his breakfast."

"Oh," said Zainab in reply, now doubled over. She looked as though she could hardly breathe as the baby started to push and shove its way into the world. "But I am rather fond of it now and it's chipped all around the rim. Please may I keep it? It's really of no other use."

"My dear girl, I have never heard you ask for anything with such well-mannered grace! Come on now, where is your fight?"

"Queen B, I pray you, stop your taunting. The baby is coming."

"I will take the jug first and then I will call for the midwife. You have plenty of time yet. May I suggest that you get on all fours? It is by far the most comfortable position. Here, chew on this cloth."

Zainab felt a sudden gush of warm liquid stream down her leg. An unfamiliar guttural panting was coming out of her slender throat. She was determined to grab the jug first. The baby would have to wait its turn.

Both women reached for the jug at the same time. They collided and their limbs entangled. Zainab bit Begum's cheek and held on to her wrist whilst Begum pulled her hair and kicked her shins. There was a sharp slap, and then another, and then a loud and clumsy crash. The jug had slipped off the table and smashed.

Zainab had gone into labour and Begum finally called for the midwife. The jug lay in shards on the floor, at once forgotten and unattended.

Four hours later, after a string of profanities so obscene that even Begum was abashed, Zainab gave birth to a girl.

That evening, prompted by no one but reacting instead to an unfamiliar feeling of affection, the Black Eunuch swept up the pieces of broken crockery and tied them in a hessian sack. He had disposed of many dismembered girls in a similar way and though they had been flesh and bone he had felt neither remorse nor pity. And yet even though this was merely a jug and not a girl at all, he felt a twinge to the far left of his ribcage. He prayed for mercy before throwing the sack high into the air and out into the sea. It sank almost immediately, leaving only the faintest trace of phosphorescence in its wake.

Area of Outstanding Natural Beauty

JAY BARNETT

I asked Mushy if he had the waterproofs. He had no idea what I was talking about.

"Borrow mine."

I handed him the sleeves. He held them out in front of him and stared at them blankly.

"Just put your arm in, and clip it to that thing there," I said, pointing to the thing.

I was in no mood for traps. My sister had visited the night before, came with a bottle of brandy bought from a man at Hornby Dock. It had been five years since I'd tried the stuff. I must have had half the bottle to myself.

Mushy managed to get the left sleeve on but I had to help him with the right. I had him check the traps by the brook. That way I could sit and do nothing while he learnt something.

"You done your water training?" I asked him.

"This is my water training, isn't it?"

"It is now." I took a step towards the brook. "It's easy. You know how to check a trap?"

"Yeah."

"Well, see that marker?" I gestured to a triangle at the brook's edge, fluorescent orange in the long grass.

"Yeah."

"There's a trap in the water just under there. There's four

along here."

He looked along the bank, at the bright triangles every thirty metres or so.

"Just see what colour the light is on them traps. You might have to get your arm in to shift whatever shit might be clinging to them."

He lifted his hands to look at the rubber sleeves.

"If the light's red, leave it. Green, give us a shout."

As I walked to the others sat on the shingle, I looked over my shoulder at Mushy.

"They won't be full!" I shouted. "They prefer open water."

Jennifer sat cross-legged, her arms propped behind her. I lay out flat next to her and looked at the sky.

"Bright," I said.

Bykes paced up and down a few metres away, trying to get a signal on his radio. He always brought it with him; it could pick up communication bands as well as commercial signals. He liked to listen in on the monitoring depots dotted around the coast, hoping to hear of things washed up, discoloration, suspicious water levels. For the most part it was talk of the weather, the tide and the safety of distances. After a while he would tune out to find something with more song about it. He walked towards us and spoke over the music on his radio.

"St Louis knows about the milk."

The chill of the morning had faded and the backs of my legs were beginning to sweat against the shingle. I looked around for something to drape over my eyes, a cloth, a bag, anything.

"You listenin'?" said Bykes.

"What?"

"St Louis knows about you stealing milk."

"Bullshit! We all steal milk."

"And soap. And sweetener. And toilet roll," said Jennifer. "But it's you an' milk that got the mention."

This was rich coming from her.

"Where've you heard this?" I asked.

"Depot. Last night," said Bykes. "Steve told me. Said he heard from horse's mouth."

"Fuckin' Steve."

At the bottom of my pack I found a clean entry-rag. I draped it across my eyes and lay back down on the shingle. I arranged myself on the stones with tiny shimmies, trying to mould a small dip to rest in. Once I was comfortable, I stilled myself and listened to the brook.

"You'll be all right," said Jennifer. "Just lie your way out of it."

"Fuckin' Steve," I said.

"You're not gonna drag us down if they fire you, are you?" asked Bykes.

I didn't answer, just listened to his radio. An advert about giving blood, an advert about land insurance, something about food. A song came on that reminded me of school days and of the Fenton Recreation Ground on winter nights. We used to drink cider there, and smoke, and scratch our names in the see-saw. It was fun until the older boys started bringing airguns along. They fired in the dark, aiming at the sound of laughter by the swings. A well-placed shot would break the skin.

I struggled up from my recline in search of something to drink. Over by the brook I saw Mushy starting back, his rubber arms held out by his sides.

"All empty!"

We gathered our things up from the shingle. Mushy unclipped the waterproofs and passed them to me.

"Keep them till they're dry," I said. "Don't want them wettin' my bag up."

"Where'm I supposed to put them?"

"Stuff them through your belt."

With no great urgency we walked towards the overgrowth. Somewhere in there were traps Forty-Nine to Seventy-Two. Our boots had trodden the path more days than not for the past fifteen years and now a dark arch welcomed us where weeds and wildflowers should flourish. We passed through and edged down into the path.

"This is Dog Holloway," I said to Mushy.

The holloway was a quarter mile long on a slight gradient; to walk it west, as we did, meant downhill. It was an ancient, dank place no wider than three metres across. Either side, mud walls reared above our shoulders, while trees formed shelter overhead.

"Why's it called Dog Holloway?" asked Mushy.

"Don't know."

He looked to the others for answers. Jennifer shrugged. Bykes wasn't paying attention.

We walked down the holloway towards the first trap. It was burrowed into the bank so that it was flush with the earth. The indicator showed empty so we moved on to the next. There were six altogether, laid and set in the mud walls. Bykes was between stations on the radio, filling the narrow space with white noise. He settled on something old and tried to whistle to it. He didn't know the song.

The second trap was in darkest shade, nestled in the roots of a stump. We couldn't see the indicator for a thick web that had formed over it. Jennifer put her gloves on to pull it away.

"Wasn't here Tuesday," she said.

Her hand knocked a root and some loose soil fell away. Beneath it the very earth seemed to move with millipedes and woodlice. The creeping things were in good number. She removed the web. Underneath it the light was red.

"Are they mostly empty, the traps?" asked Mushy.

"Pretty much. They don't like our bait," said Jennifer. "The only thing they like is . . . well, you know. And nutmeg, of course."

Jennifer bought nutmeg a few years ago from a pop-up in Camber. It cost her a month's rent. "Christmas isn't the same without it," she'd said, then managed to sell some at a premium back at the depot. A sprinkle goes nice in the traps.

We walked the rest of the holloway without fuss, glancing at the indicators as we passed. All lights red.

We came out into the opening by Kingsley Bank, where the Hide is. The sun hit us flush, quite something from the cool dark of the holloway. Jennifer unzipped the top half of her suit, down to the vest, to let her arms warm in the glow. Somewhere a few miles away we heard three intermittent bursts. Probably the guys over in Heathfields, messing with charges. They're meant to blow holes in the ground for new traps, but they wouldn't have been laying new traps. Who'd waste time laying new traps?

"Fucked up," I said. "They're gonna try me for milk, while

that lot steal explosives?"

It was easy to steal from the store. Tell one of the old boys you need a form then go in and take a bomb. We once strapped six charges to the base of a young beech tree. When it blew it left the ground and near flipped three hundred and sixty degrees.

"Milk?" asked Mushy.

"You'll not need to pay for milk again," said Jennifer. "Just take it from fridges at the depot."

"None of you'll be taking anything if they do me," I said.

The Hide sat twenty feet above the forest floor, built on eight great legs of cedar pine. It was a place humans could hide from nature, built for the days when people watched birds. It was closed to the public years ago, then used by our company for research by night. It's used for nothing these days. Night work was cancelled indefinitely after Longden Lane. The Hide had become unfit for purpose, left to the elements. We weren't meant to go near the thing but would always use it to sit out the rain, or the wind, or the job. Wasn't much point in heading up that day, the weather was too nice for the shade of the Hide. I decided to show Mushy anyway.

We took to the steps, waterlogged and soft underfoot but still equal to the weight of a man. The trees had become so unruly that some branches reached in through the viewing points. Mushy grabbed at one and shook it. My walkie-talkie let out two short blips, the sound it makes when the batteries are dying. I leant out of the north opening and looked down. Jennifer was poking the ground with a small knife.

"I got the beeps!"

She looked up from whatever fungus she was probing, then at the walkie-talkie on her belt.

"Well I haven't."

Down through the trees I could see patterns in the dirt, traces of them. Thin, entwined markings circling trees or heading direct into outcrops of bush. I could also make out three traps, all of their indicators red.

I turned around to see Mushy half leaning out of the south viewing point. He was facing up towards the sky with his back resting on the timber frame. With both hands he grabbed at something out of sight and with a pull, disappeared through the opening. I walked quickly towards him, looked through the gap to see nothing but blue sky.

"Proper sunny up here!" he shouted.

None of us had ever climbed onto the roof of the Hide. I could hear Mushy testing the timber's strength above me. His body moved and the wood creaked. No one saw to the maintenance of the thing. Its rivets and joists moaned in the damp. One day it would give up.

"I'm going down, Mushy. Be careful."

Jennifer stood by a tree, a limp thing, its leaves unseasonably dry. She dragged a scraper along its bark and it came away like paste. She put it to her nose and grimaced. Bykes was sat on a mud mound in the dappled shade, his suit half undone for the heat of the day.

"All empty here," I said, "but I couldn't see Fifty-Eight's."

Bykes stood up, stretched his arms overhead.

"I'll go check it."

I sat and leant against a cedar leg. Lots of leaning. Lots of sitting.

"Is he safe up there?" asked Jennifer, nodding towards Mushy.

"Probably not."

I took the batteries from my walkie-talkie then rubbed them in my hands. I switched their positions, as if tricking the device that they were new. It killed the beeps at least.

From beyond the sound of the leaves, Bykes yelled over.

"There's a half in here!"

I pulled myself up from the forest floor using the cedar leg as grip.

"Mushy! Come down and see this."

The three of us made our way to Bykes. He was stooped by the trap, prodding it with an extendable baton.

"Well, it's half of sumit," he said, "but not half of what it's meant to be."

Some mammal or other had sniffed out the bait. It was hard to tell what it was, now gelatinous and tangled. Bykes poked at its innards; they were moist and reflected the sun. He cleared the mess then I had Mushy reset the trap. He forgot about the bearings but I didn't correct him, and I didn't care. We still had the Holes and Bonisall. Damn Bonisall. We moved on from the Hide, the midday sun on top of us.

"OK, Mushy," I said. "These are the Holes. If there's anything caught, it's likely caught here."

The foxes had long gone but their holes were still used, so much so that the ground had hollowed out and taken on a spongy honeycomb effect. A run of dips and mounds, dry in open air. Nothing grew at the Holes. Bykes stood at the edge of the area, the forest behind him and the blue sky in front.

"Shame to waste the sun checking traps," he said, then peered into one of the small dark openings. Down there was trap Sixty-Two. Behind him, a great buddleia loomed tall as a house, heavy with cones of white flowers. He squinted and cocked his head left.

"Gonna need to shift this a little. Can't see it."

He picked up a stick from the forest behind him, then shoved it from sight, down into the hole of trap Sixty-Two. He appeared to be exerting some degree of force down there; at times it looked a struggle. Jennifer, Mushy and I looked on. Tired. Not bothered. Hot. We'd all unzipped the top halves of our suits. Bykes wedged the stick to a satisfactory point then planted his feet either side of the hole and pulled. And pulled. And we watched. Mushy spat on the floor and Jennifer wiped her brow. Then Bykes pulled some more, pulled until the stick broke free and he fell straight back, right into the buddleia. The whole thing wavered, shaking loose from its flowers a swarm of butterflies we hadn't known were there. Maybe a thousand, the colour of milk. They fluttered into our group and bounced around our packs, some stopping on the damp of our skin to taste the salt then move off. As they flew in and about us we held our arms out from our sides, as if swimming in phosphorescence. Most returned to the buddleia, others to the forest behind; some took to the sky above the dry, open Holes. They had dispersed to less than a quarter when Mushy reached out and grabbed a straggler in his fist. He held tight then opened his palm to look at it.

"Dust," he said.

Bykes was still by the hole in the shadow of the buddleia,

looking down at trap Sixty-Two. The stick must have worked because he looked up and said: "Empty."

There were three more at the Holes. Trap Sixty-Three was empty. Trap Sixty-Four was empty. Trap Sixty-Five was empty.

"Fucking Bonisall," I said.

I looked at the others.

"Let's sit here a while."

Jennifer lay burning her face in the heat. Mushy walked about, testing the strange terrain underfoot. He stopped by every hole to spit down into dark. Bykes sat on his knees, his legs tucked under his bum. He tuned into a monitoring depot over on the coast, the faint sibilant voices of people at work. We lay in the sun picking up fragments of conversation. Some fault in an engine room near the Hanagan Channel. It was solved, apparently, by the push of a button.

There were two ways to Bonisall. Through the Mess, or up Chorley Way. The Mess took fifteen minutes, maybe less. An overgrown place rank with dangerous weeds, the sort that weep and hurt the skin. We had our suits for such things but it was so nice in the sun. Chorley Way was the longer path. A flat track of mostly dirt. There were no traps on either route. The Mess was considered too poisonous. Chorley Way, too flat and open either side. Most days we took the Mess, quickest option preferred. Bykes began to zip up. He looked at Mushy.

"You got goggles?"

"Think so."

I stared at the tangled entrance to the Mess, considered the relative dramas in there. Then I looked east towards Chorley Way. As plain a track as I'd known.

"Let's go Chorley Way," I said.

"Don't be stupid," said Bykes.

I grabbed my things up and moved east.

"I'm going Chorley Way."

Jennifer rubbed her goggles with a rag. She frowned at me.

"You'll hold us up."

"That's the idea. If we get back to the depot a bit later, maybe St Louis will have gone home already."

"I got no problem with St Louis," she said. "It's not me he wants."

"Let it be known. If this St Louis bollocks is true and I'm dragged over the coals, I'm naming names."

The three of them looked at me. Jennifer put her goggles back in her pack.

"You're a bastard."

"True," added Bykes.

Mushy said nothing.

I'd forgotten the charm of Chorley Way. Just some fields with a path running through them. Sometimes dirt, sometimes tarmac. So flat and open is the route, that its skies are big. They are empty, but they are big. If we were to see a bird on the job, it would be there. I walked purposely slow, turned twenty minutes into thirty. The others walked ahead, eventually out of sight. I thought about what I might say if confronted by St Louis: *Shit job anyway.* I walked on, burnt my skin a little along the way. I saw no birds.

By the time I got to Bonisall they had checked all traps. Empty, of course. The three of them, perched by the truck, waiting. Seph sat with his leg out the driver's side door. He was the depot's oldest driver; a fat man, more gum than teeth.

"Milky, milky," he said, as I walked from behind the silo.

The Heathfields lot were on the truck.

"Hey up, Mushy!" one of them said. "Was Jenny good to you?"

He must have trained with them earlier in the week. After us, he was likely on to Canton. Poor bastard. At the start of it all.

I sat alone at the seat without windows. As we moved off there was nothing to look at but the inner wall of the truck. It was covered in coarse polyester lining, warmer than glass to rest against for sleep during transit.

Chorley Way hadn't helped, St Louis was still at the depot. All I could do was avoid eye contact. There were thirteen minutes left on the clock and he wanted to make sure no one left early. I filled in my day's report form. Nothing to report. I moved my pen across the sheet, circling the same marks I'd already made just to eat up the time. I looked across at the others doing the same.

"Can I have a word?"

It was St Louis. I pretended not to hear. Kept my eyes on the sheet. Circling. Circling again.

"Yeah, no worries," said Mushy, and went into his office.

Jennifer, Bykes and I looked at one another.

"What's that about?" asked Jennifer.

"Maybe our Mushy's a spy," said Bykes.

I tossed my report form in the pigeonhole; it was still attached to the clipboard.

"Now's as good a time as any to get out of here." I hurried to the changing rooms.

I was down to civvies in record time. I looked at my watch. Two minutes past finish. My hands were filthy. I'd wash them at home. I grabbed my bag and went to leave through the fire exit.

"There you are!"

St Louis, the bastard. He'd appeared like a ninja; sly. He walked up close, my back against the steel of the locker. His tie tangled with a lanyard proudly displaying name and title: *Daren Bell. Enickford Department Supervisor.* Can't remember why we called him St Louis. Bell-end would have been better.

"Can I have a quick word?"

He had me enter his office first. A stuffy little place; tiny high windows. A pile of boxes stacked in the corner concertinaed under their own weight.

"Sit down," he said.

The chair was surprisingly comfy; static, without wheels. I scanned his desk. He was the only person in the company to bring a briefcase to work. It sat with his keys on top. Next to that was a carton of milk.

"You're in the frame," he said.

My trapping days were up. The land of milk and sunshine crumbled all about me.

"You know Don's leaving at the end of the year?"

"What?"

"Don. He's off in November. It's likely they'll be shifting up top. I'm looking at his position, which leaves this desk free."

"Oh."

"You're in the frame."

"The frame?"

"For my position. This position. I put your name forward."

I stared at the milk carton. Judging by its moisture it'd not long been taken from the fridge.

"Just had John in here. Said he liked training with you the best."

"John?"

"The lad. Said your team's the best."

'Cause we do nothing.

"Well, what do you think?"

My elbows were on the armrest, hands interlocked across my belly.

"About what?"

"About this, sitting here." He tapped the desk. "You'll not be getting out in the sun as much, but you'll not be getting out in the rain, either."

I couldn't take my eyes off the milk, fresh out the fridge and sat by his briefcase at home time. The bastard was stealing the stuff.

"I'll give it some thought," I said.

"Better pay, too." He opened his briefcase, threw his keys in, then looked at me across the desk. "You can go now."

The depot was silent. Everyone had cleared out, off home for teas and beds. I stood washing my hands in the boot sink. *St Louis. St Louis.* What nickname would they give me, should I become supervisor? I watched the day's mud swirl the porcelain. Quite the gyre. Funny, really, all that dirt for so little work.

Aide-Mémoire for the Long-Distance Swimmer

KIT DE WAAL

You may want to take this with you.

You may need reminding.

You may have woken at six and broken the ice on February water.

You may be well prepared.

You may become numb, forcing arm over arm for mile after mile.

And you may hurt.

You may hear the sea so close in your ears that it becomes the blood in your veins.

You may want to stop.

You may have counted on calm water and found none.

You may find your resolution wavers after the ninth mile.

You may wish you could forget.

You may need reminding.

You may swim with one picture sitting square on the horizon.

You may find it helps.

You may begin to feel nothing.

You may be glad when you become tired, when the water becomes warm, becomes friendly, becomes home.

You may wish to take this with you.

Disco Phil

TOM NORTON

Phil lines up the next track and leans back against the wall, sipping at a bottle of cheap lager and looking out onto the near empty dance floor of the Albert. How many times has he played this shithole now? Too many to recall. Count how many he's enjoyed, that'd be easier. The wall at his back vibrates with each electronic kick and, eyes closed, he allows the pummelling four-four to shudder through him. It's a twenty-first tonight and he's spent the last hour building away from the R'n'B tracks the birthday girl requested into the more accessible house tracks of his collection. No objections so far from the kids, though most of them are too pissed now to know the difference. He might hit them with some early nineties rave before the night is out, just to show them what they missed. Phil takes another swig. Forty-two and still doing this. Whatever, get this set over with and head back for some sleep. And no more bottles of this cheap piss. Need to be fresh for Caroline in the morning.

The girl in the purple dress is back from the bar, a colourless drink in her hand. Vodka and lemonade, Phil guesses, probably a double. She bends forward to sip it through the straw and raises one arm in the air, that tight dress hugging her arse as she shuffles to the beat. She grabs the birthday girl sitting at the edge, sings right up in her face and kisses her on the cheek, pulling her onto the centre of the floor to twirl her in a badly improvised one-armed salsa.

Caroline is coming tomorrow. It was every two weeks Phil used to see her, after Jackie split with him. That was back when Caroline was six, but they'd kept to it all through her school and sixth-form years. Every two weeks: their weekend. Now she's up at Newcastle, English Lit, and barely makes it down every three months. Sometimes Phil can feel the distance, suddenly, and be breathless at how far away she is. Nineteen, an adult, she delights and surprises in so many new and different ways, but Phil still hurts for the child now gone.

The track is coming to an end. He sets his lager down and pulls the headphones over one ear, starting the second turntable and putting the brakes on the vinyl with his fingertips. Finding the start of the track he counts eight bars and releases, listens and pushes the speed control a few millimetres, bringing the record into sync with a single gentle spin. The vocals in the first track have finished and the beat will now see the last centimetres of the record out. Phil fades the lowest register of the existing track and flicks the crossfader a third of the way across, bringing in the new bassline. The girls cry out in recognition and start jumping ecstatically about. Purple Dress dances up to the decks, pointing at Phil and mouthing "Fucking yes." Spurred by her standing before him, he brings in the treble and the mid-tone, snapping off the bass as a few bars of high-pitch synth and snares build to their inevitable climax. Then, showing off – shameful at his age – he suddenly kills the sound with the crossfader, surprising his little fan with a fraction of a second of complete silence, before slamming everything back in, the bassline driving it all on again. Purple Dress gives him an over-the-top nodding grin then bounds up to her table of friends to pull more of them onto the floor. They're always useful, girls like her. No one's going to resist a dance with such a hot, spirited little thing. Dance floors grow exponentially, and sure enough there's soon a good twenty people bouncing and shaping away.

Phil tables the headphones and squats down at his record box, flicking through the multi-coloured sleeves, knowing that one will select itself automatically when he chances upon it. It's ten thirty Caroline arrives, on the morning train from her mother's. He'll pick her up in the Volkswagen Golf he's borrowed off Joe. He's not had his own wheels since the supermarket reduced his hours, but

Joe's a decent guy. There's still a few good people left at that place. Ten thirty he'll pick her up and the first thing they'll do is get out of this town. Drive somewhere with at least a bit of life. Over to Guildford or maybe to the coast. When he gets home tonight he'll google something cultural she will appreciate, something literary. Christ, he wouldn't know where to start.

A decision made, Phil stands with the selected record, removes it from the plain black sleeve and positions it on the free deck, sliding the empty sleeve beneath. He settles into the next mix, bringing in the new track plainly, no frills. When he looks up, the dance floor has swelled with new arrivals. Must be kick-out time at the other pubs. At the top of the steps that lead down to the floor a group of lads stand hard-faced, brazenly surveying the talent beneath them. The tops of their gym-thickened chests are on display in the openings of white, scoop-necked tees, printed with factory-faded designs. One chews gum open-mouthed, sneering confidently down at the dance floor, and Phil can tell from the way the others cluster around that he's their leader. A striking face, with eyes sharp above pronounced cheekbones, he almost has a model's features but for a pinched, slightly crooked nose. In his arrogant swagger there's a wildness that suggests he is the sort of animalistic twenty-something who opens conversations with fists.

Phil gets the odd glimpse of Purple Dress through the crowd. Now there are blokes around she's taken to a more sexy style of dance, dipping herself up and down, moving that arse of hers away from and towards them all. Phil thinks of Caroline up in Newcastle. Student central, party city. Does Caroline go around presenting herself like this? Purple Dress moves in front of the lad, raising arms above her head and pouting in his direction. In response he chews his gum, hateful eyes fixed on her gyrating shape. A current of anger pulses through Phil, a violent, remembered feel, of his knuckles thudding flesh, kicks directed into bunched, fetal shapes as street lights blur wet tarmac, a lost thrill of dominance. But with eyes half shut and a trained, measured breath he dispels the surge, which disappears as quickly as it came.

He leans back against the wall. The dated disco lights flash red, yellow, green and blue onto a thick pond of gurning faces. Lost kids inebriating themselves to escape the Friday-night monotony of a nowhere town. A mass of dark shapes undulating as one, each is given individual clarity by sporadic flickers of the coloured light. Phil knows a lot of them will manage it, before too long. Escape. They'll find their way to London with all of those who flocked before, where they'll soon be sitting around wearing hats and talking about coffee. Some of them will end up happy, or at least do something interesting with their lives. The rest, unlucky or undeserving, will end up here for good before they even realise what has happened. Just like their DJ who looks over them. Forty-two and still scratching around the town he grew up in, stitching together a living from reduced hours at Tesco, doing the odd pity job for friends and playing dodgy, desperate places like this for the hundredth time. Phil's gone backwards, he always has. Jackie had been bang on about that. But Caroline is coming tomorrow.

Behind the bar, the assistant manager looks in the direction of the booth and Phil raises a hand to get his attention. Andy gestures back – *One minute* – and saunters out of sight. "Fucking good set, mate," he shouts into Phil's ear a moment later as he hands him a fresh bottle.

"Cheers, Andy." With an index and middle finger, Phil puffs at an imaginary cigarette, his other hand on Andy's shoulder as he leans in to be heard. "I could use a smoke. You mind watching this for five?"

"'Course, mate." Andy goes all business-like. An enthusiastic faux geezer, his sculpted hair side-parted and studs in both ears, Andy slides into the booth and pushes up the sleeves of his T-shirt to better display his gym-toned, tattooed arms.

"You're a star." Phil taps a stack of records he's pulled out from the box. "These'll work. I won't be long."

Outside, Phil settles onto the only empty table in the smoking area, a large concrete yard penned by high brick walls. Between each cluster of wooden picnic tables there are tall metal heaters beating down upon the well-oiled clientele. He takes his time to roll a cigarette, knowing Andy will be in his element, a decent DJ and fond of a crowd's attention. As he rolls, he is aware of a group of youngsters bundling raucously through the double doors. One gives a laughing shriek and Phil looks up to see the girl in the purple dress. The group of four girls, all dressed to the nines, scan the yard and stagger their way over to Phil's table. "OK if we sit here, mate?" says the tall blonde at their head, a tray of drinks wobbling in her skinny arms. Phil shuffles along the bench, tensing his stomach into a more appealing shape. "Cheers," she says and sets down the tray in front of him, packed with Jäger shots, glass tumblers and cans of Red Bull. There's purple in the corner of Phil's eye as he licks the Rizla, and he watches peripherally as her shape moves around to his side of the table. A pair of black-heeled feet swing over the bench beside him, followed by slim, youthful legs, at the top of which Phil gets a glimpse of black lace stockings when the tight purple dress pulls up. Making no attempt to right it as she settles, she instead puts her hands on him. One rests on his bicep, the other gives his thigh a squeeze.

"Do us a rollie, Deejay," she calls into his ear. There's a shade of posh in her voice Phil reckons she is trying to suppress. Her friends laugh and Blondie starts administering the energy drink into the empty tumblers, dropping the shot glasses inside, where the dark-brown Jägermeister swirls into a rusty gold. Phil turns to his new neighbour, cool as he can, her face inches from his, perfume filling the narrow window of air between them. Heart hammering, he studies her closeness. She's gone to town on the eyeliner, sharpening the edges of her dark eyes into an exotic, almost Asian look, and thin strands of her dyed-black hair stick around her temples with dance-floor sweat. The fiery light of the nearby heater shimmers on the gloss of her lips, which are pursed at him, but on the very edge of laughter.

"You can have this," he says, offering the finished roll-up between finger and thumb. She gives his thigh a firmer squeeze and removes her hands from his body, plucking the ciggie drunkenly from his grasp. Placing it between her shining lips she sways a little as she waits for him to lift his lighter, then looks at his eyes as the flame ignites. She blows the first drag to one side and mouths a silent, sultry "Thank you," before planting one on his cheek and turning back to her mates who are all creasing up. "Fucking hell, Anna," says the blonde, distributing the do-it-yourself Jägerbombs.

As Phil rolls himself another he listens to the four of them launch into a wildly overlapping exchange of "she said"s, "he did"s and "oh my God"s, punctuated throughout with their noisy pissed-up cackles. He swigs at his lager, taking every chance to glance sideways. Anna. Pretty enough from the front, in profile she is stunning. He guesses there is Mediterranean in there, possibly a dash of Middle East. Blondie catches him looking and raises her eyebrows. *"Really?"* her face says. Phil returns it with a miniscule *Only human* shrug, but he is having a quiet go at himself – double her age and smitten, the only proper adult at the table and completely stuck for words.

All of a sudden Anna raises both arms and calls out "Ricky!" in the direction of the pub's doors, elongating the word as a football fan would shout the name of their team. Phil frowns at the near moronic accent she's put on and looks to where her lacquered nails are pointing. Strutting towards their table is the gum-chewing lad from the dance floor, cigarette half smoked between his fingers, a small, arrogant smile curling his mouth, arm muscles tensed to show their size.

"All right, gels?" he says to them, though his eyes are on Phil.

Phil looks away to the pub doors, resting his focus there and taking a long drag of his roll-up to convey his distance from the group.

"What's happening, Ricky?" Anna asks, her drunken voice retaining the feigned intonation.

Ricky ignores her. "On the fucking Jägers, gels? How many you had?"

"Three or four," says Blondie.

Phil looks at her briefly. There's a wariness in the way she's looking at the newcomer.

"It's all happening back at Jamie's house, remember," says Ricky. He nods his head in the direction of the Albert. "After this shithole."

Phil's surprised when he feels riled by this. He flicks eyes to Ricky, who is lit red beneath the heater. His face is finely shaped, skewed nose the only upset to its symmetry, shadows falling from the down-lit cheekbones, and Anna's eyes are hooked upon it.

"Yeah, probably see you there," she pipes up, swaying, straining to be casual.

In response Ricky half turns and spits his chewing gum in a high arc into the plants that line the brick wall of the smoking area.

When he turns back he looks at her for the first time. "See you inside," he says, almost an instruction. He gives a final glare at Phil, who holds the stare for a couple of seconds before looking straight ahead, then Ricky ambles to the pub's back doors, flicking his cigarette against the wall so it explodes in a shower of orange sparks.

Phil meets Blondie's eyes regarding him enigmatically across the table. Next to him, Anna grabs a Jägerbomb and chugs it back, downing a second in quick succession, slamming the empty glasses one after the other onto the wooden surface. She wipes her lips with the back of a forearm and suddenly spins on Phil, her dangerous eyes now properly glazed.

"Hey." She grips his arm with both hands, more for balance than seduction. "Deejay. What's your name?"

Phil looks back at the confused seriousness of her expression. It's the same face Caroline gives him when she's pretending to be cross. "I'm Phil," he says, straightening out like a grown-up.

"Listen." She points a finger at him, peering along it as though lining up the sights on a gun barrel. "Disco Phil. Get your arse back in there. I wanna *dance.*"

At this the four of them crack up, shrieks reverberating off the brickwork and turning every head. Out of breath, Anna doubles forward, reaching across the table to clutch at Blondie's hands. "I wanna dance," she repeats, stroking at the pale skin.

"Come on then," says Blondie and starts to rise.

The girls manage to extract their short-skirted legs from beneath the table, Phil helping to release one of Anna's heels when it snags under the bench, consciously averting his eyes from taking in the perfect view just inches from his face. Standing under the heater, Blondie shoots Phil a steady look with fire dancing in her eyes.

"Bye, Phil." It is a statement.

Phil holds the stare, feeling a muscle tick his tight-clamped jaw. "Look after her," he says.

The girls totter back towards the double doors, Anna holding on to the others for support. When she passes underneath a tall garden lamp, Phil gets a perfectly illuminated impression of her from behind. He takes a long draw on the rolled-up cigarette, its bright-orange cherry lighting up the space ahead and obscuring the flawless purple shape. He juts his lower lip to release the smoke directly upwards, clouding the vision, banishing dark thoughts, and when the smoke clears she is gone.

He takes out his phone, googles *exhibition guildford saturday* and scrolls through the results. He doesn't have a clue. Pressing on a link called *Corners and Curves* he reads, "A collection of human and architectural images exploring the subtle beauty of form, how organic and made subjects complement each other." He copies the link and texts it to Caroline, wincing as he types:

How about this tomorrow love? xx

He takes another slow pull of his smoke then presses it out in the ashtray. Come on, Phil, let's finish this off and get the hell out of here. He gets up and picks his way back through the people to the doors of the pub. Inside, he ducks into the gents, splashing through piss and lager puddles as he makes for a urinal. Through the open door of a cubicle he can see someone has vomited, projectile pieces spattered around the toilet bowl, speckling the yellow-tiled floor. He turns his face from the stench to examine the advertising board before him on the wall. "C'mon England!" it says in bold red letters, above pictures of a shouting face painted white with a red cross, and details of upcoming football games showing here. The door bursts open.

"Fucking stinks in 'ere," says a voice.

Phil closes his eyes. He knows it belongs to Ricky.

"Some cunt's chundered," says another.

Phil can hear the footsteps of the two lads stop at the set of urinals on the wall behind. One of them lets out a loud belch.

"That girl you've got is *fit*, mate," says the second voice. "Fucking nice arse on her."

"Yeah," Ricky breathes, almost solemn. "I'm gonna ruin it."

Ricky's mate laughs. "Looks fucking pissed, though," he observes. "Useless slag'll probably pass out on ya."

Phil feels his mobile phone vibrate in his pocket, a sudden heat behind his eyes.

"That doesn't fucking matter," Ricky says. The two of them laugh.

"That's fucking *better*, mate," the second lad carries it on.

"Means she'll shut the fuck up."

Phil's heart is thundering. He's staring into the shouting face of the England fan inches from him on the wall, imagining driving a fist right into it, breaking the teeth. The younger lads finish up and turn to the sink alongside Phil. Ricky's washing his hands, laughing at the other's comment. Phil can't help himself. He turns his head, face hard as stone, and glares into the mirror.

"Couple of her mates are quite tasty 'n' all, Jamie," says Ricky, still looking down at his hands. "We'll get 'em back to yours. Blonde one at least."

Phil snaps his face back to the wall the moment Ricky looks up. There's a fraction of a second of eye contact. He feels his blood rush. He can sense Ricky turning fully to him. Phil braces his body against the shove that may be coming, fixing his eyes on the face of the England fan, imagining the repeated impact of his fist upon the bone. He hears the door open, Jamie calling back from the corridor, "Come on, Rick." Someone else has entered the bathroom, a tall, broad-backed rugby type who chooses the urinal next to Phil. On his other side, Phil is still aware of Ricky stood there facing him. There are another six or seven heartbeats before Ricky turns, in silence, and exits the bathroom.

Phil finishes and stands for a while with hands on each side of the sink, staring into the drawn, red-rimmed eyes of the face before him in the glass. He has been clamping his jaw so tight it clicks painfully as he tries to manoeuvre it. His phone vibrates again, a reminder of the unread text. He takes it out.

Dad, can't make it, going to London. Thought mum told you, Caz x

"For fuck's *sake*." He throws the phone into the sink. His right hand forms a tight fist and ploughs into the soap dispenser mounted on the wall, sending the plastic housing scattering onto the tiled floor. He shouts out, hands tensed in the air ahead of him, a desperate pair of eagle claws clutching at invisible prey. The stacked rugby boy looks up in surprise.

"You want a fucking *photo*?" Phil hears himself say. The guy raises eyebrows, shakes his head, and returns to his business. Phil grabs his phone, hearing the guy say, "Easy, dude," in a quiet voice behind him as he heads back into the pub, pushing his way impatiently through the groups gathered near the bar. The tech-house is charging and the dance floor has dissipated. Andy has gone off-piste. There's no way the Albert's crowd will bite at this heavy underground hook.

"They're loving it, mate," shouts Andy back at the booth.

"Nice one," Phil says through gritted teeth, clapping an arm round Andy's bulging shoulders. "You're a legend."

"Need another?" Andy points to an empty bottle alongside the decks.

"Yeah, go on. What is it, half hour or so?"

Andy lifts up his chunky silver watch and goes wide-eyed. "Jesus, yeah! Half hour. Cut it at one, Phil, yeah?"

With pleasure, Phil thinks as Andy scuttles back to the bar, now jam-packed with the manic cramming of last-hour drinkers. Ducking under the counter, Phil finds the record he is looking for and puts it into place. *You Got the Love* by the Source – try not flocking to the dance floor to this at twelve thirty a.m. Shamelessly, he completely fades the volume of the existing track, Radio One style, a late-night trick in places like this to give the punters the impression the council are on the phone. Some moments later, when enough people have turned their disappointed heads, he brings in the instantly recognisable synth pads and a cheer goes up. As expected, people get last-song syndrome and fill the floor. They're grabbing each other and pointing at Phil. Fuck you, Phil thinks as he nods back.

He scans the crowd for Anna, eventually seeing the purple of her dress at the dance floor's edge. She is out of it, being held upright by Ricky, her head lolloping almost unconscious against his chest. He has an arm firmly around her back and he looks down steadily at her inebriated face, her dark hair stuck in sweaty strands to her flushed forehead and cheeks. His other hand is tight on her behind, groping across the surface and clutching at it intermittently. Her head rolls back, eyes closed to the ceiling, and he touches his lips up and down her exposed neck. When Jamie swaggers across to the pair, Ricky pins Anna's fluid form into his side with one arm, freeing the roving hand to give his friend an upturned handshake. They give wide, nodding smiles and exchange some words into each other's ears, as Phil stands watching from his cage, filled with something long buried, a forgotten power that threatens to spill.

In the thick of the crowd he sees Blondie, picking her way through the dancers, straining tall, head above the surface, searching this way and that. Before she sees them, Ricky points her out to Jamie. Some quick words in Ricky's ear, then Jamie takes something from his pocket, a set of keys, placing them in Ricky's free hand and giving him a firm slap on his shoulder. Grinning, Jamie plunges into the crowd towards Blondie, putting on some enthusiastic dance moves when he reaches her, deliberately turning her to face in the opposite direction to Ricky and her friend. In response to her enquiring gestures Jamie shrugs and shakes his head. Phil can easily lip-read, "Not seen her," when he moves his mouth. Ricky begins to lead his prize away, towards the steps leading up from the dance floor, in the direction of the pub's front doors.

Phil's hands are shaking as he takes out his phone and thumbs in a text, the sharp black characters mixing like spilt ink through a sudden film of water gathering in his eyes. The flashing coloured lights kaleidoscope when he jumps down from the booth and strides across the dance floor. *It's all I can do sometimes to keep it together.* Candi Staton's voice rings clear as he pushes through the groups of drunken dancers. *But I know you've got it.* To the subsequent euphoric refrain he catches Ricky at the steps, ripping the probing hands from Anna's body, his mind on Caroline as he pushes the lad away, as the first of the heavy punches lands in return. He can picture the little black words on the screen as he is shoved from behind, as his head hits the floor and the rain of kicks begin.

No worries Caz, be careful. Miss you love, speak soon xx

The Real Africa
SALLY HINCHCLIFFE

"Tennis?" Hannah asks. "Are you mad? I can barely contemplate moving off the porch in this heat. How about a swim?"

"The hotel pools will be full of South African tourists and their kids, swapping horror stories about the locals." I lean back against the wall of the house and pull my legs out of the sun. Even Hannah has moved out of its glare today and is sitting in the shade with her legs stuck straight out in front of her, looking no older than she did when we first met. Side by side we gaze across the valley at the tiny figures moving through the pineapple fields. Over the shoulder of the hill the clouds are building but they're in the wrong place. The storms come up the valley, I have learned, not over the mountains.

"I always thought pineapples grew on trees," Hannah says. She has said this before, has said it, in fact, every single time that we have sat here and contemplated these fields. I have shown her everything in Swaziland, driven her round the whole tiny kingdom. I have taken her to swim and play tennis, and to meet my colleagues who grinned and shook her hand and told her how wonderful I was. She has bought everything: carvings, baskets, mats, cloths, all of them lying arrayed on her bed in my spare room while she tries to work out how to pack it all to take home tomorrow. A Sunday-afternoon stillness has descended and now we have nothing left to do but sit and nothing left to talk about but those damned pineapples.

Hannah rubs her peeling nose. "I've still a few pictures I'd like to take," she says. "And I wanted to go back for one of those little elephants at the market for my mum. And you promised me you'd take me up to see your friend Bongani's farm."

Ah yes. My friend, my real Swazi friend. We'd sat up late last night, drinking too much gin, and I had poured out the real frustrations of living and working in paradise. I have been here eighteen months and I have made precisely one Swazi friend.

"He was the first Swazi I really met – he picked me up from the airport. He used to be the driver here. For something like three weeks, when I was setting the project up, we must have driven together over every inch of this country." But he'd been more than a driver, of course. He'd ended up translating for me when my basic *siSwati* ran out, and when the women whose small businesses I was supposed to be supporting proved too shy to talk to the white woman. He was the one who quietly told me I shouldn't wear trousers in the rural areas, and the one who taught me to sit patiently under a tree outside a homestead while the chief in the area decided whether to greet me or not. Whenever I needed him I'd always find him there waiting, parked up in some shady spot, at the appointed hour and place. Even after he'd taken severance and set himself up in business on his farm, the one he'd always spoken about starting, the easy pattern of our friendship had continued.

"You know, so many people who come here find it hard to make friends with Swazis," I'd told Hannah as the smoke from the mosquito coil drifted up in one unravelling skein between us. "Really, we're all the same under the skin. I get on as well with Bongani and his family as I do with half the English volunteers out here."

"And he's the real Africa, eh?" Hannah said. She did it to wind me up because I had been correcting her all fortnight. Africa is a continent, not a country, and Swaziland was no more Africa than Switzerland was Europe. But even as I corrected her again it struck me with the clarity that alcohol can bring that Hannah did have to see something real, not just the tourist version of Swaziland she was taking home with her. And not the sullen young men who gathered around when they saw our white skin, the children begging for sweeties.

I had planned it out, the perfect way to round off her trip: Bongani showing her his dam and his sprinkler system, the new shoots coming up from the expensive hybrid French beans that were destined for the South African market. We could sit on his porch instead of mine and take in his view while he told her about the tractor he was saving up to buy, the truck he would hire to take the first crop down to Johannesburg.

"Bongani is the real deal, anyway," I said to Hannah. "If this country has a future, he's it. He's really making something of his life. Investing in his farm, educating his kids. And all off his own back, no handouts or projects, never asking for a penny. It just goes to show it can be done. It's possible."

The people at work, I told her, the ones who'd shaken her hand and told her God had sent me to them, are the same ones who sit with their feet on the desk and read the newspaper, disappear off with the project vehicles for hours on end, the ones who rush out the door when *shayela* time – four forty-five – comes around. They are the ones who forget meetings and lose letters and vanish to sort out the woes of some cousin or aunt up in Sidvokodvo when they are supposed to be working. They are the people who have never let the surface pleasantries of office life deepen into any real intimacy, not with me, anyway. They are the people who return every weekend back to their families and houses that I've never seen, leaving me alone here among the pineapple fields.

Hannah was still asleep this morning when the phone rang. We'd sat on too late talking and drinking, letting the mosquito coil burn itself out in the velvet night air. The ash was still there, a perfect undisturbed spiral, when I picked up the phone and heard Bongani's voice apologising for calling so early.

"Stephanie, how are you?"

"Bongani, I'm fine. We were talking about you last night, me and my friend from England."

"Oh yes, your friend. I hope she is enjoying Swaziland." He sounded listless.

"What's wrong, Bongani?"

"*Sisi*" – sisi, sister, the way he always addressed me – "it has been bad this week, very bad. That chief I was telling you about?"

"The drunk."

"Hawu, that man can drink! He left his nephew's son to put the cattle away into the kraal and the boy forgot."

I knew what Bongani was going to say next. Last time I'd been at the farm we'd gone out to look at the field of bean seedlings poking through the earth. Hundreds of pairs of heart-shaped leaves, fresh and green, glistening from the spray of the sprinkler. His youngest boy, Mandla, had been swinging on the loose fence post and Bongani had pretended to scold him.

"I should have fixed that fence post." But he had been busy and the chief had been a drunk and the boy had been forgetful.

"The beans?" I asked

"All of them." I could hear over the hiss of the phone line the deep breath he took as he nerved himself. "Stephanie, I must ask you please to help us. We must pay Mandla's school fees very soon. And he needs a uniform. But we need to plant more beans and the school money is all I have. Three hundred rand. Please. I will pay you back, if you will lend it to me now."

Thirty pounds. The price of a boy's education. The cost of a friendship.

After I had put down the phone I went out and swept up all the ash from the mosquito coil, scattering its poisonous dust to the winds. Hannah – sleepy-eyed, fragile-faced – came out and asked me what was wrong.

"Nothing, nothing, nothing," I muttered, and she wandered back inside, used to my moods.

Hannah suddenly takes charge, the way she always has done, the way she did when we met aged fourteen through an accident of surnames, seated side by side in double French.

"Come on, we can't sit moping on the porch all afternoon on my last day. Let's go and see this famous Bongani of yours and then I'll try and blow the rest of my holiday money." The three hundred rand burns in my pocket. I'd nipped out earlier to fetch milk, taking it out of the cashpoint without Hannah to witness. I will slip it to him discreetly when she isn't watching. He will be grateful and humble, and Jabulile will come out and bless me for my generosity. Hannah will take everyone's photograph and go home, happy that she's seen the real fucking Africa.

Bongani's farm is at the end of a track that's no more than two paths running parallel across the side of a field. The house is in a grove of banana trees and papaya trees on the side of a terraced hill. It's not the usual cluster of little huts but a three-roomed house, square, with a pitched tin roof and unfinished render. I have to take the track slowly because my little car hasn't much clearance and I lean forward, peering for rocks that could take its sump out.

As we make the turn from the road a little girl I don't recognise stares at us as we pass. Another one, younger – four years old maybe, it's hard to say – in a torn, dirt-coloured dress runs beside us as we bump carefully along. She isn't smiling or waving or even looking at us, just running, seriously, as if it were her job to run alongside the car, keeping pace with it. She is so close she makes me nervous I might hit her and that's how I take my eyes off the track, just long enough to miss seeing the tortoise. When I do see it I take it for a rock and shift my approach so that the wheel goes over it, to save the car's underside. Only at the last minute do I see the swift tuck of the head into the shell. To swerve again would be to hit the girl, to brake would send me into a skid on the loose dirt surface. We hear the thump and clatter as we hit it and then I come to a careful stop. In the silence after I switch off the engine, Hannah clears her throat.

"Millennia of evolution undone by the invention of the motor car."

"Thanks," I say.

When we get out, the children are gathered round the cracked shell. The tortoise is still waving one leg feebly. Its eye opens briefly, and then its mouth. The little girl goes to poke it with a stick and I want to slap her.

"We should put it out of its misery," I say, but I have no idea how.

The tortoise lays its head down and I can see it panting. Bongani comes striding over, a tall man, still striking.

"Bongani, you have to kill it."

"*Sisi*, no one can kill a tortoise," he says.

"I can't bear to watch it."

Bongani laughs and picks it up in one big hand. The tortoise tries to retreat into its ruined shelter. "Next time don't drive over it then." He makes as if to throw it and I wince but then he takes pity on me and calls Mandla over to take the tortoise away behind the back of the house. The two girls follow him, the older carrying the younger on her hip.

"Anyway, I am grateful for the visit." He reaches out with his hand. I have learned to do the local handshake smoothly now – first the conventional hold, then moving to grip the thumb, then back down to the hand. I have taught it to Hannah and she tries it now.

"Ah, you are a real Swazi," he tells her, as he always used to tell me. "*Sawubona, sisi.*"

"*Yebo,*" she replies and he laughs again.

"A real Swazi, *sisi*, a real Swazi."

We slip off our shoes and sit on the porch, and Bongani calls to Mandla to get us some roasted mealies, corn cobs. "I have picked some soft ones, the way you white people like them." The two girls watch us from the gate, silently. Bongani tries to beckon them over but they simply stare and he laughs.

"They're from the rural areas, the lowveldt. They haven't seen many white people and they're frightened."

"Who are they, Bongani?"

"They are my daughters – well, you would say I am their uncle. My brother's wife died last week and her family has sent them here. They say my brother made her ill, that he brought the illness into the family. He died and then she died and so they are here."

I have learned not to ask what people die of.

Hannah takes her corn and wanders over to the girls, who creep forward slowly until they can touch her hair. She sits down in the shade of a tree and pulls one dark strand in front of her face and starts to plait it. Encouraged, both the girls join in, one on each side of her, working away with busy fingers.

Bongani and I get down to business. I give him the cash and he puts it away uncounted.

"I will pay you back, *sisi*." He shifts on the porch, talking to a point somewhere beyond my left ear, awkward in a way he has never been before. "I will plant again next week and the beans will be ready in four months. If I get a good price I will have enough maybe for school fees for these two next year. Those beans can fetch a good price."

The money from the beans was supposed to go on improving his irrigation pump, but I just nod. I look at his feet, stretched out in front of him. They are caked with mud from the dam, hard-soled and cracked. Beside them, mine look as soft and pale as the underbellies of fish.

We walk up to the ruin of the field, Bongani and I, and look at it in silence. There is nothing to say. The plants had come on well since I saw them last but now they lie scattered and trampled, creamy flowers broken in the dirt. One sprinkler still spurts madly until finally I can stand it no longer and go and kick it off the hose. We both watch the water pouring out onto the ground and draining uselessly into the soil.

Hannah comes over, her hair stuck out at crazy angles from her head. The braids are already unravelling but she holds a girl with each hand. Bongani shuts off the hose and we all walk back to the porch. Hannah sits down with the smaller girl on her lap while the larger one sits beside her.

"Why can't you kill a tortoise?" Hannah asks. "Is it bad magic or something?"

"Oh no, nothing like that. It's just that they're not easy to kill, in their houses like that. Even a jump from heaven couldn't kill Mr Tortoise. Did you not know? That's how he got the pattern on his shell."

Hannah laughs, the girls laughing uncertainly along with her. "Serves me right for assuming everything in Africa has some sort of magical significance."

On the drive home I am silent and irritated. Hannah is holding a bundle of spinach and four ears of roasted corn that Bongani has given her for the flight tomorrow. She still has a few plaits unravelling in her hair. I say something sour about white tourists coming back from Africa with their hair in braids and she pulls them out, yanking with her fingers at the tangles. We have strained the normal boundary of our friendship, these last two weeks. I am sick of her company yet cross with her for leaving, flying back to England with her souvenirs while I have to stay on, single-handedly trying to make everything in this country work. When we get back, I go to sit on the porch and pour the last of the gin into my glass, and Hannah goes to pack. The tonic ran out a long time ago.

From my seat on the bare concrete of the porch I can see the dark clouds massing, not over the hills but down the valley, building in earnest. It is the time of day when the cattle egrets gather to fly back together to their communal roosts. We have made a ritual of it, Hannah and I, watching them circling, catching the last of the evening sunlight, white against the darkening sky. For a moment I think about not calling her, but then I knock on her door and she comes out to watch them disappear for the last time, both of us standing together, leaning slightly into the strengthening wind. The storm is rushing towards us, sweeping up the light from the fields below. We can see great bursts of lightning and count out loud the seconds until we hear the thunder. In the fields, tiny figures run for shelter but we stand out until the bolts come so thick and fast we can no longer tell one peal of thunder from the next, until the storm is almost overhead and darkness rushes over us. We run inside laughing to unplug the phone and light the candles before the electricity goes off.

We have cold roasted corn and warm beer for supper. Hannah's face glows in the flicker of candle light.

"This is the real Africa," she laughs, as the lightning illuminates the house in a stark burst. I open my mouth to correct her but don't rise to the bait for once. I have forgotten my irritation with her, have forgotten even what it was about. "Which reminds me." She rummages in her bag and hands me a bundle of money. "Give it to Bongani for those poor girls," she says as I count it out. It is almost three hundred rand. "I can't carry anything more back with me and I'd like to see it stay in the country."

"This will send the oldest to school for a year," I say.

"I can't think of anything I'd rather spend it on. Imagine just taking in two kids like that, no fuss or bother, when you've barely enough for yourself. You're so lucky to know a man like Bongani. Oh, and there's another thing." She darts off to her room, half colliding with the door in the gloom. She comes back with a little package, surprisingly heavy for its size.

"I got you an early Christmas present. I wasn't going to give it to you, actually, after this afternoon, but then I thought what the hell."

It is a little soapstone tortoise, beautifully carved. It fits my hand exactly, like a charm.

"You don't have to give me anything," I say.

"Oh but I do. I've had a wonderful holiday, and I owe it all to you."

I shrug. "What else are friends for?"

"Exactly. What else are friends for?"

I say goodbye to Hannah in the airport car park. She'd told me not to wait, busy arranging her luggage on the trolley, homeward bound already.

"It's been great having you," I say, and at the last minute she turns and reaches out to hug me, an awkward collision of shoulders, my hands still half caught in my pockets. By the time I have freed them she is gone, but I stay all the same and watch the plane climb, white against the clouds, glinting once in the sunshine before it disappears.

I should go back to the office but I don't, I go to Bongani's farm, and find him standing in the ruined field with a hoe.

"*Sisi*, I am happy it has rained," he says.

Jabulile, Mandla and the two girls are pulling up the broken plants and piling them by the side of the field. I join in. Every so often we find an undamaged one and surround it with a handful of straw as a mulch. After the storm the air is gin clear and the sun nicely warm on my back. Hill after hill surrounds us, striped with brown as the terraces are ploughed to greet the rain. Bongani tells us about some man he read about in the paper who used his own children as oxen to pull a plough.

"They are saying it is cruelty, but how else can he feed them? These government tractors don't come, or if they come they are broken."

Jabulile says nothing but smiles her secret smile. I stand up and stretch my aching back.

"I feel like you've used me as an ox, Bongani."

We stand at the top of the field and survey our work. I count ten, fifteen, twenty little mounds of straw. The rest of the field is empty and waiting.

"Tomorrow we will plant again."

We sit on the grass together and Mandla pulls out an old mineral-water bottle from the ditch where it has been keeping cool in the shade. He passes it to his father who drinks and then passes it on to me, wiping the mouth of the bottle first with his hand. The water is a cloudy suspension, drawn directly from the dam. Normally I drink only tea at Bongani's house, knowing that at least the water would have been boiled. But I receive the bottle with both hands, as is polite, and drink. What's a little dysentery between friends?

Tomorrow, I think, I will go back to work and worry about the state of the world and the state of the country and the state of my project. I will fret and scold and write reports and take it all upon my shoulders. Today I'm happy just to lean back in the shade of a tree and rest and talk, among friends.

As I stretch to put the bottle back in the ditch I feel something shift, and reach in to my pocket to find Hannah's soapstone tortoise, the warm weight of it, a comfort to my fingers.

"Hey, how is that tortoise, Bongani? The one I ran over?"

He smiles a long slow smile.

"It was delicious, *sisi*."

the original one-foot freedom ride

DANIEL BOURKE

. . . cool and in the breeze the hedgerow is lurching and I try to keep a lid on this panic.

The night is cool and in the breeze the hedgerow is lurching and I try to keep a lid on this panic.

I can hear the sea, just. The lane runs black to where the waves are hissing and breaking and headlights now will be like a midwife's head torch shining in.

In Ilfracombe a deckchair boy once punched the Kaiser.

The bone and muscle of my leg hurt between knee and hip. I can feel a tapping in my pocket; I have felt it for a while.

I hop down from the gate and feel into my jeans, find a blue tobacco tin, faded, with an image of a spoked wheel inside a cogged wheel. It's the Rotary logo. Grandad was a Rotarian. You couldn't smoke in the meetings and when he came home he used to sit in his chair and draw on his cig so deeply you'd think the smoke would never come out. He had a Rotary ashtray, too, lifted at all four corners in the glass-blowing, and you stubbed your lit end into the emblem. A lot of smoking merch, for a place that didn't let you smoke.

I give the tin a shake. The tin goes mad. Something bounces up and down and all around inside the tin. Definitely something alive. Or something charged.

I check my other pocket and find a pocketknife and a head

torch. I put the pocketknife back in my pocket and the head torch on my head and turn it on.

I lift the lid. I lift the lid a little more. There is lots of green grassy muck. It smells wet and earthy inside the tin. There is a toad. A small toad. Thumb-size. It is facing almost away from me so I can only see one of its black eyes. It turns. The wide mouth is set in a stoic frown. He is a scaly khaki with black spots, glistening with wet and slime.

OH, GOD! He leaps somehow towards me, his downthrust pushing the tin into my hand and his head hitting the lid into my fingers and my heart punching my chest and the lid snaps shut and my stomach punches my ribs and there's not enough blood getting to my head.

I met resistance when I closed the lid, I swear it. More than from the ridges on the corners, the ones that keep it shut. Different resistance, a harder kind, and I fear I have caught some part of toad. I fear I have trapped arm or tongue or even head between lid and tin.

The clouds have cleared to unveil a perfect disc of moon, as if an invisible giant is wearing a head torch.

What am I doing here? How did I get here? Did I find the toad up past Hartland Point, near that toadstool-shaped radar station, in one of those gardens that overlook the cliff? Who lived in those houses back then, when people were here?

Was I sitting by a garden pond eating rabbit?

Did I absent-mindedly move my leg and disturb the rushes where a toad, this toad, was happily sat? Did this toad leap for cover, hide under a leaf? But what if his arse was still visible? He thought he was hidden – but with his arse on show.

I always wonder about that radar station. Did it watch for missiles? Or aliens? Or storms? On that headland you used to be washed by the beam of the Hartland lighthouse, and see the distant sweeping flashes of those across the Severn, on Lundy and the coast of Wales. Now you can only see the lights of the town, like a long flat ocean liner. How long will they last? Ilfracombe, where a chair boy once decked the Kaiser.

If I have killed the toad I will force a hole into the tin's bottom and poke my dirt-grey thumb through. Paint black eyes on it and a stoic frown. Who would know the difference?

Easy prey never realises it's easy. That's the point. The light under that leaf would have been soft for the toad, diffused by the foliage he thought was protecting him. He would have sensed a dimming as the lid bore down on him. Would have felt the disturbance in the bank as the tin itself forced up through the muck to trap him from under.

In my hand the jumping in the tin resumes. Not dead, then, although there can't be much oxygen inside. My fingers are pressing down in a fear grip, a C chord, the natural angle of the human clasp. I lift the tin to inspect the damage and the jumping stops. This side, some fronds of grass straggle down but there is nothing that seems to be part of animal. The jumping starts again, concentrated on the other side. I turn the tin.

A three-pronged foot of toad, on a leg snapped and trapped by the lid, dances.

I clench my hand even tighter and the tin starts to buckle. I rest the tin on the gatepost and walk away, go down onto my haunches in the lane. My dirty temples sweat.

I stand. I take out my pocketknife, unfold its blade, pick up the tin, and as I cut off the limb the knife loudly scrapes on the metal. The leg falls onto my T-shirt; I brush it off with the knife. I open the lid a crack to free the toad's stump then squeeze it shut, put the tin back on the gatepost. I am back down on my haunches in the middle of the lane.

The clouds are thinning around the moon, a blurred glow in the sky. I open my thumb and forefinger to crush its face. The flap of skin on my hand, the webbing, is much bigger than it ought to be. Overstretched.

I need to put some air holes in the tin if this toad is going to survive long term. I could use the pocketknife. But I need a rock to hammer the blade so the knife doesn't close on my hand.

The night is getting colder. I can feel it where my T-shirt doesn't quite reach my arse. But my head is still hot and slimy in the hair.

My forearm, the inside, the side that's not hairy, seems greeny yellow in the sky's maternal light. I should sit down again. I might not be well. But I see what looks like a good rock in the ditch by the lane. It holds perfectly, fits my hand like a breast.

The clouds are moving fast and the light is changing: paler in some places and darker in others. Time is passing.

I hit the knife with the rock to punch holes in the lid for the toad.

I hit the knife with the rock to punch holes in the lid for the toad.

I hit the knife with the rock to punch holes in the lid for the toad.

The moon is casting pools of white on the lane. Clouds hang in the distance, uplit amber by Ilfracombe, where a deckboy kiboshed the punch-chair.

Down the lane a light or some lights are approaching; light or lights have appeared down the lane. There are lights on the lane. There is light on the lane and it is heading here . . .

\ \ \

signal on the headset gets a bit clearer. Fragments of sentences come through now. It's like the first time you wore headphones, the sounds not in your ears but inside your head.

". . . and I remember cycling very fast down a hill, aware of the danger of falling off but thrilled by . . ."

You're pulled again and you shuffle again. And then you are falling. The headset noise pitches up like a churning river but the voices are louder, too. Words bubble out at you.

". . . was in the antechamber and this guy said . . ." . . . ". . . generally you know he is going to be at his worst when . . ." . . . ". . . candles . . ." . . . ". . . seventeen . . ."

\ \

driving into the sun – what you assume to be the sun – which is shielded by the clouds but still manages to hurt your eyes because they are already pained with the tiredness of driving. There is so much light; the cloud must be really thin, or the sun really bright, or near. You can barely hold your eyes open as you look up. You are driving these dales in this white van and your eyes and the foot are tired. You pull over so you can rest and eat a little rabbit. Your stump has a dull throb of pain. Thank fuck the van is automatic – the original one-foot freedom ride. You put on the handbrake. It is a nice spot, a lookout with a wide view west but sheltered in other directions by the dip. On the horizon it looks like rain, but the fields in the foreground are bright with sunlight.

You cannot stay long because you need to finish this journey, to get off this road. You pinch your Adam's apple. It feels soft – in fact your whole throat feels soft, or rather tenderly tough, like when you had mumps.

You hear jumping in the back of the van; your passenger is restless, perhaps because you've stopped. You are relieved you made air holes. Old Transits can leak fumes.

You need some air so you get out and hop over to a gate. On the ridge by the horizon the flat empty line of a motorway hovers. The van has a blue cogged wheel painted on it, with a spoked wheel inside. There are toadstools by the fence. At the top of the short hill behind you is a stone burial chamber, three upright surfboard shapes and one balanced on the top.

The day is getting brighter. It's like the light from one place has shifted and is concentrating in clusters elsewhere, leaving dark patches behind.

There was definitely some resistance when you slammed the door of the van.

There was definitely some resistance, something soft yet tenderly tough crushed in the door.

The light dips, a dark cloud comes over the hill behind you. An engine. To the east in the dusk the glow of what must be headlights is

\

The Girl in the Glass Tower

ELIZABETH FREMANTLE

I s the hammering inside my head?

Tap, tap, tap, in the soft place beneath my temple, in the matter where my thoughts live.

Something, someone, tapping, wants to be heard, to escape.

It is a subtle and prolonged species of torture, this noise, reminding me of the impossibility of freedom.

I am the pane in the window overlooking the courtyard; I am cracked in two places but still manage to hold my form. Through the glass the world is distorted, divided into three parts, each with its own perspective, none of them quite true.

Tap, tap, tap.

It is the sound of my youth. For months and months they have been renovating the rooms beneath mine. I try to keep my mind on the clean smell that drifts up: whitewash and freshly sawn timber. My maid surprises me on the floor, nose pressed to a crack in the boards to breathe it in. It takes me far into the past, and somewhere back there I believe I will find a way to make sense of things, of the shape of my life, the shape of me.

I am taken back to another tower, the little Stand Tower at Chatsworth; I was nine. I know that because it was the year the boy to whom I was betrothed died. He was the Earl of Leicester's son, not even out of babyhood; I never met him but there was much talk of it among the servants. They said that since Leicester, despite all his efforts, never achieved the throne by marriage to the Queen, then his son might instead, by wedding the Queen's most likely heir – that was me.

The walls inside the Stand Tower were cool to the touch and left a powdery residue on the tip of my finger. The door was propped up to one side, waiting to be fitted. Everything was coated in a film of fine sawdust and the stone flags were scattered with pretty curls of shaved wood. I picked one up and threaded it on my finger, holding up my small hand to admire it. Noticing the dirt beneath my nails, I imagined the fuss Nurse would make later, glad Grandmother was away in London on business, otherwise, never mind my grubby nails, I would not have dared to be up at the Stand Tower without permission and with only a stable lad for company.

I poked my head out from the entrance to ensure Tobias was not peeping, but he was seated on the bottom step humming tunelessly, with his back to me, as good as his word. The ponies were tearing at a tussock of grass nearby; everything was green and full of promise. Or was it? Surely it was late summer then and the land must have been parched – though perhaps there had been rain, for I feel sure I remember the soft squelch of mud underfoot.

Memories are like that cracked pane of glass with its subtle distortions. *Tap, tap, tap.*

I stepped into the shady interior and unbuckled my satchel, pulling out a crumpled pair of breeches pilfered from the laundry, giving them a shake. Little eddies of dust danced and wood shavings skittered over the floor.

I remember clearly the thrill that passed through me as I held those breeches up to my body. "If only you'd been a boy." Grandmother's refrain circled about my head. I stepped into them, tugging them over my shoes, not caring about the mud that smeared my white stockings. Bunching my layers of skirt in one hand, I tied the breeches' tapes as best I could. They were much too big, puffing out wide, and were cuffed above the knee.

The idea had come to me from a troupe of players that had visited Chatsworth in the spring. I was allowed to stay up that night and watch them perform a comedy with a girl disguised as a boy – though truly it was a boy actor pretending to be a girl disguised as a boy – which had us all, even Grandmother, laughing until our cheeks ached. I had thought a good deal about it, tried to imagine what it might be like to be a boy, to go about unencumbered by skirts, to ride astride, to be at the heart of things instead of on the edges, to be listened to even when you spoke nonsense, like my baby boy cousin whose infant burblings were a source of wonder for Aunt Mary and Uncle Gilbert.

I fumbled with the fastening of my skirt; the knot was too tight, tied double and wouldn't undo. I was tempted to ask Tobias for help but didn't dare; it was enough, already, persuading him to go up there with me, though he didn't seem to mind that it might have caused him misfortune if we were caught. Exasperated with the stubborn knot I yanked hard. Something gave, with a crack of broken threads, and the skirt – petticoats, bum-roll and all – fell in a heap at my feet.

I began to experiment with my new-found liberty, striding back and forth, one hand on my hip as if perched at the hilt of a sword, drawing it, lunging forward with a jabbing motion towards an imagined adversary. Girding myself then, I sidled out to stand at the top of the steps. Tobias was busy scraping mud off his boots with a penknife. I hollered, a kind of battle cry, as much as a nine-year-old girl can make such a sound, and took the steps two at a time, making a final running leap to land before him.

He jumped up in shock and then, seeing me, clapped a hand over his mouth. Only then was I aware of the sight I must have been, my boned satin bodice atop the voluminous creased breeches and my filthy stockings all wrinkled about my ankles.

"Highness!" was all he could manage.

"Don't call me that. Just for today can you not pretend I am any old girl playing dress-up?" I secretly wanted to tell him to call me Charles, to make believe just for an hour that I was a boy and named after the father who was an empty space in my memory.

He looked aghast, as if I had asked him to denounce God. "What should I call you, then?"

"Call me whatever you want, anything but *that*."

He opened his mouth to speak but said nothing.

Not knowing what to do with the awkwardness, I sprang at him, thrusting with my imaginary sword. "*En garde!*"

He laughed then, drawing his own pretend blade from its pretend scabbard, raising it to meet my own. We danced back and forth, slashing and swiping until he saw his chance and pounced forward. "*Touché!*"

I collapsed to the ground with a terrible howl, clutching my chest.

He was still laughing, quite red-faced with it, as I prepared to mount my pony. Dancer tossed his head, rattling his bridle, sensing my excitement.

I whispered into the hollow of his ear, "Just you wait, boy. Together we're going to fly," then realised with a thud of disappointment that of course he wore a woman's saddle. There would be no flying, just the usual sedate lumbering canter. I began to unravel, as if a thread had been pulled somewhere inside me, and didn't know what to do so I did nothing, just stood looking into the valley, fighting my distress.

I had a clear view of Chatsworth. I could see Uncle Henry in the mews with the head falconer; I recognised his bright-blue cape. I liked Uncle Henry. He said he had "magic hands" and could make things disappear. When he got his cards out and began flicking and flipping them, people were drawn to wager he couldn't, but he could; I had seen it with my very own eyes.

Someone was shaking a red Turkey carpet from one of the windows like a flag and wisps of pale smoke rose from the chimneys in the forbidden wing where the Queen of Scotland was housed. Her convoy had arrived from Wingfield a few days before, under heavy guard, and the Chatsworth staff were all grumbling about the extra work. I could see the day-watch in the courtyard below her apartments and a mounted pair, with muskets slung over their shoulders, patrolling the east entrance. All at once I knew what to do. I unbuckled Dancer's girth strap, lifting that wrong-shaped saddle off, propping it on the steps.

"Are you sure?" Tobias had the same look of concern he'd worn when I'd asked him to accompany me to the tower. "What if some harm should befall you? Riding bareback is –"

"You may be four years my senior, Master Toby, but I am at least as good a rider as you and you know it." It was true; I was a natural in the saddle, everyone said it. "Besides –" I was about to remind him that he was obliged to obey me but stopped myself, for I had stepped into a place where the normal rules didn't apply.

I led Dancer to the steps and swung my leg over his round, piebald rump, marvelling once again at the freedom the breeches offered. "Good boy." I leaned forward, resting my cheek against his neck, whispering, "You'll fly like Pegasus."

Once out of the copse and onto open land we picked up our speed, galloping faster and faster, hooves thundering, the wind in my face, hair streaming in my wake. Pleasure simmered in me. It was as I had imagined, exactly: being a comet shooting over the sky, an arrow fired from a bow, a bird soaring, a lead bullet whistling. In that moment I was untouchable. I wanted to wrap the feeling in my handkerchief and keep it in my pocket for ever. The sensation returns to me across the years – the illusion of freedom is so complete I feel as incorporeal as a current of air that could blow through the crack in the window.

We eventually slowed to a walk as we reached the cover of trees. Tobias, who had been following on his own horse in anxious pursuit, drew alongside me, saying, "Why did you want to do this?"

"I don't know . . . To know what it would be like." I couldn't find adequate words to describe the sensation of joy, of liberty, of vigour, but he seemed satisfied. I realise now, after all this time, that the thing I always sought above everything, above the crown, above love or matrimony, was freedom.

"You won't tell anyone?" I said, but didn't really need to ask, for Tobias had already pledged his silence and he was good at keeping secrets; he had kept secrets for me before. He'd said nothing when he found me once on the roof leads after dark. I had gone up there to look at the moon, or so I told him, but truly I had gone there out of curiosity, and too much curiosity was not supposed to be a good thing in a girl, or so Grandmother liked to remind me. I hadn't thought to ask Tobias what *he* was doing up there, when he belonged in the stables. Nurse said I was a secretive child. Which I took to mean that Nurse thought me dishonest, but there is a difference between keeping secrets and telling lies.

"You have my word," he assured me.

"Let's not go back just yet." We were already at the Stand

Tower once more, dismounting. I wanted to eke out that moment of stolen freedom before having to truss myself back into my skirt and return to the house where my tutor awaited with his book of Latin verbs. "Let's go up!"

The staircase was tightly spiralled and steep and unlit. I mounted cautiously with one hand on the wall, which was chill and damp as pastry. I imagined I was a knight rescuing a maiden. Round and round the stairs went, until we arrived at a chamber flooded with light from four large curved windows. There was a rotten stench from the corner.

It was an ordinary, small, brown-speckled bird, lying belly up, its twig claws clutched into tiny fists.

"Nightingale," said Tobias. He picked it up firmly as if shaking someone's hand. "Must have flown in through an open window and not found its way out again."

I couldn't get the thought of that small bird out of my head, flapping wildly, bead eyes swivelling, flying terrified at the panes, mistaking the glass for sky and eventually losing all hope. *Tap, tap, tap.*

Tobias opened the window and threw the little carcass out. For some reason I had expected it to float down like a feather but it dropped hard, as if its bones were filled with lead. We stood for a while in silence.

"You been up here before?" he asked.

"Yes." I could see the guards searching a delivery cart in the Chatsworth courtyard. "Before this tower was built. With my mother." Remembering Mother felt as if someone had tied a rope about my heart with a slipknot. "She's dead."

Tobias lowered his head and, after a silence, pointed towards the house. "She's your aunt on your father's side, isn't she?"

I didn't understand immediately that he was talking of the Queen of Scots until he added, "It's a terrible thing that she should be shut away for all those years and her own son sitting on *her* throne."

It was not clear to me how the Queen of Scots' situation had come to pass; I only knew what Grandmother had told me, with lips pursed in undisguised disapproval: "She was foolish in love and paid insufficient heed to good advice. Given half a chance she'd push our Queen off her throne and take it for herself."

What I did know was that she had been in my step-grandfather's custody, at one or other of his houses, for a very long time. She used to have greater freedom and walk in the gardens, even ride out and hunt occasionally, under guard. But things had changed and she was now kept under close watch with no visitors and had to take her air on the roof leads. Those were the orders of Queen Elizabeth.

"She'd like to see you" – Tobias was whispering, despite the fact there was no one to hear – "I promised I would bring you to her."

"But it is forbidden –" I stopped. Was this why he had so readily agreed to accompany me up to the Stand Tower; he wanted a favour in return? "Do you serve her? I thought you served my grandmother."

"In a manner of speaking."

I didn't question him further, for it was clear from his crossed arms and floorward gaze that he wouldn't say more. Suddenly I felt very young, too young to understand things, but I could not deny my desire to see the Scots Queen, and what greater temptation is there than that which is forbidden?

As I slunk across the great high chamber, a sound startled me, sending my heart thudding as if it had a mind to burst right out of my chest, but it was only a log falling in the fire. Once in the long gallery I moved faster, keeping close to the wall. I stopped, holding my breath as I heard the unmistakable slap of slippered feet. Ducking behind a tapestry, I waited as the steps moved past, their rhythmic *pat, pat* punctuating another sound, a *clickety-click* that conjured in my mind the chink of the fat pearls Grandmother wore in four heavy strands to below her waist. But no, Grandmother was in London. All sorts of imagined scenarios assaulted my thoughts: a change of plan, a lost wheel on the coach, plague in the capital. Only as the sound was receding did I dare peep, and saw the back of one of the laundry maids with a creaking basket of linens. Relief gushed through me; but I sensed myself drawn to the danger and the idea of having a proper secret, something real and important.

As Tobias had told me, there was only a single guard outside the forbidden apartments. I suppose, now I think of it, it must all have been carefully arranged, but at the time my understanding was slight. He knocked on the door with the butt of his halberd: three sharp knocks in quick succession, a pause, and then two slow ones. It opened and a hand reached out, beckoning me into the room. The latch clicked shut behind me.

The chamber was dimly lit and there was a general rustling as the women, who were scattered about, put their embroidery frames and books to one side and dropped to the floor, heads bowed. I felt a laugh pressing at my throat. I was used to the servants' deference but these were well-born ladies and I a mere child. Unsure of the correct way to behave, I stood gawping at them for what seemed an age, wondering if I was supposed to give some command, a gesture, to indicate that they were free to go about their business. Then at some invisible cue they all rose and returned to their needlework or whatever it was I'd interrupted.

I cast my eyes around for the Queen, who was said to be a great beauty; one or two of those women were comely enough, but I reasoned that a queen got on her knees for no one, save God. A pebble of disappointment dropped into me. I had expected to find her glorious, seated beneath a canopy of state, festooned in jewels and haloed in gold light, like in the cobwebby paintings of the saints that were stored away in the cupboard at the back of the chapel. Grandmother had scolded me for "putting my nose where it didn't belong" when I asked her what they were doing there. I was puzzled by those paintings, for I knew it was wrong to revere the saints, and supposed that must have been the reason they were gathering dust in the dark.

There was a movement in the corner and a woman I hadn't noticed heaved herself up from a prayer stand, stepping into view. She was tall as a man and stout with it.

"Ah," she said, opening her arms wide. "Let me look at you. Come, my eyesight is not what it was." Her voice was odd, not quite French like the dance master and not quite Scottish like the head falconer, but a mixture of the two.

I stood rooted to the spot, again unsure of how to behave. This great lumpen matron dressed in black was surely not the beautiful Queen of Scotland? That pebble of disappointment seemed to swell. But then I saw something, a haughtiness in her demeanour, a spark of pride in the eyes, that made me drop in a curtsy all the way down to the floor.

"Up, up," the Queen said. "Come and sit with me."

The ladies hustled round, procuring a pair of chairs, which they placed by the hearth. The Queen lowered herself into one, fitting her bulk tightly between its arms, and patted her lap with the command, "Up, Geddon," for a small dog to jump onto it.

"Mary, would you bring us something to drink," she said. "We have three Marys here: Mary Devlin" – she pointed to a woman who was filling two cups from a ewer – "and two more there" – she waved an arm in the general direction of the embroiderers. "And *I* am Mary, of course. There is your aunt, Mary Talbot, too, though we never see her these days. It's a shame. I was fond of her." She crossed herself, something I had only ever seen done once, by one of the stable lads; the head groom had cuffed him for it. "All named for the blessed Virgin." She pointed towards the prayer stand, where a painting of the Virgin, puce-cheeked with a brilliant-blue gown, dandling a plump, haloed baby, was hung. Only then did I notice a large jewelled crucifix in a corner and the rosary beads that hung from all the ladies' girdles. Everybody knew the Scottish Queen was Catholic but, seeing those prohibited objects, things the household chaplain denounced in his sermons as the tools of heresy, reminded me of the strangeness of that other faith.

I couldn't help but think about the stories I had heard the servants whisper, of Catholics who tried to poison Queen Elizabeth, who sought to destroy all we knew to be good and right, and the priests being dragged from hiding places hardly bigger than rat holes and taken to the Tower for interrogation. When they sat in my bedchamber and believed me asleep my maids often discussed what happened there. I would spread my limbs out in the bed and try to imagine what it might be like to be stretched on the rack. I had never questioned the wickedness of Catholics, but the Scottish Queen, smiling and petting her dog, seemed as far from an enemy as a robin from a raven.

"Your parents chose a Scottish name for you. Not really a name you think of for an English queen, is it? But just as well you are not a Mary, too. That would be most confusing, though I would like to think you had been named for me. I suppose that would have been too much to expect, given that I am such a wicked woman." She emitted a small, bitter laugh. "But I am so very glad to have this chance to see you, Arbella." She reached out and squeezed my hand tightly.

My first instinct was to snatch it back. It had been drummed into me from infancy that I, as royalty, must never be touched without permission, but I reasoned that would not apply to a queen and so left it sitting limply in hers. She smiled openly and warmly. Grandmother never really smiled, though she often told me she loved me; she said a smile made a person seem meek. I wondered about that, for the scriptures said meekness was a virtue, that the meek would inherit the earth, but Grandmother was not to be questioned. She was strict and inflexible and capable of turning a whole room to her attention just by clearing her throat. By contrast, the Scottish Queen's smile made me feel safe and, in some peculiar way, though that royal aunt of mine was a complete stranger and an enemy of sorts, profoundly loved.

"I am to be moved to Tutbury and it occurred to me that we might never be under the same roof again." She sighed, sinking into her seat, like an ancient house settling. "Tutbury is hell itself." She crossed herself once more.

Leaning in close enough for me to smell the aniseed on her breath, she continued, "You see, I have always thought of you as something like a daughter. My son" – her voice cracked as she said it and I was aware of all the women craning in to listen – "I fear my son is lost to me."

"I am sorry for that." I meant it from the bottom of my heart, thinking of my own mother and how even death could not break our bond.

"My little James, your cousin, the King of Scotland" – her tone was momentarily hard and then softened – "what a bonny infant he was." She gripped my hand very hard. "His mind has been poisoned against me."

I didn't know how to reply, just repeated, "I am very sorry for that."

"Now, I *know* you have been raised in the new faith, my dear, but you are yet young. What age are you? Nine, I think. Am I right?"

I nodded.

"Fresh as a new shoot." There was that tender smile once more. "I want you to remember this. Whatever you have been taught to believe, the Catholic faith is the true faith. It is the only path that leads to the Kingdom of Heaven." She placed her palms together as if in prayer. "Despite what has befallen me, I know it is God's plan and I have faith in His wisdom. If He had meant for me to have the throne of England, then it would have been mine – I suspect He has other plans for me."

I had never heard anyone talk of God in such a way; it was as if the Queen knew Him intimately, as if He were her own father. God for me was something intangible and frightening.

"It is my hope that one day, my dearest child, you will see what a comfort the true faith is. Ask your Aunt Mary, Mary Talbot. She will tell you."

"Aunt Mary?" My head had begun to churn with all that new information.

"If the English throne was not my destiny then it is surely yours, and when you have achieved it, I will be up there watching over you and your Catholic England." She had a beatific look on her face as if she had been visited by a host of angels. "You are my hope, Arbella." With that she released my hand again and took something out from beneath her gown, a small wooden box, which she opened, removing a flat elliptical object from it. "I want you to have this, as a reminder of our meeting."

I took it. It was like a ring without its shank. One side was a smooth disc of red stone; on its other, set into a bed of gold, was an oval of translucent milky substance bearing the impression of a lamb. I didn't know what to say; it seemed so very precious.

"It is an Agnus Dei," she told me.

"The Lamb of God."

"You know your Latin. Good girl." There was that smile again, deep and inviting. "It has been blessed by His Holiness the Pope," she whispered, "and will protect you. But do *not* let anyone see it. I'm afraid these days an Agnus Dei can visit trouble on its owner." She sighed and the smile disappeared. "But earthly trouble is sometimes the price we must pay for heavenly grace."

I wanted to ask what she meant – how could it at once protect and visit trouble? But I said nothing.

Less than three years later the Queen of Scotland was gone. I wondered if she had been executed because she no longer had the protection of her Agnus Dei.

Tap, tap, tap.

My fingers wander now to the silk purse that hangs from my girdle containing my treasures: the weighted die that Uncle Henry gave me once, to remind me things aren't always as they seem; the tiny bell from Geddon's collar; the fold of parchment containing a lock of my husband's hair; the smooth crystal drop from the glassworks at Hardwick; the scrap of paper bearing Mistress Lanyer's poem, which is about me, but a me I no longer know. Right at the bottom, beneath everything, is the Agnus Dei, blessed by the Pope. It has not protected me very well.

Tap, tap, tap.

"The Girl in the Glass Tower" is the first chapter of the novel of the same name (Michael Joseph, 2016)

Thinking About Sleep

JOHN FORDE

Mornings are my favourite time with you.

This morning you are quiet and still. You lie on your back, solid and unmovable as stone, but not so cold. Your body is warm, the lines in your brow softened into marble smoothness. It's early yet; the only sounds are the whirring of the heat pump, programmed by you to switch on in the night. I curl into you, resting my head on your shoulder, and blow softly on your ear, bidding you to wake.

Your ability to fall asleep, no matter where you are – the armchair, front-row seats at the theatre, the red-eye from a conference in Sydney – is both a wonder and profoundly irritating. On good nights, I manage three or four hours, flickering between sleep and waking like a swimmer struggling to break through the water's surface. Mostly, I stay awake into the wee hours, staring at the hairline cracks in the ceiling, and polishing the punch lines for the jokes I'll tell at your funeral, while you lie beside me, snoring like a bassoon.

You always wake up clear-headed, cheerfully oblivious to the possibility of life without eight hours of restful sleep. "Morning, Tiger," you say, leaning in for a kiss – always full on the lips, your stubble tickling my cheek. You swing your rugby player legs out of bed, and slip on the threadbare bathrobe you won't let me throw away. "Off for a pee," you announce, as if this will surprise me. I hear the thundering of the toilet plumbing, and you return with the breakfast tray. Your tea is white and milky, with three heaped spoonfuls of sugar. My coffee is dark and oily, brewed Turkish style, the grounds nestling at the bottom of the cup like sand.

"Dark and bitter – like my soul," I say, as I take my first sip.

"There's nothing wrong with your soul." You bite into your toast, the honey and butter running down your chin. "Your arse is getting saggy, though."

Then you collect the cups and plates and slide the tray under the bed, disturbing the dust balls that we're too arthritic to reach. "Time for a cuddle," you say: a brisk but affectionate round of fellatio. By nine, you're out the door to walk Oscar. He waddles behind you, a tree branch in his mouth, with a look of well-bred outrage when he realises it's just to the corner store and back. "He learned that look from you," you say, as you close the front gate.

On Sundays, Oscar is left to scratch and yelp at the bedroom door as we stay in bed – you with the weekend paper, still an evangelist for the printed word, while I flick listlessly through my iPad. We still manage a fuck once or twice a week, laughing as we negotiate the cruelties of old age: your sciatica, my creaking joints, the occasional failure to get beyond half-mast. Then you fall asleep, always facing me, one arm stretched out as if grasping for something in your dream. When I turn away, you pull me close again, your chest hair scratching my back, your cock pressing sleepily against my thigh. In our early days, I wriggled away from you – you were too hot and hairy, like a fur coat on a summer's day. Now the bed feels cold and empty until you clamber in beside me: naked, barrel-chested, furry, still schoolboyishly excited to find me next to you. I can count on one hand the times we have slept in separate beds. Otherwise, here we have slept and fucked, argued, eaten, watched television and grown old and tired together.

This morning there is no need to move. Pale light peeks through the folds of the curtains. In the garden, a tui starts its melancholy song. I turn away from you and push my legs into the cooler depths of the sheets, my toes searching for the edge of the mattress.

The bed was our first joint purchase: breathtakingly expensive, especially for you, the dedicated budgeter and clipper of supermarket coupons. You came home from the climate-change conference in Wellington, brimming with nerdish excitement.

"The hotel beds were amazing. Super King size. The mattress was so thick you could sleep through an earthquake."

"There was an earthquake?"

"No. You're missing the point."

The point was always clear. You'd been raised a rung or two above poor white trash in South Auckland – living in your school uniform, sharing a room with younger brothers, contorting your six-foot-four frame into a single bed until your wretched mother kicked you out at sixteen. How thrilling it must have been for you to find a place to fit in, without apology or discomfort.

The next weekend, we walked to the furniture warehouse on Stuart Street, our hands stuffed in our pockets against the cold. You thumbed through the catalogues like a bookie searching for a sure bet. The mattress would be shipped from overseas, the walnut base so big that it would need to be dismantled to get through our front door.

"It'll be worth it," you said. "We spend a third of our life asleep."

"Well, *you* do."

The salesgirl peered at us through kohl-rimmed eyes. "Which one of you is it for?"

I stared at her coolly. "Both of us."

"Oh, ri-i-i-ight." She grimaced, then turned back to her computer and jabbed viciously at the keyboard. "It's going to take weeks to get here. Are you sure I can't interest you in a futon?"

"No thanks," you said, smiling at her as you wrote out the cheque. "Just call us when it's ready."

We wove our way through the beige lounge suites towards the exit. "What a little cunt," I muttered. "Has anyone told her the law's changed?"

You shrugged your shoulders. "She's young, that's all."

I was testy and itching for a fight. "Why do you always have to think the best of people?"

"You're cute when you get angry."

As we approached the sliding doors, you turned and waved

her goodbye, then dropped your hand to my arse and gave it a firm squeeze.

The day the bed arrived, I darted around nervously, offering the delivery men cups of tea that they left half drunk on the windowsills. You chatted with the hot younger one, helping him lift the frame into place, double-checking the angles with your spirit level. "At least something here'll be straight," you joked, making him laugh. You always had the knack of talking to straight men as equals, not rivals or potential conquests, and they were drawn to you as easily as I seemed to repel them. I stalked into the back garden and smoked a resentful cigarette, burying the butt in your vegetable patch.

When they were gone, we made up the bed with orange floral sheets gifted by my mother: hideous, but roomy enough to stretch over the giant mattress.

You put your arm around my shoulders. "What do you think?"

"Let's go to Ikea."

"Good idea. Then we can christen this big fella tonight."

I sat on the bed and looked up at you. "Ikea can wait."

We met in a bed – in the dying hours of Gemma's end-of-term party. I'd arrived with my boyfriend, Adam, a rock-climbing instructor with killer abs and perpetually dirty fingernails. Like most of my exes, he was intensely angry, which made for great sex and a lousy time anywhere else. He hated Gemma's clique – the Cool Kids of Death, he called them, in a rare display of wit – and was gorgeously out of place at her parties. It wasn't until the bottle opener went missing and I went to borrow his Swiss Army knife that I realised he'd gone.

"Fuck," I said, half to myself. And then I noticed you – leaning against the fridge in the kitchen, a full foot taller than the others. You were staring at me, a perfect poker face: composed and alert, revealing nothing.

I put down my wine glass and walked up to you. "Got the time?" An unoriginal line, though in my defence, I didn't actually know the time. Gemma thought clocks were bourgeois, and my ironic Thomas the Tank Engine watch had run out of puff that morning.

You raised your wrist silently and showed me your watch – a simple round clock face with Roman numerals, the kind a grandmother would give for a birthday present. Tufts of your arm hair clustered around the strap like overgrown shrubbery.

"It's getting late," you said. Your eyes were huge and brown, and vaguely plaintive, like a concerned Doberman. "Reckon I'll head off shortly."

"OK, thanks," I muttered. I was uncertain about flirting with you, but now I was annoyed to be deprived of the opportunity. I pushed past you and went in search of a bottle opener and an easier source of distraction.

An hour later, Gemma and I were snuggled together on her bed. Her mirror ball twirled softly in the half-light, as the Cocteau Twins trilled their exquisite misery on the turntable. "*A-lice, A-lice, A-lice, A-lice, Alice,*" she murmured, clutching a half-empty bottle of Stolichnaya to her chest.

You appeared at the foot of the bed, bearded and unkempt: Jesus in a duffle coat.

"I'm going now," you said, solemn as an executioner. "Want a lift?"

"Sure." I wanted to sound nonchalant, but without Adam I had no easy way of getting home.

"C'mon then." And then you smiled. Your bottom lip was big and fleshy, and I could see the gap between your front teeth. *Dents du bonheur*, the French call them: happy teeth. I smiled back.

"Is she gonna be OK?" you asked. Gemma was asleep, regally beautiful with her Louise Brooks bob and milky skin.

"She's in a K-hole. She won't be back for ages."

I eased the bottle out of her grasp. You rolled her onto her side, and pulled the duvet over her, stopping to brush a lock of hair away from her face. It was strangely moving, to see a man of your size and old-school butchness act with such tenderness.

"C'mon then," you said, more firmly this time.

I slid obediently off the bed, and padded behind as you cut a path through the shadowland of dancing bodies.

It was a clear winter's night. The frost had turned the grass to icicles. In the orange glow of the street lights, the car windows glistened like jewels.

As we inched down the icy footpath, you stopped and wrapped your scarf around my neck. "Here," you said, your breath making ghostly shapes in the air. "Till we get to the car."

"Th-thanks," I said, through chattering teeth.

You unlocked the passenger door first, then walked around the front to let yourself in. "No central locking."

I smiled, unsure if this was a joke or a source of embarrassment. We sat with the motor on, waiting for the engine to warm up. I put my hands over the heater fan, trying not to shiver.

"Didn't that outfit come with a coat?"

"I should've come as Paddington Bear, like you."

"Come here, you cheeky fucker." You pressed yourself into the gear stick and kissed me, holding my face between your big paws. I kissed back, tentatively at first, then with a jolt of excitement as you slipped your tongue into my mouth.

You pulled away and looked at me, a spider's web of saliva dangling from your lips. "I've been wanting to do that all night. Wanna go back to my place?"

The car creaked and rattled as we took the icy corners. You made no small talk, but kept a reassuring hand on my leg between gear changes. It was nearly two by the time we reached your flat. Your room was predictably tiny and monkish, and so cold that our fingers trembled as we peeled off each other's clothes.

"Let's get some sleep, eh?" you said, as we crawled under the blankets. "I'm knackered. We can have some fun in the morning." You kissed me again, and we lay together in the darkness, your arm around my shoulder.

"Thanks very much," I muttered, but you were already asleep. I was too tired and drunk to find my way home. There was nothing else for it but to try and sleep, and hope that I would remember your name when we woke.

In the morning, you fucked me with a thrilling savagery that nearly collapsed the bed. We stayed in your room for most of the weekend, scuttling to and from the kitchen with cups of tea, and working our way through your Blue Note jazz LPs.

By the end of the year, we were still a pair – a milestone baffling to me, former king of the one-night stands, but unremarkable to you. When your flatmate graduated and moved out, I moved in, without even a conversation.

My parents adored you. You were the level-headed, unswishy son they'd always wanted. You loved them back, spending hours in the garage with my father repairing his vintage cars, and complimenting my mother on her indigestible vegetarian meatloaf. After Sunday lunch, you'd help her with the dishes, listening sympathetically as she complained about my father's snoring until I pulled you away, making excuses about needing to go to the garden centre.

"Funny that you both ended up with snorers," you said.

"I'm amazed she hasn't stabbed him in his sleep."

"Don't be dumb. Your parents are great."

"I suppose." I knew you were right, but basking cosily in my family's beige middle-classness always left an uncomfortable void. You had never known your father, and your mother was best left where she was, watching daytime television through the prism of an empty bottle of whiskey.

"Are you going to stab me when we're old?"

"Maybe. If you're lucky."

We closed escrow on the yellow wooden house on Clifford Street the month after you landed your post-doc fellowship. I sat in the sunny front room, pretending to check the proofs of my novel, eventually reviewed in the *Herald* as "a harrowing account of homosexual self-loathing and promiscuity". In the back garden, I rolled endless cigarettes as you explained your renovation plans. I cringed, remembering our straight friends' disastrous DIY projects: tears over late deliveries, warped floorboards, furniture covered in sawdust and fabric swatches. But you were a master of calm and order: removing dry rot, laying down floorboards, plastering ceilings, and supervising a pack of shirtless hotties to landscape the garden.

Finally, you laid down your tools and let me throw a boozy house-warming party. It was a grand affair: caterers, a team of waiters, crisp as their white shirts, a DJ, and a 2 a.m. noise-control warning from two implausibly hot policemen.

We crawled into bed as the sun was rising.

"Jeremy wants to feature us in *NZ Home and Garden*," I said. "We might even get the cover."

You wrinkled your nose. "Nah. This place is for us."

"He wants us to get married."

"No wonder you're smoking so much," Gemma said.

We were sitting under the apple tree, on the bench you'd made from reclaimed wood. Gemma was skinny ("My post-divorce diet," she said), hiding bloodshot eyes under huge aviator sunglasses. We watched you through the French doors, wrestling with the pork belly.

"I don't smoke," I said. "Give me one of yours."

Gemma passed me her silver cigarette case, the last remaining evidence of her husband. "In all the time I've known you," she croaked, "I don't think you've ever paid for a cigarette."

"So should I?"

"Buy your own?"

"No. Get married. Well, poof marriage."

"I'd marry him in a second."

"*You're* advocating marriage?"

Gemma took a long puff on her cigarette. "He's perfect. He cooks, he builds things, he doesn't mind you drinking. You guys still have sex, right?"

"Every day. Unless one of us is sick."

"He *is* perfect. Do it before he changes his mind and dumps you for a twenty-year-old."

"He won't." I sighed. "It's so depressing."

"I know, honey. Life sucks."

We sat in silence for a moment. "But why get hitched?"

"Easy," she said. "All the free shit you'll get from your friends."

We pushed the civil partnership forward by six months, before Gemma got too sick to leave the hospital. We kept it small and low-key, as you'd wanted – the ceremony at the Town Hall on Moray Place, then dinner at Etrusco, our favourite Italian restaurant. Gemma was shrivelled and bird-like, her skin blue-veined and translucent as Murano glass. Her ice-blue Versace dress hung off her ravaged body like sackcloth. Undeterred, she coiled tinsel around her portable IV drip, and you twirled her around the dance floor as the band played Wham!'s *I'm Your Man*.

After the funeral, we collapsed on the bed, still in our suits and shoes, and held each other. "I want a child!" I wept into your shirt, coughing up a whiskey burp. You said nothing and stroked my head until I fell asleep. In the morning, I was too embarrassed to mention it, and you, thankfully, too diplomatic. We brought Oscar home from the shelter a few weeks later.

Marriage didn't change you much. You still baked bread and changed the washers on leaky taps and offered the neighbours first pickings from the apple tree. You drew a blank at irony, sarcasm and sexual innuendo, and tried without success to make me appreciate the comic genius of Jim Carrey.

By forty, you'd gone badly to fat. "A sign that you're too happy," my mother sighed, grim as an Old Testament prophet. The doctor prescribed exercise and less red wine – a diagnosis that would've sent me over a cliff – but you shrugged it off, jogging in the mornings with Oscar, and weight training at the gym with a perky young buck who looked shockingly like a young Adam.

I found it remarkably easy to cheat on you. I've never understood why adultery is supposed to require great effort. The mechanics are relatively simple. A book-reading out of town, a moderately expensive hotel; a stranger at the bar with a smile that lingers a moment too long. A drink or two, a discreet exchange of room numbers, then separate elevator rides to the tenth floor. A knock at the door: another drink, a partial undressing; a brief, frenzied exchange of body fluids. Finally, the relief as the door clicks shut behind him.

You sat on the bed, stony-faced, as I unpacked my bags.

"What was his name?"

"Dan." In truth, I couldn't remember. He'd left me his business card, which I'd chucked in the rubbish after he left.

"Did you use a condom?"

"I used two."

"Good. At least you were safe."

"We don't have to talk about this now."

"No, we don't." You took a pillow from your side of the bed and walked out, pulling the door closed behind you.

You stayed in the spare room for a week, walking stiffly and rubbing your back as you went to and from the bathroom. We crept around each other carefully, like visitors in a cancer ward, avoiding eye contact.

When I came home on Friday night, you were in the kitchen, surrounded by steam and bubbling saucepans.

"I'm making soup. Butternut squash."

"Smells amazing. Need a hand?"

"Nah, I'm good. There's a bottle of Malbec open on the table." You picked up the meat cleaver and continued hacking away at the squash.

We sat on opposite sides of the table, the silence punctuated only by the scraping of soup spoons against bowls.

"This isn't poisoned, is it?" I said.

You arched a bushy eyebrow. "Only one way to find out."

"You're a botanist. You know which plants are poisonous. Just a few leaves in a bowl of soup and I'd be gone."

You said nothing, and continued slurping, steady as a metronome.

"You've got black circles under your eyes," I said.

"You know I can't sleep unless it's next to you."

I had expected not to sleep that week, which seemed somehow fitting. I wanted to sweat out my purgatory alone in our bed, in solidarity with you. But I have always been a useless penitent. I slept like an infant, long blissful nights of oblivion, my limbs stretched luxuriantly across both sides of the bed.

I was nearing sleep when you came into the bedroom that night. You perched on the edge of the bed, still fully dressed.

"I don't want us to split up."

I rubbed my eyes and reached for my bifocals. "Neither do I."

"But you're going to do this again, aren't you?"

"I don't know," I said. "No. Maybe."

"I've thought about it. You can see other people – if you want."

"Is that what *you* want?"

"It's not about what I want."

"Of course it is."

You looked down at your hands. "I don't mind. But we need some rules."

I folded my arms in front of me. "OK."

"No one we know. No friends."

"That's easy. I hate most of our friends."

"Always use a rubber."

"Of course."

"And no one in our bed."

I said nothing. You leaned forward and put your arms on either side of me. "I mean it, Tiger. No one in here but us."

"Agreed," I said. "Now can you please come back to bed?"

I waited for a month before plunging again – a fun and mostly guilt-free fuck with a dreadlocked guy from my yoga class.

"So, what's the routine?" I said, when I got home. "Do I put a dollar in the change jar?"

Your eyes were sad and full of love. You kissed me gently on the forehead, like a priest anointing a disciple. "We'll have enough for a Rolex in six months."

We drifted along like that for a few years. You looked the other way, or pretended not to mind, and I pretended not to notice when you did.

As I neared fifty, the gentlemen callers faded away. I was forced to contend with the slackening and thickening of my body, the sudden horror of my first grey pube. "Don't pluck it," you said. "Ten more will come to its funeral."

And then it was just the three of us again – you, me and an ancient, incontinent Oscar – all of us with bad hips and worn-out patches, bruised but still staggering along.

The sun is higher in the sky. The curtains glow golden and orange as if about to burst into flames. Your body is colder now, your face the colour of chalk.

The end happened as you predicted, years ago, on a Sunday afternoon drive to the garden centre. We were discussing my new book, a historical romance. The reviews had not been kind – my old friends at the *Herald* called it "sentimental and clichéd" – but it had been a modest bestseller. After two decades of equal rights, gays were apparently mad for the good-old-bad-old days of clandestine lives and anguished love affairs.

"Do you think it's too sad?" I pressed.

"I always think your writing is too sad."

"No one wants to read about how happy you are."

You shrugged. "I do. You always leave out the good stuff."

"What good stuff?"

"Like us. This."

We drove on in silence for a while.

"I want to die before you," you said.

"That's macabre. Too much Tammy Wynette." I pushed Eject on the ancient disc player and slipped in *Maximum Dance Hits 2*.

"Turn that down. I mean it."

"Why you? What about me?"

"You'll be fine on your own. You'll potter around. Get a new dog. Scare the neighbours."

"I'll start by telling them to stop taking our fucking apples."

"See? You'll be fine."

"So would you," I said.

"No, I won't. I want to die first, Tiger."

It was unlike you to get the last word. But all things considered, it was the least I could do for you.

And so, this morning, I will get out of bed, check again for a pulse and gently lower your eyelids. I will pad down the hallway, past Oscar's old basket, and call for an ambulance. The paramedics will arrive and compliment me on my presence of mind, and offer me a sedative, which I will decline. When the undertaker arrives, we will wash you and dress you in your best suit. At the funeral, I will make jokes at your expense. I will not cry, but I will drink heavily afterwards. I will force myself to speak to your trashy relatives, and thank them for their Cellophane-wrapped condolences. Then I will ask to be driven home to sleep here, alone. I will keep to my side of the bed, and lie in the darkness, wondering where our love will go after I die.

And I will never sell the bed. They will have to carry me out in it, kicking and screaming, like a lunatic. It may even make the local evening news. You always said I should have been on television.

Kim

EDWIN DIXON

Every now and then I think back to Kim. The first thing I remember is the dancing. Dancing with a glass of whisky in hand, whisky spilling over onto the carpet. I remember thinking it wouldn't be cleaned up, even in the morning. I remember I was sitting with Liam and Joe, side by side on the couch, three of us watching the dance. And of course I remember Kim's toplessness. That's only the beginning of the story. I don't go on much further than there. The best bit, the middle – I haven't dwelt on that in years.

This all went down in my home town of Dartford. My life began here, I'm still here, and I'm sure Ladbrokes would offer short odds it'll end here as well. We don't have much – a market on Wednesdays, a Norman church, a high street with a weekend cinema – and what with Bluewater dwarfing us down the way you could say we've got even less. But this is where it happened. Not in London. Kim was here, in Dartford.

As I recall, it started in the Flying Boat. Still going today, it's as good a place as any for a bit of all-day breakfast and a drink. Me and Joe were sat near the door for the breeze. Big lads need that after beating fifteen hundred calories of grease. It was late November and the punters swinging the hinges was basically free AC.

Later today, when I'm perched by the second Carling tap with my paper, I'll think back to Joe. We never needed the chat, us two. Best friends at school we didn't talk much even then, just sat at the back on day one and kept on till final year. He departed last autumn, too young at thirty, a car crash you probably won't want the details of.

Back on the day with Kim, Joe was sipping his pint, smiling, content with life. Then Liam walked in: skinny, red-faced and Irish. He came straight for us and I remember he was grinning so wide Joe couldn't meet his eyes.

"Fellas, I got one staying over tonight," Liam said. He said, "She's called Kim."

"Why's she coming here, to Dartford?" I was trying to imagine why anyone would.

"That's the beauty of my brain," Liam said. He winked. "She's coming on the Eurostar. I told her Ebbsfleet was the best station for London." He laughed.

Around three or four months Liam had been living with us. Joe and me shacked up straight out of school but the third room was always a merry-go-round of loose personalities. These days I've got a couple of Slovakians who don't speak English.

I looked at a strip of bacon fat on my plate. Liam said, "I've stocked up with a crate and a bottle of whisky. You lads help yourselves." I ate the fat. "But leave a little for me and the lady, OK? I imagine we'll go for a few but we'll need some when we get back." We nodded. "Enjoy your drinks, fellas. I'm gonna pick her up." Liam left.

Joe gulped down nearly half his pint. He looked right at me. He said, "Girl coming over tonight?"

I drank my Carling, nodded.

"We ain't had a girl round since Abi," Joe said. "Must be seven months."

"Five," I said.

"You feeling all right?" Joe said, and his thumbs went scratching his arse. It was awkward but I appreciated the concern.

"I'm fine," I said. See, Abi went to school with me and Joe. She was my girlfriend for three years until I was eighteen. She left Dartford and she left Joe and she left me. What more can I say? She may come back into this later, if I can face the telling of it.

In the pub I said to Joe we should get going. "Might as well have a head start before this Kim arrives." We grabbed our jackets and left.

Liam had been using this website called Couchsurfing. He'd told us about it at the Flying Boat one time. I can't remember which night, or if it was an afternoon, but Liam had this coffee with some stuff called Cointreau in. I'm sure it was quiet – I recall the looks we got on account of the decibels. Anyway, Liam had said, "It's for strangers, yeah. But it's for travelling. It's free, see. No fucking money. And you take whoever. But I take the girls and they stay on your couch. Strangers. But they're travelling, so, you know, they're good fucking people." He was leaning further back on the bar, his coffee tipping further towards the floor. "And girls is what you do. Try to do. That's why you pick the women." It went something like that. Me and Joe left him soon after when he got talking to some woman in a parka.

Kim was a bit of a surprise – the first of these Couchsurfing girls. We'd had a couple months of nothing then this. Maybe we could have stayed in the Flying Boat with our empty breakfast plates, but truth be told, with a girl in the house, some stronger volumes would need drinking, and Liam's stash was free.

Temple Hill is where we walked to, a maze of joined-up houses. As you can imagine there's an incline. I can't tell you why they put the "temple" in; I've never seen anything looks like a church. Maybe the last generation of Dartfordians felt closer to God up here. Some people need Him round this estate.

The house looked then how it looks now: basic, the same as the ones on both sides. Past the front door I put my keys in the cracked Batman mug on the sill. That mug still hasn't split yet. I wiped my feet on the then orange carpet. Nowadays that carpet's become a kind of brown colour.

Me and Joe didn't bother going up to the bedrooms. I wouldn't go up there all night. We've got the pisser downstairs, see. Good for boozy nights, not for showering mornings. Priorities.

One thing I remember about Liam is he loved the Eden channel. He was into all that – faraway landscapes and igloo people and animal shagging patterns. The Eden channel was on when I settled into the couch with a warm Żywiec. Liam didn't drink Carling.

"Fuck is this?" said Joe. He sat down next to me.

"Fuck is this," I agreed. He might have been talking about Żywiec or Eden. It didn't matter to me; I kept the beer and switched over to UK Gold. Joe had dragged the crate from the kitchen to between our stretched legs. We kept that couch occupied till the dancing started.

Kim still hadn't arrived by eleven, a good five hours after our first Polish lager. Me and Joe were pouring healthy measures of Famous Grouse.

"Long time," I said. I thought a minute more and added, "Maybe they won't come at all." I was on only a slight buzz from the drink.

Joe kept his eyes on the telly, some repeat of *The Good Life*. Laughter hadn't sounded from us once. Joe finally said, "Wouldn't be so bad."

"Maybe not," I said, and I meant it. I said that as the key turned in the front door.

Laughter sounded from the hall. I heard Liam say, "Come on in and meet the lads, Kim." He walked in and was followed by a little Asian bloke, drunk and topless. "Boys," Liam said, "this is Kim." Liam sat down on the couch. Kim staggered to the whisky, poured himself a measure in Joe's glass, and started to dance. The whisky spilt over onto the carpet.

Like I said, I usually finish the story here. I told this first bit once, after a few pints, to a bloke at the bar who found himself in the Flying Boat by chance. His car had broken down south of the Dartford Bridge. There was no one else so he introduced himself, this grey-haired matey, as a travelling holiday salesman from Norfolk. He didn't try to sell to me. When he found out the dancing Kim from the beginning was not a bikini model but a Korean man, he slapped my back and called Liam an "imbecile" for saying yes to a profile with no photo. Story over, I felt I'd contributed enough. I didn't need to say another word as he shared a story or four with me. It was nice just listening. The grey-haired man's car was ready before sundown. He shook my hand before leaving.

But today I'm not much in the mood for just listening. The words keep coming. Maybe it's Joe's ventilator being switched off a year ago today. No matter, all I know is I want to carry on.

Kim looked at me, then at Joe, and back. His shoulders were

swaying in circles round his hips. Wherever the amber wall light had him I couldn't see an inch of fat. He looked younger than us at that time, but I know he was twenty-three.

"OK, Liam, I've got it. I know which one," Kim said. His voice was more American than the telly. "You're Joe, definitely Joe. So, so, sooooo Joe. And you, you're thingy. You're the other one. I know your story, brother, and I love you." He pointed to me, gave me a hug. I sat still, confused.

"You got it right. He got it," Liam said to us, not looking but pushing Kim off me. "I'm bringing your bag in." He looked at us. "I'm bringing his bag in." He brought in a weighty backpack with a metal water bottle clipped outside. A Hawaiian shirt with ripped buttons was draped over the top. Kim saw it and held Joe's glass up to the ceiling. He nailed it in one.

Leaning over the back of the couch, Liam said, "He's a bit fucked, fellas. And as you can see he's a bloke. He's a bloke, which is my mistake. But we had a good time. Good time. Nearly got lucky, too. But the shirt, you know . . . We were in the Boat. Thought we'd see you there. But anyway, it didn't happen. It didn't happen. Night, fellas. Looks like Kim'll be all right there, lads. Night."

Kim had collapsed across both arms of the dusty armchair. His head blocked the bottom of the telly. I picked up the fallen whisky glass and poured Joe another. We'd only missed five minutes of *The Good Life* so we kept at it. Nothing of Kim was said. Joe went up after the episode finished and I fell asleep on the couch after three more Żywiecs.

I opened my eyes to the damp of the front room. My back hurt from sleeping sitting up. The floor was clear of empty cans and the whisky was back on the shelf, next to Liam's old rap vinyls. Kim was opposite, wide awake with showered hair. His skinny neck and arms poked out of T-shirt holes I would have ripped trying to get into.

"Hi," said Kim. "Liam's gone to work. I tidied up." He said it as a fact, not looking for thanks, and I didn't give him any. The clock said nine. Joe wouldn't be up.

"Do you want some cereal?" Kim said. "Liam showed me the amenities."

I shook my head. My mouth felt like dried mud, the same as every morning.

"Water," I said. I meant to fetch it myself but Kim was up to the kitchen and back before I could mention it. I gulped down the whole pint and got myself another. From the kitchen frame I looked across the living room to the hallway, thinking about heading upstairs, but Kim was watching me from behind his cereal spoon. I mean it when I say I don't think anyone's ever looked at me that long right in the eyes. Even Abi.

"Have a seat, dude," he said. "Bring your water and have a seat." Perhaps it was the American accent, but I sat down. "Man, I was fucked last night. I apologise. How was your night?"

Now this I won't forget about Kim. The eagerness of his eyes, the belief in my mind that he wanted to know everything I had to say about my afternoon, evening and night in Dartford. He had that look every time he asked a question.

"Fine," I said. On the cushion next to me I saw the remote. I moved my hand towards it and stopped just short.

"Liam and I, we went to that pub of yours. What's it called, the Ship?" I nodded – ship, boat, same difference – and sipped my water. "He told me all about your girlfriend leaving and all. I'm real sorry, man."

I'd never told Liam about Abi, and I'd definitely never had her brought up so openly in conversation. Reckon I hid the shock well when I wiped the matter away with an air swipe of my hand. The thing is, me and Joe never really spoke of it either. I got to thinking how Liam and Joe must have had a few drinks and how Joe must have been open and talkative, open and talkative about me. I put the thought out of mind.

"Anyway, it's a real nice pub, don't you think?" He had half a smile, not daring, but encouraging. I actually wanted to talk with him.

"It's nice," I said. Kim waited and his eyes didn't flinch. His elbows leaned forward to his knees. "I go a fair bit," I said.

"I'm not surprised. It's a beautiful pub," Kim said. "Quite a history too, right?"

"Oh yeah?" I never knew anything about the pub's history.

"Dude, I was talking to the – what do you call them over here?

Landlord? He told me all about it. Said it used to be some navy barracks for officers. I asked him about the pillars and the high ceiling and the cool staircase. He said it was for them, the officers, that whole grandiose look."

I'd never really clocked those details before, but ever since Kim told me all this – about the pillars and the wooden stairs – I've sat in the pub and looked at my establishment and agreed – after checking the word – that my surroundings are absolutely very grandiose.

"Well that I didn't know," I said.

"And this was the last place the officers would stay before setting out into the world. They'd start at London, dock for the night in Dartford, then sail away to distant lands. Dude, Dartford would be the last place they'd stay before travelling away for years."

I never knew Dartford had had a docks, and I've spoken to Gary, the gaffer, about the history of the pub, and he never confirmed Kim's version. He said the Boat was built in the nineteen hundreds as a car showroom. Never been a place for officers. But even so I still believe Kim. He had no reason to lie. Plus it put us on the map, having Dartford visited by officer types.

"I didn't know that," I said to Kim. "I never knew Dartford was visited by officer types."

"You travel much?" Kim said.

"Never appealed." I leaned back on the couch. "You?"

Kim smiled and slapped his leg. "All over, man. All over. I just came from Paris. Liam was nice enough to meet me at Ebbsfleet, from the train. We were on the drink pretty quick, though. Yeah, I been all over, man."

"Why do you have an American accent?"

Kim laughed. "I get that a lot. Moved to the States when I was six." He laughed again and shook his head, probably at the confused look on my face. "I was born in Korea."

I knew a thing about Korea and said, "North or South?"

"Jesus Christ," Kim said. "South." He stood up and went into the kitchen. "You want a coffee, bro?"

After making coffee Kim took out his camera, a big black weight that he could have filmed telly on, I'm sure. "Come here.

Let me show you some pictures." I sat on the arm next to him and watched him flick through these images on an LCD screen. They started off in these modern cities, glass-tower skyscrapers with Kim's face in the corner, then some of what looked like museum stuff inside clear cases. They soon became greener as he whizzed through and he stopped on a lake. "This is Canaima," he said, "in Venezuela." Kim talked me through this lake. It had a red tint to it which apparently was caused by iron. And these palm trees, four of them, were sticking out from the shallow water, their leaves shadowy against a blue sky. In the distance I could see these tall mountains which looked like Tetris blocks. "They're called tepuis," Kim said when I pointed them out. Some of them had waterfalls. At the front of the picture there were three dark women washing rags. "You see those women? They're Pemon women, native to the country. In their whole lives, and some cases whole generations, they've never left Canaima. You can't even get to this village except by small plane. But look how beautiful this is. Angel Falls is just up from this lake." He said, "Live a place like there and you'd never want to leave."

It all seemed very Eden channel to me, but looking with Kim I believed this was a beautiful place. Knowing that Kim, this real person who was sitting on my armchair in Dartford, had been to Canaima, I even imagined myself there too. "Beautiful," I said. That might have been the first time I said that word in this house.

"Let me show you something else." Skipping forward what seemed like a thousand images he paused on a wooded mountain. "This, my friend, is Seoul. Right in the city centre." I squinted my eyes. All I could see was a hilly green landscape, taken from up high. These green hills rolled downward towards some yellow dots at the base. If I'm honest, I remember it looking like rural China, which I'd seen on one of Liam's documentaries.

"There's no buildings," I said. "How's it a city?"

"Looks that way, yeah. It's a small screen. But when you're there, on top of this mountain, you can see this forest cascading down into small buildings, then high-rises, then skyscraper spikes." He zoomed in on the photo and the yellow dots cleared themselves into buildings, more and more of them as the mountain flattened and disappeared between the concrete.

Kim said, "It looked like Seoul was just litter dropped on this national park. But I stayed at this viewpoint all afternoon, and it got me thinking. I thought, You know what? I really do feel a connection." He turned his head from the camera and looked right at me. "See, I was born in Seoul, and hadn't been back. And this place was everything I loved most, all in one. Crazy cities and beautiful landscapes. I felt this real connection, deep down, in here. You know what I'm saying?"

He kept at me for an answer. "Yeah, of course," I said. I wanted him to think I understood.

"Of course you do," he said, and tapped my back.

There were more photos. Europe was his favourite. Cobbled squares in Moscow, Venice rivers with floating houses, spiky cathedrals in Spain – places I'd never known of. "Europe's so close, man. You've got to go," Kim said.

"Just keep flicking," I said.

At one point Joe came down. His bed clothes were a mess, his grey T-shirt spotted with suspect yellow stains. There was no hiding the surprise on his face when he saw me on the arm of the chair. "Didn't know you were still here," he said.

Kim looked up. "Hey, man," he said, and went back to flicking. I kept on with Kim. Joe spent a bit too much time making his tea. He went upstairs silently. I still had the thought of him and Liam talking about me and didn't feel for his absence.

When he was all done commentating on Paris, Kim put the camera back in his bag. I was sorry for it to finish and moved back to my side of the room. I stared and this time he found me looking. "You feel it, don't you?" he said.

"What?"

"The bug. The fucking travel bug, man."

He was half right. I never imagined myself in Venezuela or Moscow, but maybe a trip to Amsterdam would work. "A bit," I said.

"I knew it. I told Liam last night I could persuade you. You know it's not even that expensive. Liam's travelled a lot too, man."

I wasn't sure to be offended, but looking at Kim's face, smiling like he'd won an accumulator, I didn't think on it. Instead, I thought of Abi. This is where she comes back into it.

"You know I could've travelled," I said.

Kim picked up his coffee and took a sip. I knew it must be cold. "Go on," he said, and I spoke, the whole thing with Abi. With Kim I didn't have the same heat that I get talking to others, when all you're thinking about is the faces of the people you're talking to – if they're bored or not – rather than the words that come out your mind. Kim wasn't judging me, unlike Liam, and he understood the feelings, unlike Joe.

"She left me to go to university," I said. "She went 'cause she knew I'd never follow, not to Swansea. Nursing, studying to be a nurse. She left at the start of summer, before the course even began. Said she was sick of Dartford and all it had. Sick of me circling jobs for porters in Darent hospital and never even paying for us to go to London." I wasn't emotional. I said it flat to Kim's nodding face. "A few trips to London might have saved us," I said. "Still, probably for the best."

I drained my cold coffee, too. I wasn't sure if London was the same as travelling and Kim didn't speak. I know it might not sound like a long story, but those words felt freeing. Every sound out my mouth made my shoulders fall further back in my seat. I didn't feel things would get better, but it was good to talk.

We sat in silence for a moment after. All I heard was a knackered Ford Escort drive by the single-paned window. They're all knackered Escorts round here.

"Listen, I've got to go catch my train to London. Next house," Kim said. He stood up, collected a few things and put his pack on his shoulders. The water bottle he reached round to clip on the side. I was surprised by the disappointment I felt. Surprised that I felt insulted, too.

I stayed seated. Kim walked over, standing well above my head for a short guy. He grabbed my shirt and pulled me to my feet. "I don't know the way to the station." He grinned. "You're coming with me. Let's go. And bring your wallet. You'll need it for the return ticket."

"What?"

"Your ticket. Come with me. It can't be more than a tenner. I'll show you there's nothing to be scared of."

I hadn't been to London since Mum took me to a hospital

appointment, back when we were on speaking terms. Maybe it was the photos, or maybe it was that Kim wanted to spend more time with me after all, but I agreed. I didn't tell Joe as I ran upstairs and changed and ran downstairs and washed. There was a lightness in me, like four pints of Carling. I'd call it excitement.

"Proud of you, man," said Kim when I was ready.

I followed him out the door. I remember it had rained and the wet tarmac glared in the sun, like snow. I wanted people to look out their windows, for them to see me next to this Asian fellow with a ripped Hawaiian shirt over a white vest in late November. I kept up with him past the dead communal grass areas where no kids were playing.

"We got the whole day," said Kim. "Buckingham Palace, Big Ben. The lot. I'm not meeting my new host till six in some place called Mary le Bone. What is that, French?"

I didn't know. It didn't even bother me that another person needed meeting. It seemed a lifetime away. We carried on down the hill as Kim talked of everything he wanted to see and showed me pictures from a guidebook he'd downloaded onto his phone. The places I didn't recognise. It filled me with wonder, like we were going overseas.

It was at the bottom of the hill, just a couple hundred yards from the station, that I felt this strange tugging, a weight slowing me down, stopping me. I stood still.

Kim carried on then turned when he saw I was gone. He looked at me and came back. "Come on, let's go. We're wasting time." He looked behind me. We were outside the Flying Boat.

"Quick pint?" I said.

"Are you kidding?"

"Come on, just a swift one." As I said it I felt the words falling away from me. The light-headedness was gone; my legs felt stiff. People breakfasting behind the window of the pub were looking at me and I suddenly wanted away from this guy in the Hawaiian shirt and white vest. "Drink," I said.

Kim smiled and shook his head. It might have been disappointment. "Come with me. London," he said.

"Drink," I said.

One last shake of the head and he went, "I guess Liam won."

He hugged me full on and held it tight without me returning the gesture. I saw the people laughing inside and faced away. "Nice knowing you," said Kim, and he left for the station. The flowers on his shirt flapped in the wind.

From here, things get hazy. When I try and recollect this scene I sometimes see it as a sad farewell, like I didn't want Kim to go. Other times I swear I'm shouting, asking for him to come back. All I know for certain is the journey ended with me in the pub at eleven in the morning. Joe came down and saw me soon after. I can't remember what was said between us, whether I was off with him or not, but I'm sure by the end the company was good and the beer was sound. The last clear thing I remember is noticing the emblem of the pub dangling under the name outside. I reckon this was the first time I studied it. It was a massive old warplane with huge floats to let it land on water. Still today, I imagine Kim flying the boat over those – what do you call them? That's it. Tepuis. Funny, the further the bookends go from Kim the fuzzier things become.

New Materiality

STELLA KLEIN

Jimmy stands up. His giant hands dangle at his sides; his ripped jeans sag halfway down his bottom. His underpants are pale blue today and already Frankie can taste his liquorice breath, feel the prickle of his chin, and it brings on a tremor just beneath the surface of her skin. The last time she saw Jimmy she was walking down the hallway past her own kitchen. And there he was, standing at the window, his mouth full of Sugar Puffs, milky-lipped but beautiful. He slips onto her radar now and then like this, shimmers before her eyes like a fox in broad daylight, and then he's gone again.

So today is feast day. The boy with no name is here and so is Babette. Jon Devlin is ready to start and he's passing round the register. *The* Jon Devlin, who sold a lot of neon art in the nineties (Frankie checked on Wikipedia – *Temperance in White* and *Shite in Neon Blue*), who told her at her interview there is something fresh about her paintings, something visceral, that they smack of New Materiality.

"So. Jimmy," Jon Devlin begins. "What do you have for us today?"

What Jimmy has for them today is anyone's guess. Two Polaroids appeared last week on the walls of his studio – the face of a platypus and a pool of blood on a glossy white dish. And this morning those strips of blue foil were still hanging from his ceiling like a floating wig.

Jimmy's stepping inside the half-empty ring of paint-spattered chairs. He's laying out sheets of grey sugar paper in a spiral formation on the pocked red floor. Slowly, purposefully, he's pacing from one sheet to the next, towards its centre.

"These . . . are . . . the . . . footsteps of . . . my life," he chants.

Frankie shivers at his melting Dublin notes, tries to focus on the progress of his black plimsolls, round and round, inwards and then backwards, outwards, as the sheets grow twisted and grubby with the spearhead pattern of his rubber tread. Jimmy hops off the centre of his spiral, rubs his hands together, ready to start all over again, and Babette gouges the silence with her Californian drawl.

"Coo-ool," she says, bobbing her head slowly up and down like she's having deep thoughts. She pokes her tongue through a pink gobbet of gum and stretches one torn-fishnet leg out to the side. Frankie surveys the low cut of her vest, the thickly pencilled eyes, the cuff-chewed cardigan that hangs limply off her shoulder. All those impossible moves and signals. And here he is, just inches away, a Celtic god, standing on one leg, not once looking in Babette's direction. But all Frankie can do is stare at his foot and the coffee rings on his sketchbook, imagine the kind of drug-induced state it would take for her to move in on Jimmy.

Seriously, respectfully, Jon Devlin is examining Jimmy's paper spiral, and seriously, respectfully, No Name is looking at Jon Devlin, his head cocked to one side.

"Right. So. Anyone?"

"It is mark making," says No Name.

"Mark making, yes. We're looking at *process* here."

Jimmy wobbles at the centre of his spiral; a flop of black hair hangs over one eye. He swivels sharply, making a messy tear on the paper, and facing outwards, swinging his arms for balance, evolutionary, he retraces his steps.

"Subject-object merging," says No Name.

"Aha!" says Jon Devlin, tugging at that tawny beard, loosening it like a ball of wire wool.

London rain has started to pelt against the windows and No Name is scratching beautiful wispy characters down a page of his tiny green notebook.

"Are we not witnessing here . . . some kind of *becoming*?" says Jon Devlin. "In the Deleuzian sense, no?"

Deleuze, thinks Frankie. Fuck. Check it later. Like *becoming* when she was small, maybe? When she'd *become* a chicken, crouching in the egg-warm straw, down in the ammonia stench of chicken world, pressing her palms against those folded velvet wings and tiny feathered skulls, letting them strut around her, suspicious, one-eyed, demented.

Jon Devlin rests his elbows on his parted knees, presses his knuckles against his lips as if in prayer, and Frankie remembers waking this morning from a Jimmy-infused dream – the length of him against her back, his bony hands creeping up inside her T-shirt and across her shivering ribs. In the cracks of the shower tiles she'd seen faces – slanted eyes and long noses, grinning and winking – and taken them as an omen that this would be the day that Jimmy falls at her feet. She'd dressed quickly and stepped outside, crossed the quadrangle, past the Cultural Theory woman fishing in her bag, past the students on benches sipping Starbucks, puffing on their first roll-ups of the day. The sky was yellow-tinged like old bruises and she was light-headed with the Jimmy dream and thoughts of paint: fast-water white, banana white. Thin smoke, old snow.

By the time she reached the studio, silver clouds were billowing in, filling her with the dark, deep thrill of later, this two o'clock convener. She checked Marcia's status: "tranquillising sheep", standing beside another veterinary student in long galoshes, his hands around the jaws of a ram. And thinking of home, Frankie got hot chocolate from the machine, and began smearing new globs of paint on yesterday's palette.

"So," Jon Devlin's asking, "can we say whether this piece would continue to exist if we left the room?"

Frankie wonders how it feels to be Marcia, whether it's possible to get romantic around needles and damp animals. She's thinking about damp and dry, about the grass at home turning yellow in summer, the hills dotted with sheep turds, round and hard as bullets. She's thinking about the time she sat by the castle wall drinking cider with that boy called Stan, how she stopped him because she only half wanted him. But Jimmy's eyes are sparkling; she would like his hands on her.

"Will there remain here some *trace* of Jimmy's performance?"

Babette busts a small pink bubble with the tip of her tongue and exposing the cones of her little white breasts, she leans forward to inspect Jimmy's tread marks up close.

"There, indeed!" says Jon Devlin.

Jimmy hops off his spiral one last time and slopes back to his chair. He straightens out like a plank, thrusts his hands deep into his front pockets, and Frankie wonders if he steps on spirals of paper when he's all alone, if he smiles in the dark, if she's ever crossed his mind.

"Perhaps you'd like to . . . *re*trace the history of this piece for us, Jimmy? Share with us your thoughts, experiences, during the making of it?"

Jimmy takes a stretch and looks up at the ceiling, locking his hands behind his head.

"Last night I had spaghetti hoops for tea," he says. "And I read a book about bees."

It's hard to tell if Jimmy is being insolent or deep, although the flicker of lines across Jon Devlin's brow is softening into a warm smile, and it looks like he's settling for deep. Maybe people were kind to Jon Devlin, too, when he first tried neon art.

"OK. Well, thanks, Jimmy. Let's keep those reflective journals going, hmm? Capture process, find connections." Jon Devlin slides a finger down the register. "Right. And so. Today, we also have Babette, yes?"

Babette reaches between her legs and pulls out a black bin bag from under her chair. She's rifling around in it and Frankie's thinking, Please, not the ashtrays and half-pint glasses she's been collecting under her bed. She can picture Babette in the Union last night, sat in the far corner, stuffing more beer mats under her man-size shirt, telling that boy with the bicycle clips about this latest work of hers, her *Matter out of Place*. Frankie didn't actually see this because she was on the other side of the bar, trying to block out the sound of Babette's voice rising over the babble, watching the door for Jimmy, with that girl on the next table talking about needs – felt needs, normative needs, public-sector needs. And Frankie had tried to work out if Jimmy was a basic need or a higher need.

But no. It's not the beer mats. Babette is bringing out something

Frankie's not seen before. A wire construction. She didn't know Babette was into wire. Babette snatches a glance at Jimmy now and glorious, basking, she sends her thing around the circle. No Name turns it about in his hands and holds it to the light.

"It is a wire heart. Valves and ventricles," he says and passes it to Frankie.

It's neat. It's perfect. The wire is decorated here and there with little strings of red wool tied in bows. And something is rattling inside it: a flat strip of aluminium cut into the shape of a word. *Neglect*, it says, and Frankie remembers she forgot to return her mother's call on Sunday. ("Are you *there*, Frankie? It'd be nice to hear your voice.") But she prefers not to think of her mother alone at home and talking to the dogs.

Frankie passes the heart to Jon Devlin who holds it between his knees, frowns and looks inside. Hmm. Is this perhaps . . . some kind of a – knick-knack? He doesn't say those words but Frankie fancies he might, and already he is passing the heart to languid, beautiful, inscrutable Jimmy who lays it to rest on his divine crotch and refastens his hands behind his head, and she's trying to remember life before Jimmy – surely she was only half alive back then. She'd like to climb inside him, all over him, know him better than herself.

Frankie wonders what this silence means – if everyone likes the wire heart, or maybe they're just thinking about Jimmy, too. The splinters of rain against the wired glass make her crave a softer, Welsh kind of rain, and she imagines for an instant that when she steps outside it won't be these wet brick viaducts and screeching trains, the four-lane swish of the A13, but the smell of rotten leaves on mushy ground, the damp November logs of home.

"The heart is a cage," says No Name. He looks pleased with this and writes it down.

And because Frankie can't stand up and walk across to Jimmy, touch him, run her hands along his legs, she sits completely still, eyes fixed to the floor. She's thinking after-rain green and glisky silver-grey, the purple-brown of mud and bracken moor. She's thinking later she will spread across her canvas these dark and shiny colours of desire.

Blue

NADIM SAFDAR

E ach boy Salim had known like a younger brother. Now, watching
them march away, he whispered a prayer, "*Bismillah ir-Rahman
ir-Rahim*," and began, in his heart, the process of forgetting.

Slowly, they were diminishing into the distance, and as they
lifted their heads towards the grey impenetrable wall of the Great
Karakoram, Salim heard a cry, "*Allahu Akbar*," and from that
moment on their backs seemed to stiffen into their journey and
their feet spurred to a hastened pace.

He turned away from them and walked the short path,
bordered by wildflowers, back towards the high-walled seminary.
It was almost dawn and above, thin spears of treacle sunshine
broke through the restless clouds. For a moment, the air was
perfectly still; the overpowering scent of night-blooming jasmine
was fading fast. What replaced it was a sweet dryness, a mixture of
yellow warmth, of irrigated earth and of the sand beneath his feet.
From the rear of the compound, a diesel generator started.

As he reached the gate, he glanced at the infant's cot bolted
to the ground to one side. It was weathered from the frost that
came down off the mountains, and sodden and misshapen like a
pregnant ewe. Some mornings Salim would discover inside the
crib a swaddle of dirty rags and, nested within, a tiny doll-like
figure – almost too pathetic to be human, and deathly still – in need
of reviving with warm milk. Other times, shrouded in morning

mist, God had willed them an infant grown too big to fit the cot, roped instead to a bar in the gate; shivering from the night's cold, he'd chirp for his mama with dewy, pleading eyes. Passing shepherds brought in feral-eyed older boys, and sometimes the seminary was bequeathed unwanted newborns – their stricken mothers emptying their bellies, without cry or fuss, in the west field that was kept fallow. Upon issue, for a healthy boy, the master parted with a fistful of rupees. He paid a further stipend to a wet nurse from the village who collected the babes, returning them to the seminary when they reached the age of four.

Strong in discipline, the seminary raised the boys and five times a day they were made to turn their heads towards Mecca. By the age of thirteen, at the pitiless mercy of the master's stick, most pupils had committed to memory the entirety of the Holy Book and the celebrated graduates were afterwards known as *Huffaz*.

It was also God's will that with the monsoon rains came disease that threatened to empty the compound. The dead were buried, with little ceremony, to the west in the unharrowed field. Others, whom the master took to his chambers at night, would often wish they too had died. But they knew better than to escape into the night lit only by the whim of the moon – to the fierce blast of cold, thick like granite, to the roaming chaos of wild dogs or across the border to the litter of rusting Soviet landmines.

Salim briefly cast his eyes towards the distant range, its snowy peaks emerging into chalky white. In the foreground, the spreading sun cast long shadows around the seminary's former pupils and the disturbed dry earth sprang up in great clouds around their newly issued marching boots. Within minutes, the sun's relentless advance would illuminate the yellow plain that extended for about a mile, ending abruptly as the land climbed steeply into the dark mountains. But by then the youths would have disappeared into silhouettes and blended into the view. Not one of those they sent out had ever returned and on the lips of each boy, Salim knew, hung a prayer. A prayer he had put there. "*Mashallah*," Salim cried. "*Mashallah*, you lion cubs of Allah."

He put a hand on the empty crib and rocked it. It creaked at the joints. Then, pushing open the gate, Salim gazed up at the minaret, his uncle, the master, at his station within it. Pocketing his prayer beads, the master put his thumbs into his ears and leaning fixedly forwards as though about to transcend into the breaking clouds, his fine voice rang out the dawn call to prayer.

Educated in a seminary in Arabia, the master alone understood the words that filled the air above them and although Salim, too, had engraved the Holy Book into the fibres of his heart, it remained a foreign language and allowed him the space to imagine what it might mean. Only on Fridays would the master translate his sermon, and even then only the master knew what he chose to edit.

Seeing Salim enter the compound, the remaining boys hurried barefoot into the courtyard, flopping out their prayer mats before them. Salim offered a perfunctory nod and took his place at the head of the assembly. He prayed slowly, the boys following his movements, and behind them stood the master, ready to pounce on any boy who miscued the ritual. With his back to them, Salim shuddered at the crack of the master's stick followed immediately by the puppy-like squeal of a pupil. Salim couldn't disagree with the master when he explained, as he often did, that, "The boys would do well to acquire a familiarity with pain." He understood, also, that those they sent out, "We would need to forget." Salim would, however, have liked to have completed at least one prayer, lost in his own personal grace of communion with Allah, without the interruption of the stick.

Seven boys the master had sent out that day to a camp in the Karakoram, and if, like a test, their feet had carried them that far, their handlers would be waiting for them. Salim knew that at least seven more would be left to the seminary in the next month or so. It took fifteen years to bring a boy to sufficient strength and the institution amassed more than were ready to let go, the compound growing a storey in height every four to five years. Money would come. Small change, like a tax, from local people. And thick wads of cash delivered by strangers on motorbikes – American dollars and British pounds, donated by whom or payment for what, Salim wasn't told. The master kept the money next to a Kalashnikov in a trunk in his study, guarding it jealously with a beady-eyed watchfulness.

After every prayer, the boys were arranged in neat lines with the Holy Book resting on a wooden *rehal* in front of each of them. Rocking back and forth, the boys would recite loudly over and over again, committing the words to memory. The master paced up and down the line, listening out for intonation and pronunciation, and Salim would be instructed to follow, holding his uncle's stick.

The pupils had grown more resigned to the stick than fearful of it, but the unspoken threat of close supervision alone with the master in his chambers would quicken their minds and reverse the rote-learning of the page they were stuck on. Salim would often plead on behalf of a particular boy but the master, his thick fingers spread across his large belly, would cryptically retort, "It is well a boy knows hunger."

On the second morning after the boys' departure, God willed a new pupil to the seminary. Next to the cot he swayed on his haunches, his arms encircling a pot belly. His shoulder blades bordered deep hollows and ribs stretched taut his skin. He looked at Salim through large doleful eyes and with a clawed hand, motioned to his mouth. Alerted by the guards, Salim had brought with him a plate of white rice and pinching some between his fingers, he put it to the boy's lips. Salim watched him chew, the bolus of rice flattening against his tongue and palate, and with that, a transformation overtook the boy, his eyes now eager and alert, and a smile spread across his face. He was a white-skinned child from the hill tribes, with freckles dotted above his cheeks. He had full lips, a short, snub nose, and a gentle almond-shaped gaze.

As though suddenly imbued with energy, the boy rose to his feet, broke free of the thin rope that bound him, dusted down the dirty rags he wore and followed Salim, and the plate of rice he held aloft, into the compound.

Salim named him Blue, after the colour of his eyes. Having examined his teeth, he wrote him into the register as aged seven. Salim took him to the ablution chamber, a stone slab to stand on with a cold tap above, and washed him down with carbolic soap. Still cold from the night spent outdoors, the boy made no sound or protest. Salim shaved off his hair, ridding him of lice.

Blue was given small but frequent amounts of plain rice and settled on the uppermost floor with boys about his own age, overseen by older boys. There Salim left him, turning abruptly away from the child's piteous look of abandonment.

Salim found the master in his study. He was seated cross-legged before a low table. He reported their new intake.

"Blue is no name for a child." The master took his beard into his fist and thought for a moment.

"His eyes are the colour of the midday sky," Salim said brightly.

The master leaned back against a bolster cushion. "In winter the noon sky can be a very cold blue."

Salim shook his head. "He has pale skin and fair hair."

"Then he will be from the tribes on the other side." The master thought for a moment. "Or the bastard son of an infidel."

"He is no infidel. His face is carved like ours."

"Under the hot sun," the master said with a deep sigh, "a white boy would be a burden to his family." He reached for a book from a shelf behind him. "Bring him to me."

Salim started for the door.

"Not right now." Thumbing through the book and without looking up he added, "Leave him outside my door after night-time prayers."

Salim stopped perfectly still, his hand halfway to the doorknob. Something inside him suddenly turned. He felt it strongly, but whether it was in his heart or his head, he couldn't say. His chest rose and he stood straight and tall. God didn't will them a boy like Blue only to have him spoiled at the hand of the master. Salim turned to face his uncle full on. "He has a fever," he lied. "Of the skin."

With a flick of his wrist the master dismissed his nephew.

Sleeping against the wall at the far end of a long room, Blue seemed undisturbed by the cacophony created by the others as they read from the Holy Book. Like the flapping wings of a trapped bird, their bodies pitched about wildly. Blue opened his eyes as Salim approached, stood up and raced over on thin spindly legs. His cheerful face buried into Salim's side and bony arms clung around his waist. Easing him gently away, Salim gathered the boy up and carried him to his room. He weighed little and still smelled of carbolic soap.

Salim placed him flat on the bed. The boy smiled. The trust he held in Salim was almost overpowering and it occurred to Salim that, just as he'd done with the others who had arrived before him, he should leave Blue to his fate. It wasn't lost on Salim that by interfering, he was altering the balance and disrupting the natural order of the seminary. For the first time, he was defying the unchallenged will of the master, and that, to Salim, was a dangerous leap.

"Shhh." Salim put a finger to his lips and stared coldly into the boy's eyes. He suddenly understood that there was a difference between the two things that ran their lives in the seminary: God's will and fate. Fate was a roll of the dice. Fate was the whim of their leader. Fate was malice and perversion. Fate was anger. Fate was jealousy and scorn. Fate was an occasional act of kindness but fate was always the stick dangling close by. Salim said to Blue, "For what I am about to do may Allah forgive me."

Uncoiling his turban, Salim stuffed one end into the boy's mouth and wrapped the remainder tightly around Blue's small head. The boy struggled, his eyes suddenly white with fear. Salim began to chant to him softly, "*La ilaha illa Allah, la ilaha . . .*" and the boy, breathing hard through his nostrils, softened under his grip. Salim climbed on top of the mattress, his legs straddling firmly the child's sides.

The first movement was the hardest and the boy's pale fragile skin yielded to the rusty metal rasp that scraped it, bursting readily into tiny pinpricks of blood. And in his eyes – although Salim tried not to look at them, his glance would still scan across, for the briefest of moments – Salim saw only confusion and pain. Yet still he worked his way across the visible parts of Blue's body: his neck, arms and feet, and marked just enough each cheek and his forehead. He worked in a frenzy and fury and lost any account of what time had passed, and although it must only have been a minute, when he next glanced at his little face, the boy's eyes were closed and he was unconscious.

Just as Salim had taken Blue in open view of the other boys, so he returned him to the corner of the infants' dormitory. The pupils said not a word and cast their eyes downwards to the Holy Book in front of them, but they knew and understood and no report would be made.

Blue made no protest as Salim picked him up after the last prayer of the day. With a fearful foreboding he carried the boy down three flights of stairs and across the compound. As his uncle had instructed, Salim propped the child against a wall outside the master's bedchamber and put a blanket over him.

Salim slept little and returning before dawn, he found the boy unmoved, shivering and mercifully untouched.

Blue offered sad vacant eyes and Salim could not help but think that unlike many of their intake, who had known only the indifference of birth and existence, the child had, in his short life, known joy and love. Salim felt a growing panic that Blue's arrival had been some sort of mistake. Perhaps the boy had been separated from his people and, found somehow by a wandering shepherd, he had been deposited at the gates of the seminary.

Bending low to kiss Blue on his now scabbed forehead, Salim returned him to his dormitory, placing him between two others for warmth.

Salim entered the kitchen, stirring Cook who was dozing on the hard floor.

"Has the milk boy come?" Cook rubbed the sleep in his eyes.

Salim shook his head.

"Then why did you wake me?"

"You sleep too much, you lazy fat bastard."

Cook was a beardless, middle-aged man who had recently been found crouched low by the compound gate. When he was asked his business, the man said he was looking for work. It was the beginning of the fighting season and their regular kitchen help was due to lead a group of local farm boys into the Karakoram. God willing, he would return for winter, but until then, the seminary would have no one to prepare the tea, breakfasts, lunch and dinner.

"What type of work do you seek?" asked the master.

"Only what God wills." Cupping his hands together, the man looked up towards the heavens.

It was a statement the master approved of. "In return for your labour we can offer only food and shelter."

Salim was instructed to station the cook's wife and daughters under tarpaulin at the rear of the compound; the man himself was permitted to sleep next to the warmth of the ovens.

Sitting upright on the floor, Cook covered his face with his hands and shook his head.

It was a cold morning and Salim pulled the thick woollen shawl tight around his shoulders.

Cook spoke. "A newborn girl its poor mother strangled in the west field overnight."

Through a gap in the man's fingers Salim could see his eyes water.

Shivering involuntarily, Salim quickly said, "Who told you that?"

"What kind of God . . . ?" Cook let out a muffled sob.

Salim was conscious of standing tall over him. He stammered, "Only an infidel would question God."

"My wife says the mother carved out a shallow grave with her bare hands, and buried her still warm."

Salim kicked the man in the stomach, which seemed to arouse some sort of reality for he removed his hands from his eyes and looked up at Salim as though offering himself up for another blow. Cook had been instructed to wear a beard and several days' stubble covered his greasy face. His large cheeks wobbled uncontrollably. His eyes were dark, as though rimmed by kohl, and his peppery hair was matted against his scalp.

"You tell your wife just be thankful that her daughters are still warm."

Cook wiped his eyes and nodded.

Turning, Salim added bitterly under his breath, "And that the master prefers boys."

Silently, he went from floor to floor, watching the boys as they slept. Some had mattresses, but not all. Although they went to bed in an orderly fashion, with each boy allocating a space for himself, by morning their bodies had unconsciously shifted, their arms and legs entangled with those of their neighbours.

Each floor was basically one long rectangular space where the intake ate, prayed and slept. On the ground floor were the older boys and the *Huffaz*, and attached to that level only were other rooms: a study and bedchamber for the master, a kitchen and ablution block, and a store cupboard Salim had appropriated as his bedroom. He rarely used it, preferring to sleep communally on the third floor where he could keep an eye on the infants.

Having himself been left in the care of his uncle, the master, at the age of six, the first space Salim slept in was where he still felt most comfortable. He had expected his father to come for him and remembered three younger sisters. Stepping carefully in the gaps between the sleeping boys, he tried to recall the names of each of his siblings but found he could not. Salim could no longer picture his parents either, adopting instead images painted on the trucks that often belched past the compound, of Indian movie stars and actors advertising Nestlé powdered milk. Salim remembered a small walled compound and a cow the family would draw milk from. He recalled his mother cutting fresh grass for the cow with a scythe and her figure bent low in the long foliage, dressed in green, a shawl covering her head, and the birth of a sister, the same day his father took Salim out to the bazaar on the back of his bicycle. He recollected the rear wheel of the bicycle slipping on the rutted road and having to hold on tightly. Flashing past, he had seen rifles for sale and shoulder-borne rockets and turreted box-like vehicles on tracks, and at one stall thousands of brass bullets sparkled in the sun.

Now, Salim gazed at Blue, sleeping soundly. Where he had scraped it, Blue's skin had burst into blackish welts and swollen, and for a moment Salim allowed himself to think about the seven they had let go. By now they would be three days deep into the mountains. They would have braved the relentless daytime sun and a peculiar night freeze that hollowed out their bones and, eyeing the vultures circling above, a boy would be asking himself if such hardship was a fate of birth or whether the master was right – it was God's will. Each had set off with a dry cake of flour saturated with sugar, sustenance that would be spent by now. Salim whispered a prayer, "*Inshallah*, you lions fight until martyrdom. *Inshallah*."

Juma prayer took place in the freshly swept courtyard with the sun boring down on it directly above. At the front, cast in a long green robe falling to his feet, was the master. His glorious robe was studded with sequins tracing colourful rose patterns and depicting the deep-red pomegranate fruit. On his head spiralled a dazzling white turban. He sat in an elevated position on a short flight of wooden steps used only on Fridays. Before him was seated, cross-legged, the entire pupil intake, the cook, the laundryman, the housekeeper, the guards and about a dozen elderly men from the village for whom chairs were provided at the rear.

Their leader was reading short passages from the Holy Book followed by a translation orated with a forceful anger, at times tears streaming down his cheeks. It was a familiar theme and fatigued from a sleepless night, Salim found it hard to concentrate, hearing only the words that seemed to command the master's greatest effort: *infidel, jihad, Allah.*

Bent into himself, Salim rubbed his eyes and, absent-mindedly, he yawned loudly.

The master stopped mid-sentence and stood up. He grunted. His stick was always nearby and he reached for it.

Salim felt a tightening knot strangle his gut and his heart pounded against his chest. He looked up.

The boys scattered to make a path as the master strode, in long steps, towards Salim. It was the hottest part of the day and the sequins on his robe glittered in the sun.

Salim chose to cast his eyes downwards, to his knees. The master's stick made a rut in the ground as it spiked into view and the fall of his robe brushed against Salim's cheek. He could hear the master's long diatribe as he towered above him – accusing Salim of siding with the infidel. Salim was aware of the sweat from the master's brow that dropped onto his own forehead. He remained perfectly still, observing in close detail the small pieces of coloured glass that made remarkable patterns on the master's robe. He swallowed hard to prepare himself for a blow and concentrated on taking long deep breaths. Finally, the noise above him seemed to abate.

Slowly, Salim dared to look up.

The skin on the master's cheeks and forehead steamed with perspiration from the great effort he had expended. With a loose tail of his turban he wiped his brow. His lips trembled and cold eyes glared down at the younger man.

In both hands, the master's stick drew back, like a cricket bat, far behind his shoulders.

As though about to pray, Salim put together the flat of his palms and raised them towards the master.

Suddenly, from somewhere near the front, there was a shriek.

Blue stood up, a white skullcap concealing his blond hair. His face, grotesquely swollen from when Salim had last seen him earlier that morning, contorted into some sort of agony and again the boy screamed.

The master's stick dangled at his side, coming to a gentle rest against Salim's knee. With an impatient expression, the master turned towards the men at the rear and one, a compounder, stood up. The boys parted to let him through, and picking up Blue, the old man left.

The master returned to his place at the head of the assembly and continued with the prayer. Looking up at the perfect blue sky, Salim communed silently with Allah, asking Him to forgive him for what he had done to Blue.

After *Juma* prayer Salim avoided the master where he could. However, on the occasions when they happened to meet whilst crossing the compound, the master spoke to Salim cheerfully, as though nothing untoward had occurred, or that now he had publicly established his authority over Salim, for the master, that was enough.

Salim took to sleeping in his room and, diligently, he carried on with his duties: teaching the rote, instructing the cook, the laundryman and guards. Salim was neither the master, nor a pupil, nor was he part of the staff. He was conscious that he alone had been left to prosper beyond the age of fifteen without being called to jihad. Salim felt awkward at times and, physically, he towered above the others, not least his uncle.

Another week passed.

Salim was woken from a deep sleep by what he thought was someone pulling at his leg. Startled and confused he reached for the light but before he could switch it on, a flashlight illuminated a circle on the peeling plasterwork of the store-cupboard ceiling. At the foot of his bed crouched the cook, his white teeth luminous like tombstones under moonlight.

"Come," Cook instructed, getting silently to his feet.

Rubbing his eyes, Salim sat up in bed and drew a shawl around himself.

"Come. Now." Cook's gesticulation was panicked and urgent.

Salim followed him out of the room and across the hallway. The heavy double doors that guarded the seminary creaked as they drew open. Outside, a green electrical lantern hung in the portico, thick with flies. The colour green was a beacon for the faithful and the only visible night light for miles. The sandy ground thankfully yielded little noise as Salim and the cook made their way to the street side of the gate. The seminary's two night guards stood at a distance from the wooden crib, smoking. Above, and stretching flat into the horizon, the black sky was crowded with stars. With wildly excited eyes, the cook gestured that Salim look in.

Cook's flashlight led Salim's gaze to what looked like a bundle of bloody rags. His eyes accustoming to the light, he could make out a mat of black hair and a short nose. The swaddling trembled from the movement of the newborn's tiny birdcage chest.

Salim turned towards Cook and shrugged his shoulders.

A cigarette met the floor and was stamped underfoot by a guard.

Cook shook his head.

Again Salim gazed into the crib but this time, something compelled him to peel away the bloody cloth. He recoiled in horror and stepped back.

Salim's first thought was that the master must not get to know about this. His mind raced as to what to do. He didn't have an answer, he needed time. Briefly it occurred to him that the cook's wife – he could conceal the infant with her.

The master travelled in procession, always a gaggle of boys around him, and the doors had been left open. Salim heard the boys first, their excited squeals, and turning, he saw his uncle's bed robes flap in the night breeze as he made his way over to the cot.

The boys crowded silently around.

The master looked at Salim, at the crib but not into it, at the cook and the guards and finally at the boys jostling for space around his legs.

"Fuck off," he instructed loudly. "All of you."

To stop Salim from leaving, he put an arm around the younger man's shoulders.

The others skulked away and the infant in the crib stirred, letting out a pathetic cough.

The master looked in and then turned to face Salim, his lips quivering as though wanting to smile. "Perfect, isn't she, like an angel from heaven."

Salim nodded.

The master continued. "The more I study the less I understand about God."

Salim felt a cold sweat on his brow and spoke in an authoritative voice. "She might be useful – in time. We could put her to work."

The master shook his head and sucked the frozen mountain air between his teeth.

"Or could ask – One of the villagers might –"

The master broke in. "I was kind, was I not, to your boy Blue. I let him go with the compounder."

"He was sick, master."

"He wasn't sick when he was willed to us, nephew."

Deep inside Salim felt a cold panic rising, yet on the surface his skin seemed to burn.

The master's hand slipped from Salim's shoulders and came to rest at the back of Salim's neck.

Salim's gaze traced the luminous peaks of the snow-capped range. "Or maybe there is an alternative fate written for her."

"There is only God's will," retorted the master.

Salim continued. "We could offer her to the cook's wife."

"Cook will be leaving us in the morning."

Salim felt his head being pushed forward.

"She will have a price." Salim's voice was uncertain. "When she is older . . ."

The master offered an ironic nod and turned his eyes westwards towards the fallow field.

Salim felt his uncle's hand shift to his throat and close. He struggled for breath.

"Nephew, I think you know what you have to do."

"Blue" is the first chapter of a novel in progress, provisionally titled *The Journeymen*

One for Luck

MELANIE JONES

The girl hops through shafts of morning light, dodging the sprinklers. Her skin is gold.

Rose sips cranberry juice on the porch and watches her daughter. The firstborn. Rose used to think that Sarah would be the solid one. That's why she gave her a sensible name. A name for a successful working woman.

Daughter number two shies from the water, treading heel to toe. Alana. Named on a whim. Deep-blue eyes. Red hair. A wild child, Rose had once imagined. Destined for far-flung journeys, bandanas and bongs, scratching out a living in some dusty country and laughing about her sister the lawyer, doctor, teacher, whatever. But Alana is quiet. She follows rules. Rose often asks herself if she is disappointed, but that's never it. They could still be anything, go anywhere. Sometimes it feels like terror.

It's summer and almost every house on the cul-de-sac has a sprinkler maintaining a perfect lawn. The sprinklers are light activated and it is the pump hiss pump hiss that wakes Rose and the girls each morning. Their father sleeps through the scuffle for swimming costumes, through hasty breakfasts. Sarah and Alana are first out every day. They are the only children in the street. They are adored. Rose grins as Sarah runs shrieking across Mr Collins' lawn and slides under the sprinkler past a bed of peonies. Alana is slower and is caught in the face by the water. She coughs but keeps going. Her hair, more of a rusty brown now, is damp and stuck to her face. Her sister's is still dry, a flag of blond.

Rose holds cranberry juice in her mouth, letting the bitterness rest around the gums at the back where her wisdom teeth used to be. She keeps it there for as long as she can before swishing it to the tip of her tongue for a dash of sweetness. She touches the lip of her dressing-gown pocket.

These perfect mornings stretch back for ever. As if the girls have always been twelve and ten. Always on summer holiday. They float in a happy haze. Rose knows she should enjoy it, but when everything is beautiful, it starts to feel normal.

She looks up at the clouds and hopes for rain, a grazed knee on one of the girls, or her old favourite, bashing her elbow on the door handle. If she holds out for long enough, one of these things will happen. Then she'll take the pill. Blow away the clouds.

But nothing changes. It stays bright. The girls remain trapped in their magical bubble. Rose wonders if this is genuine. Or whether everyone else in the cul-de-sac has swallowed their morning pill and the glow of their collective luck is tiding her over. She drops her hand into her pocket. The bottle is there. It's there.

Mr Collins opens his door as the sound of shrieking children carries over to the next lawn. A few months back the noise would have scrunched his face into a frown and he would have muttered behind the door while his wife told him not to be such a grumpy old man. As if she'd been the angel of patience and compassion. But not any more. He waves at Rose. Nice lady. He used to think she was hysterical. Always crying or making a noise. If the car didn't start, tears. If he went over to complain about the girls, tears. Too fragile.

Now he finds her pleasant enough. It's not like he's one of those "born-again" types or anything. Just, everything's easier when you don't have back pain or when the bills aren't mounting up on the doormat. When the sun shines.

He looks down at his feet and sees the manila envelope he knows is from his daughter. It's decorated with stickers and drawings and it's fat. She sends him the local paper from her village so he can see what's going on. He tells her there's no need, that he has enough to deal with in his own little world without needing to read about hers. But she knows, he knows, the wife knows, everyone knows really, that he loves it. That it makes him feel like she's close. She never used to write. Mrs C doesn't read the letters. She says they're fake. That there's no way the kid would write to them under normal circumstances (Mrs C calls it a side effect). But she's not getting into the spirit of things. There's no good in thinking about what was. He only cares about what is. He pushes the past to the back of his mind. The time he dragged his teenaged daughter out onto the street by her hair, calling her a slut, and all the neighbours came out and watched. It flashes into his head when he touches the envelope but quickly fades. "You'll be lucky if you ever hear from that girl again," one of the neighbours had said, probably Pete. Well, lucky's the word. Once a week she writes. Curling handwriting with kitty-cat ears on the dots of the i's, just like when she was a kid.

He can smell food. Mrs C'll be calling him any minute now. Breakfast will be laid out. Boiled eggs. He hates poached or scrambled. Too wobbly. Toast cooling in the toast rack so the butter won't melt and he can enjoy the shapes he makes in it with his crooked front teeth. Marmalade. A pot of tea. And lucky red pills sitting in the shot glasses they bought on their honeymoon. He'll chink glasses with the missus. "Here's to us," she'll say, and down the pills'll go, followed with a dash of grapefruit juice. Mrs C always buys grapefruit now. No more of this nonsense about it tasting like bile. It's the small changes he enjoys the most. There's more to luck than money and glory.

Rose hasn't noticed him waving. Too busy watching those golden girls of hers. He can't blame her. He wishes he'd taken the time.

Another door opens and Mr Collins squints in the sunlight to see the gayboys in their suits. Now that's not fair, he tells himself. We don't call them that any more. Now he calls them Fred and Tony. Good lads. They've been round for dinner. Tony works in the city these days. It's not like before when there were parties and people passed out on the lawn. Fred's been good for Tony. Good for everyone. A decent young man. Mr Collins regrets being rude to him when they first met, but the regret is small. They're best of friends now. Fred knows how to run a business. He cares about the community and always delivers on time, like clockwork.

Tony gets into his car and Fred leans through the open window for a kiss. Mr Collins doesn't care. People can kiss who they like. He doesn't fancy watching, though, so he hugs his envelope and steps back into the house. He can already taste the marmalade.

"The creepy guy from Number 7 is looking."

"So?"

Tony turns away and Fred's kiss lands on his ear.

"Is that any way to say goodbye?" Fred says.

Tony shakes his head. "Hurry, then," he says. "Or I'll be late."

Fred watches the car leave the cul-de-sac. Tony should be happier. But that's the trouble with Tony. He loves to complain and so now, he does it more and more. That's his idea of good luck, something to gripe about. Fred likes an easy life, so he lets it slide, every time. Tony is one of those people who needs to feel superior. Fred wants him to have that.

He breathes the clean fresh air, still cool even though the day is starting to heat up. He listens to the waves of giggles and sprinkler spray as the girls from Number 6 bound through the sheets of water.

One day soon, they'll have a child of their own. Despite Tony complaining about the adoption forms and bitching about how they'll be grandparent age before they finally get a kid, the process has been easy. And it should have been so much harder given Tony's history. It takes time, that's all. Fred is happy to wait. He wants both of them to have the image of the perfect child in their heads before they sign the papers. Synchronised and clear. That's how it works. But Fred hasn't decided if he wants the kid to be smart. "Would you rather be smart or happy?" he asks Tony. "Can't I be both?" Tony says. Fred knows you can't be both.

It was only a year ago that Tony approached him outside the leisure centre. He was after the usual stuff and thought Fred was a dealer. His clothes were unwashed, mucky and torn. His left ear was full of piercings and his right looked like someone had taken a bite out of it. The other salesmen wouldn't give him the time of day. Told him he was asking the wrong people, that he couldn't afford what they had. Tony had shouted some abuse and gotten a bit of a kicking from Fred's boss. But Fred had seen something in Tony's eyes. Potential. Beauty. A good man in a bad situation. Just needed a bit of luck.

He took Tony for coffee, found out all about him. That his mum had died the year before, that he lived in her old house in some grotty back road outside of the city, that even though he'd never worked a day in his life the mortgage was paid off so he struggled to get benefits. Fred gave him a freebie. Soon it was clean clothes, a job in finance, dates in high-end restaurants. Fred moved in, got chatting to the neighbours and in a matter of months, grotty back road became desirable cul-de-sac. Heaven on earth.

Well, almost, he thinks, as a car in the driveway furthest from his revs and then grumbles to a stop.

The owner of the car, Karen, is Fred's final project. Karen used to be Tony's best friend but she couldn't handle him getting his life together. She said all kinds of awful things at Fred's moving-in party. He can forgive. He knows Tony misses her. She's out of the car now, screaming into her mobile phone and kicking garden ornaments. Fred smiles. This could be the perfect opportunity to smooth things over.

Karen flings her phone into the road. The screen shatters. She makes a fist and swings it into the car door. Her hand bounces back. Knuckles bruised. Her eyes are blurred with tears and she's sure the pod people are filing out of their houses to get a look at the freak show. Smug Rose. Pervy Mr Collins. Tony, who used to be a half-decent person before he started driving a Mercedes and using a ruler on the grass to check whether his gardener was doing a good enough job. She marches back to the house, picks up the stack of post that has been accumulating on the doormat and hurls it into the street after the phone.

There's a mallet on the other side of the front door. Her ex put it there during the riots, in case of looters. She'd told him they weren't in much danger this far from the capital but he'd been a paranoid weirdo. Well, she has a use for it now. She snatches it up and swings it over her shoulder.

Not as many people as she thought. Only Rose stepping from

foot to foot on her front lawn like she needs a piss and Fred, who must have just finished giving Tony the morning send-off. She gives both of them a wide grin before bringing the mallet down on the phone.

The explosion knocks her back but she doesn't fall. A black cloud of smoke rises from the ground and the air smells of burnt plastic. Mobile phones explode? Well that's a fucking health hazard. She adds phone companies to her "not to be trusted" list and looks up to gauge the reaction. Rose has started to walk her way. Karen wants to hit the mobile again but she's scared of another explosion so instead she swings the mallet back and brings it smashing into the useless piece of shit hunk of metal that her dad calls a "vintage fixer-upper". Normally she leaves the house a good hour or so before any of these creeps wake up, but now she'll have to face them. "You know," she says to the car, "I used to be the fucking respectable one around here."

She wonders if Tony's ever told Fred who helped him plan the funeral after his mum died. Or who drove him to hospital that time, in the very heap of shit that Fred is now eyeing with disdain. She'd crashed on Tony's floor as a kid, when her own mum was too blitzed to remember she had a daughter. That's where faking it leads. But Tony hasn't spoken to her since Fred moved in. Since it stopped raining. Since everyone started to get that same look of contented bewilderment on their faces. She's the only one who still takes the newspaper. Still has a telly. The rest of them all got rid of theirs in the first few months. Living on the same street, she's reaped some of the benefits. Warm weather, flowers, peace and quiet. But whatever it is they're taking doesn't extend to the rest of the world. People still die. Illnesses remain uncured. Poverty, war and everything else goes on. The street just doesn't hear about it.

Rose is walking towards her with more purpose and it looks like she's dragging Fred along. Karen rests the mallet against the side of the car and pops open the bonnet.

"Good morning, Karen," Sarah says as she skips into the road.

"Morning, Karen." The echo from Alana.

Rose smiles. They are polite girls. Good girls. She hopes

people see that this is her doing. Karen is in her driveway probably thinking to herself that Rose must be a great mum to have such well-behaved girls. Girls who would never cause an explosion in the middle of a residential area. Rose wishes Karen would move out, but her husband tells her to be more charitable. That they have enough luck to share.

She is feeling a little sick now and as she leaves the front garden she feels a splash of water that hasn't come from a sprinkler. Her knee is starting to ache again. She tries to catch Karen's eye. No luck. She touches the bulge in her pocket and walks closer. Fred's out on his lawn, too.

"Poor Karen," she says to him.

He frowns. Fair enough. Karen is a pain.

"We should give her a hand," she says.

He follows her to the edge of Karen's driveway with his hands in his pockets.

"Car trouble?" Rose says.

Karen looks up from the engine holding a spanner. She waves it around in front of her face as if that's an answer.

"Well I don't think that'll be much help," Rose says.

Karen runs an oily hand through her hair and Rose takes a mental step back. The woman is foul.

"Can't you do something?" Rose says to Fred.

"Cars aren't my thing," he says.

Karen is just staring at both of them. She hasn't said a word and Rose is wishing she'd stayed on the porch. She can't hear the girls any more and the ache has spread to her shoulders. A raindrop falls on her hand and sends a shiver up her arm.

"Is it raining?" Fred says.

He's glaring right at her. She smiles and shrugs.

Rose doesn't know how he knows but he always does. She tried to detox once, just to see what would happen, but within hours there was a little note from Fred on the doormat about the dangers of withdrawal. A free pill taped to it. He doesn't need to worry about her. It's not like she's not going to take it. She just wants to feel the benefit.

"You know," she says, a little out of breath, "I'm going to ask Mr C if he has a tool kit, or some oil, or something."

She starts to walk away and shoves her hand into her dressing-gown pocket. The pill bottle has one of those child-safety lids and her hands slip around as she tries to get it off. She jogs down the Collins' drive and bangs her fist on the door.

"Tool kit, car, breakdown, KAREN," she shouts through the letterbox.

She's still fumbling with the lid and it's definitely raining now which doesn't help. By the time she's back to her own driveway, she has it open. She pulls out the cotton wool, sticks her index finger inside, and swirls it around searching for the pill.

"RAC," Karen says, pointing at the fragments of her phone.

Fred is watching Rose skitter around the street. He turns to look at Karen as if he'd forgotten she was there. Well good, she thinks. Never wanted to be the subject of his attention anyway.

"What?" he says.

"Cunts. Told me my membership lapsed. I paid it. Now there's some new condition that –"

"RAC?" Fred cuts her off.

"Yeah. They fix cars. The fucker won't start and when it does it's just lurching around."

He smiles. It makes her feel queasy.

"Karen, the RAC is not what you need," he says. "Why don't you let me help you?"

Something red and translucent is in his hand. She doesn't know where it came from. At first, she thinks it's a jewel, a ruby earring glittering even though the sun has gone behind the clouds. Then she remembers.

"One for luck?" he says.

Karen stares and then looks up. For a second the red seems to reflect in his eyes. She looks back at the pill. It's beautiful. He's slipped it into her palm before she has time to say no.

A door opens. Mr Collins with his tool box. Rose's girls are following, nosy little shits.

"I'm not taking this," she says, but her hand closes over it.

"This better be an emergency," Mr Collins says. "I've not had my breakfast yet. Can't get anything done on an empty stomach."

Fred laughs.

"Well we all know what that means," he says so that only Karen can hear. "Why don't you let me give it a go?"

Before she can stop him he's opening the driver's door and turning the key. The engine turns over and settles to a smooth purr.

He steps back and thumps the roof.

"See," he says, "no RAC required."

Heavy summer raindrops fall and his hair is pasted to his forehead. Karen's curls start to frizz.

She's out on the main road before she has time to think about what happened. Glancing in the rear-view mirror she sees the streak of oil across her forehead, remembers her work bag sitting at home on the sofa, and the front door left wide open.

"Fucking hell."

It's raining hard now and visibility is next to nothing as she turns the car around and heads back into the cul-de-sac, splashing through the puddles that have formed. She can just make out Rose banging with her fist on her own front door. Did she lock herself out? The woman looks desperate, like the old days. Karen's still staring at her when she hits the sheet water and the brakes fail.

Rose sobs as she thumps on the door.

"I've run out of pills," she calls to Pete.

Her dressing gown is sodden. She wonders if one of the girls has a key. It's raining so hard they won't notice she's been crying. She's so stupid. All those warnings about always having a fresh supply. Pete asking her every morning if she's remembered her pill. "Think of the girls," he says.

"Sarah! Alana!"

There's a scream underneath her shout. The girls are still on stupid Karen's lawn with Fred. They wave at her through the rain with their arms above their heads.

"Home!" she calls.

Alana is the first to follow orders but she's taking the long way round, sticking to the pavement. Sarah jumps up and down on the spot a few times before sprinting across the road just as Karen's ugly Nissan Micra comes sliding back into the street. The flag of blond heading straight for the smudge of grey. Rose starts to run, her dressing gown flapping open. Mr Collins drops the tool box. Fred is running too as the car spins out of control.

Karen sees the girl and her mother racing towards each other and wonders if the car will slide to meet them. Perhaps they'll make it out of the way in time and instead she'll hit one of the cherry trees that line the cul-de-sac. She must be going fast because the world outside of the car is blurry. But things feel slow. She has time to turn her head and get a good look at the street. If the car spins again it could be Fred that gets the rough end of her front bumper. Back to reality for everyone. Or Mr Collins, the rageful drunk. His daughter would thank her. Karen wonders if she has a choice. Her left hand tries to move the wheel but it's locked. Her right is in her lap, closed in a fist around the pill. She has a choice. She takes a deep breath and opens her mouth. Swallows.

Black Box

ALIYAH KIM KESHANI

Sweat runs between Mei's eyes. She scrubs furiously, pausing only to dip the brush into the bucket of gunk water beside her. Her right hand begins to cramp but she ignores it.

The plane has been missing for twenty-three days.

She doesn't feel the sun at first, the morning warmth creeping up her back. It wakes her tired muscles. Mei closes her eyes, puts down the spray for a moment. Then she presses on, bringing up her left hand to hold her right steady. She forces the bristles into the corners of the oven and, eventually, dislodges the charred remains of a chip.

"Ha!" She throws down the brush.

From the bedroom, there's a groan. Mei freezes. She hears the spring of the mattress then Rohan's feet on the floorboards. She lugs the bucket to the sink, throws the greasy water down the plughole.

"That you?" says Rohan, squinting from the doorway. "What time is it?"

He shuffles into the kitchen, kisses her on the cheek. He smells of sleep – a musk of linen and sweat. Mei pulls off her gloves and massages the knot of muscles in her hand. She watches as he moves groggily around her and it's envy she feels. For a sleep that can erase everything in its path. Rohan steps from one cupboard to the next, opening and closing doors.

"Oh," she says, remembering. "Top left. Spoons in here. Cereal on this side now."

"Again?" He carries his breakfast over to the table. "How long have you been up?"

She'd sat bleary-eyed in front of the Biography Channel from midnight and watched the lives of Lincoln, Churchill and Houdini. Houdini had been her favourite. He'd started out as a nine-year-old trapeze artist, the self-styled "Prince of the Air". The programme had gone on to explain his illusions and how, in a theatre of thousands, he'd made a full-size elephant step into a cabinet and vanish. But he'd only done the trick once, at the Hippodrome in New York, in 1918. And the elephant was called –

"Mei, did you sleep?"

She throws the gloves in the bin. "I'm fine."

"Mei?" When she doesn't reply, he pushes back from the table, stands up. "I don't think you should go in today."

She runs the taps and washes her hands.

"I could take the time off, too," he says. "We could stay in, rest. Book our holiday –"

"Ro, I've got a billion things to do," says Mei. "Go shower."

"Do them from home."

"I have to finish my report and get it to Siobhan this afternoon. I can't afford to give her another reason –"

"You were signed off."

"What difference does that make?"

He takes her by the shoulders and turns her round to face him. "Give yourself a break, Mei. Call in, take the morning off. Your uncle –"

"Rohan." She's silent a moment. "Please."

He shakes his head, leaves the room. The bathroom door slams. Mei hears the hiss of shower water then slowly lets out her breath. She takes her coffee over to the window and watches the couple in the opposite flat as they play out the same morning routine: breakfast, shower, work. They bustle through the living room, ignoring the television flickering in the corner.

Mei had been obsessed the first two weeks, glued to the screen while her phone beeped with every update. When the information ran out, she'd followed the conspiracy theories from Putin to

Snowden to North Korea. She'd scrolled the online threads until the speculation unravelled into alien abductions. And then, finally numb, she'd stopped. She reset her filters and avoided the news, watched documentaries through the night instead. She would wait for the embassy to contact her. When they found it. When someone could explain.

She rubs her eyes, looks up over the buildings. Even the gulls are struggling today, riffing on the wind. High above the Orbit Tower, a small plane cuts into a mass of cloud. Its underbelly glints in the sun for a moment then it vanishes, its trail of plume slowly dissipating. Mei drops the blind and turns away.

The homeless man sits at the mouth of the alley, his dog huddled beside him. It's the same strange colour as the dogs her uncle used to keep. *Keeps.* The same orangey tan. Mei slows down. It's hard to think of her uncle without the dogs. The way they would press against the bars of the front door when he went inside, whining pitifully and thwacking their tails against the metal. Where had they come from? He'd never named or bought any of them. He'd just accumulated them, his strange pack of half-wild loyal dogs.

Mei drops a handful of coins in the man's bowl as she passes, then makes her way down the alley. In the wind, the trees lean into the fence, their branches crowding through the mesh. It's colder than she thought it would be, but a good kind of cold; bracing. She picks up the pace, turns onto the high street and is met by the mingled smells of coffee and pastries and petrol. It's a thirty-five-minute walk to work this way, part of the reason she'd moved from the cramped Bayswater studio. No more trains or being stuck underground, wedged under someone's armpit.

And walking was good. She'd always loved it, even as a child. When they'd visited Bentong in the summers, her parents would conk out with jet lag, leaving her uncle responsible for entertaining her. He'd fix them sugar-on-toast and iced Milo for breakfast, then take her walking through the plantation, just the two of them. He'd tie a red rag around his head and slide on his Rambo sunglasses before they left, while she sprayed herself with repellent. Even in the mornings, the air would be hot and sticky, humming with dragonflies the size of her fist. He'd chop down branches for them to use as walking sticks, hand her the smaller one and say: "Today, Ah-Mei, we are kung fu ninjas!" And they'd pretend to kick and jab the tree, yowling like cats. Or: "Today, Ah-Mei, we are old and very serious grandmothers." And they'd hunch over and wobble out through the gates, past the rows of coffee beans drying in the sun, all the while complaining of their sore backs and knobbly knees.

He would talk about the land as they walked, how many acres they owned, the price of rubber, how to tap trees. He'd show her the guavas and papayas, the rambutan and jackfruit. They'd gaze up at the clusters of green bananas, and prod the fallen mangoes until the skins pulped and crawled with ants. And, sometimes, her uncle would cut down a thorny stinking durian and they'd both pretend to hold their noses all the way back home.

One summer, when she was eight, they'd gone to stay in the Genting Highlands for a few days. She, her parents, her cousins, her neighbours and her uncle. On the way home, they'd taken the funicular down the hilltop, crowded into their two cars and driven back to Bentong. And it was only when they'd stood outside the front door, waiting for her uncle to open it, that they realised they'd left him behind.

Mei smiles.

Her mother had been furious, especially after he'd phoned to explain. He'd spent the night in a casino and had passed out under the blackjack table. He stayed on for another three nights then used his winnings to pay for the taxi ride home. She could see him now, stepping out of the car, sunglasses on despite the rain, and dressed in a new white suit.

Mei jogs up the steps to her office. She pulls out her work pass and swipes it against the sensor. That was so much like her uncle. Undefeatable. Unpredictable. Irrepressible.

Where was he now?

From the top of the stairs, Mei can see the pile of papers on her desk. She groans quietly before making her way across the floor.

"Jesus Christ, you've lost weight," says Abby, sticking her head over the divide. "Just look at you! I'm jealous."

"Morning," says Mei, and takes off her coat. She switches on her computer. Why had none of them noticed her uncle wasn't in either car that day? Two and a half hours from Genting to Bentong, and amidst all the bickering and singing and shouting, it hadn't crossed anybody's mind?

"Hey, did you hear about Steve and Collette?" Abby hisses. "Oh my *God*. His wife found the photos from the Christmas party – you *know* which ones. And now she says he has to fire her – Collette, I mean – or *she's* going to leave him. So. Much. Drama. Shall we do lunch? I can catch you up."

"Not today," says Mei, forcing a smile.

"Why not?"

Mei clicks through her emails. Her uncle had overslept, that's why he'd missed the ride. But his timekeeping had always been bad. He was always late to things. He'd miss the beginnings of films, of dinners. He was even late to her cousin's wedding –

"Earth to Mei! Lunch?"

"Abby, I can't. I have to finish my report."

"Ohh." Abby lowers her voice. "She wasn't happy about that. Wasn't it due last week?"

"I wasn't here," says Mei.

Abby shrugs.

Mei closes her eyes for a moment and wills Abby to disappear, but she doesn't. Instead she stays, lingering on the periphery of Mei's vision.

"She was asking about it so I sent her some of your notes."

"What?" says Mei. "Why would you –"

But it's too late; Siobhan is already making a beeline for her. Mei can see the bob of her dark curls over the top of the filing cabinets. Abby sits down and begins typing.

"Mei!" Siobhan pulls up a chair and scoots it next to Mei's. Her floral perfume fills the air. "I need to dash in a minute but I wanted to check how you were."

"All right," says Mei. "Busy."

"Good –" Siobhan's BlackBerry goes off. She pulls it out of her pocket, frowns at the message and types a quick reply. She pockets the phone again and smiles at Mei. "It must be a difficult time."

Mei nods, trying to ignore the semicircles that Siobhan's mascara has printed onto the tops of her eyelids.

"How's your report coming along?"

"Abby shouldn't have sent my notes," says Mei quickly. "They weren't finished."

"Don't worry," says Siobhan, patting her arm. "We're just glad to have you back." She gets up, wheels the chair to its desk, hesitates. "There is one more thing," she says, turning to Mei. "Steve's taken the week off and his report needs finishing, too. Can I leave that with you?"

"I've got all this to do," says Mei, picking up a handful of files. "I won't have time."

Siobhan's phone begins to ring.

"You've been away, Mei," she says, pulling out her BlackBerry. She groans at the screen then glances up. "I'll send it to you now." She walks away, answering the call.

Mei throws down her files. She stares fixedly at her computer until Abby finally starts typing again.

By midday, her head aches. She squints at her report, the skin of her right eyelid jumping with every pulse. A floater in her vision trails distractingly across the screen. Against the white, it's a squiggle, never quite in focus, always on the move. She blinks hard, shakes her head, but it won't disappear. Instead, it changes shape and slides, hook-like, down the page. Mei closes her eyes.

She should never have left teaching. She'd been good at it, enjoyed it. It just didn't pay anything. Her uncle had taught, too. Maths. Two years at a school in the city before she'd been born. Back before Grandfather had died and left her uncle to sort out the plantation and the debt. Her uncle had been the smart one, the one that went to university because the family couldn't afford to send the rest. But, somehow, the rest had found jobs, moved countries, changed lives. And he'd stayed on in that little town, working with the labourers. He'd never taken holidays; he refused to get a passport. He'd never even been on a plane until –

Mei opens her eyes.

What if he hadn't got on?

There had to be security footage; the passengers boarding the plane. The embassy could request it, check it. What with her uncle's timekeeping and his reluctance to leave, it was possible.

She searches the Internet for the number, then picks up her phone and punches it in. She pauses before the last digit, the tips of her fingers prickling. The keypad comes in and out of focus. She puts the receiver down, slowly breathes out. *Ang. Ang Kwan-Yew. I'm his niece.* She rehearses her lines, picks up the phone again. The burr of the dial tone throbs in her ears. This time, she forces herself to enter the whole number. She swallows; waits. The line is busy.

After twenty minutes, Mei gives up. She washes down a couple of paracetamols with the dregs of her coffee. Then she stands and stretches, wincing as the muscles in her back crack loudly. She carries her cup down the stairs to the breakout room. Abby's voice flares out through the open door.

"I can't believe she's still acting like this. It's ridiculous."

"She's having a hard time." That was Martha's voice.

"*She's* having a hard time? What about me? I'm the one stuck doing all her fucking work. I have my own reports to do, you know? But, no, we can't get Little Miss Perfect too stressed. Well, here's the truth – we're *all* stressed. But we don't go swanning off like that."

"That's not fair, Abs. Her uncle was on that plane."

"I'm *sorry*," Abby says, "but so *what*? That was a month ago. We can't tiptoe around her for ever. He's gone. She needs to get over it. End of story."

Mei clears her throat as she walks in. There's a moment of silence. They shift in their seats then switch topic – how cold it was, how good *Love Island* had been last night.

Mei puts her cup down loudly in the sink and fills the kettle. She can feel the heat coming off her face, can practically hear them mouthing, "Oh my God! Did she . . . ?" behind her back. Let them, Mei thinks. Let them think whatever the hell they want. She walks over to the table and rounds up the empty cups beside Abby.

"Done with these?" She turns away before they can answer. She runs the tap on full and scrubs at the coffee rings with her fist inside the cups.

"I was just telling Martha about the new Brad Pitt film," Abby says. "Have you seen the trailer, Mei? It looks *amazing*."

Mei says nothing. She reaches for the dirty plates piled on the counter.

"And," Abby continues, "I forgot to tell you. I tried that Thai restaurant you recommended. On Charlotte Street? You're right, it's to die for."

More silence.

"We'd better go," says Martha eventually.

"Yes," says Abby. "Some of us have work to do."

Mei waits until they're up the stairs then throws down the sponge. She wipes her face with the back of her hands. Forget work. Forget waiting for the embassy to pick up. She'll go in person. She'll demand to be seen.

Her phone rings on the way to the station. It's Rohan.

"Sorry about earlier," he says.

"Forget it." She jogs across the road, narrowly avoiding a van. It blares its horn.

"What was that?" Rohan says. "Where are you?"

"It's fine," she says, her voice trembling. "I can't talk right now. I have to go to the embassy."

"Has there been news?"

"No." She dithers at the top of the station stairs, stepping in and out of the stream of bodies. Then she tells him about Genting, about her uncle, his timekeeping. "The embassy could get the security footage. I should have thought of this sooner. He might have missed the boarding, or – or someone else used his name and got on."

"Mei, where are you?"

"And he doesn't even *have* a mobile so that could be why –"

"Mei!" Rohan's silent a while. "We'd have heard from him by now. I'm going to come and meet you –"

She pulls the phone from her ear and stares down at the screen. Rohan's voice, tinny through the speaker, pulses out of it. She disconnects the call and takes the stairs down to the Underground.

The train is busier than she expected. She shuffles along the carriage and finds a seat across from a mother and baby. She watches as they play peekaboo, the mother disappearing behind her Tube map. The baby's eyes widen, first with expectation then with worry. The frown deepens, the mouth parts, lips trembling and then – suddenly – an explosive screech of delight. The child lights up, beams its gummy smile. And who knew? Come back, Mei wants to call. Come back, please.

The train slows down, then shudders to a halt inside the tunnel.

At first, it's all right. It's routine. A red signal. Waiting for the train ahead to leave the platform. That must be it. But the driver says nothing. Passengers sigh and pull out their phones. Mei ducks her head to look out of the window but there's only blackness.

It creeps up on her. Her arms begin to itch, the insides of her elbows aching like pressed bruises. The fear takes hold, changes shape. It snakes out from somewhere between her lungs and coils around her ribs until it's hard to breathe. She needs to distract herself – something, anything. The baby. She concentrates, watching it reach up for its mother's hair. The pudginess of its hand, the tiny fingers curling in the yellow light, and the soft, oval nails –

Mei gets up. She pushes past the suitcases in the aisles and stands by the door, breathing hard. She closes her eyes and wills the train to move. She can smell the sourness of her clothes and the sweat of the passengers around her. Overhead, the carriage lights begin to flicker. Her fear expands inside her chest and rises up along the cavity of her throat. Was this how it had been? Like this? She wants to crouch against the floor, to cradle her head in her hands, and howl.

Suddenly, the lights glare and the train lurches forward. Mei snatches at the pole and steadies herself. She clenches it until the next stop and stares out the window. Her pale reflection slides against the darkness, the upper half of her face bulging away on the curve of the pane.

Two guards stand outside the embassy. Above them, the Malaysian flag flies at half-mast. Its red and white lines ripple in the wind, making and unmaking the crescent and star.

They'd come here the day after the plane vanished. The square was heaving with reporters and photographers but Rohan had pushed through the crowd. They'd been escorted to a room already full of the other families. And they'd waited, the air bristling with fear and worry. Eventually, an official came in. He talked for a short while, repeating what they already knew, then he read out the list.

People jumped to their feet, shouting with anger, with disbelief, as the names were called. The woman beside Mei dropped to her haunches and sobbed with her face in her hands. Mei stood numb. There were two hundred and thirty-nine names in all. Her uncle's was one of the last. And when it was read out – *Ang Kwan-Yew* – it sounded distant and strange, as though it belonged to someone other than him. She'd felt Rohan's grip tighten on her hand, then something inside had given way.

"Are you all right, Miss?" says one of the guards.

"Yes," she says softly and looks back up at the flag. Rohan had guided her out of the building that night. He'd found them a cab and they'd ridden home in silence.

"Do you have an appointment with someone?"

"No. But . . ." The words fall away. The list would have come from the passports. They'd have been scanned on boarding the plane. Mei rubs her eyes.

"Can I help?"

She turns to look at him. He's so young, his face smooth under thick-rimmed glasses except for a small flared pimple by his chin.

"Miss?"

"No," she says. "You can't." She leaves the square, and makes for Hyde Park.

For years, the park had been part of her weekend routine. She'd wake early and buy sticky rice dumplings from the Chinese shop below her flat. She'd eat them slowly, savouring their rich saltiness, as she walked through the park.

It feels larger entering from the south somehow. Mei steps off the path and crunches over leaves. She runs her hands over rough tree bark and takes in the smell of grass and soil. She passes the lido then crosses over the road to the western side of the park.

She hears the parakeets before she sees them, their fresh hard chatter. They burst out of the treetops and circle fast overhead, their wings a blur of lime. Despite herself, Mei smiles. She watches them soar out into the sky.

In front of her, something is snagged in one of the bushes. She bends down and picks it up. It's half a postcard, stained by grass and curling at the edges. She smooths it out: a black-and-white print of a girl standing with one arm down and the other reaching up – the card has been ripped away at her elbow. Mei turns it over and reads the thin italics:

> Dear Lloyd, I cannot tell you how touched I was to receive your letter. Thank you for your condolences and for the kind and thoughtful book. I enjoyed it very much. It has been most difficult –

Mei blinks then reads it again several times. She takes it with her, walking slowly up the Serpentine until she reaches the Peter Pan statue. It was always her favourite spot; the two benches, slightly tucked away from the path, opening out onto greenery and the waterfront. She sits down and studies the postcard again. In the picture, the girl's short hair blows up around her face. Her skirt tugs forward, pulled by the wind. She stares up at something but it belongs to the other half of the card.

Dear Lloyd . . . It has been most difficult . . .

This time, Mei doesn't stop. She cries; for her uncle, for herself, for all of them left behind to guess and to grieve. Eventually, she puts the postcard in her pocket and sits watching the ducks on the lake.

She sees Rohan some time later, making his way along the path. He sits down beside her and passes her a paper bag.

"Sandwich and a coffee," he says.

She smiles at him, squeezes his hand. "How did you find me?"

"I looked everywhere else."

Mei laughs quietly then takes a sip from the cup. The coffee is cold, but it's rich and sweet. "I was thinking about the elephant," she says, after a while. "You know, Houdini. He timed his pistol shot with the curtains whipping up so it looked like it had vanished. But I don't get why he didn't bring it back. Wouldn't that have completed the trick?"

Rohan puts his arm around her.

"Do you think it was too hard?" she says. "To bring something back that big?"

"I guess so," he says, eventually.

In time, they get up and walk.

"This is good cold, actually," she says and takes another sip. "Reminds me of iced Milo."

"Yeah?"

"Yeah. I thought you could only get it in Malaysia but apparently you can get a tin anywhere now. It's like Ovaltine. My uncle used to make it when we visited. Old style, in a saucepan on a stove. He'd pour it into this long Mickey Mouse glass I had. So it was hot at the bottom but then you'd put ice cubes in and they'd float on the top. And when you drank it, you'd have to draw your straw slowly up through the glass so you could get all the temperatures in one go."

She's silent. Just the gentle step of their feet on the path.

"I'm sorry I didn't get to meet him," says Rohan.

"You'd have liked him," says Mei. "He was very funny."

They walk around the Serpentine slowly, the sun lowering in the sky and the street lamps flickering on in the dark.

Nearly Not There

DAMIEN DOORLEY

Anyway afterwards Jimmie and me we'd still have to see each other because where else are we going to drink. It was brave of him really I like to think to say hi, pity about Billy. Said that nearly a year and then he didn't say it no more. I took Billy for his walk every morning and every evening. He was friendly and people were friendly back. Some days he'd catch a rabbit and settle down right there and eat it and then people weren't so friendly. A dog catches a rabbit the rabbit's his. I still do that walk around the cliffs and I don't see why old ghost Billy shouldn't be still chasing them old ghost rabbits.

If I drink out I like to be near home. I only take the ferry across if I'm going to have a coffee and shop or pretend to. I go around the shelves filling a trolley like I'm a lady or a secretary or some kid's mother and then I leave it all in some random aisle and walk out and I'm me again. Every now and then there's a woman with her baby like a big parcel hung from her front, a big saggy parcel of big-bottomed fruit. Sometimes there are girls who are still expecting. I bump into those ones, hard. You know that feeling? Some of them know me and they don't look and the ones that have never seen me look again and work out fast what they're seeing and you can tell that's the last time they're going to notice you. I was expecting a few times myself and I think it was mostly Jimmie. Anyway I always dealt with it.

We had a rent for a while on a converted cow stall they called a bier I think it was. You could see over the walls to that same lighthouse. I took to gathering seaweed on the beach, the rent took everything we had. I'd dry the seaweed on the walls and it had that real sharp salty and a little bit rotten smell. This is interesting soup Jimmie said, is there any more of it. Yes, plenty. That's not the answer I was looking for he said.

We grew a few flowers or they just grew we didn't grow them exactly.

Fish you expect to see dead. Hardly ever see them any other way. When you do there's something special about it, like when you find whitebait caught in a pool waiting for the tide to come back and they're flashing this way and that together in that way starlings do in a flock, they just know which way they are all going to turn. That's some kind of miracle or it looks like one. Flies don't flock like that they are just way more crazy.

Anyway you don't want to know what happened to Billy. Jimmie said he'll be better in the morning or the one after, dogs have these powers of recovery like all animals, you can do all kinds of things to them and they bounce back with a little sleep. Jimmie wasn't too cognitive at the best of times and I don't know what the best of times would be for Jimmie. He grew up in one of those stony old villages inland and his so-called parents smoked more weed and drank more booze and popped more pills before he was born than he or I for that matter will ever have time to do in all our days on this earth. They took it to Olympic level I always said to him. Slow down. He couldn't they were too deep inside him.

People round here have collies mostly but Billy was a boxer brown and cream. Some days when I dream it all better I open the door and Billy runs out and doesn't stop running over the hills and far away. A dog would do that, I've seen it when a dog knows it's time to get away and never look back.

Jimmie was outside in the lane smoking and he called Billy out to play around. Billy pricked up his ears and looked at me. I thought it was like he was saying, is this a good idea? A dog can be divided in himself, like a person. But play got the better of him and off he went and they played and played for a long while with Billy barking like he's saying come on throw the stick. I thought they'd be coming in soon because it was getting kind of dark and I was thinking I'd put on the lamp.

I thought at first Jimmie'd been hit when I heard the car and I ran out there like I never think I ever ran anywhere before or since. But he was leaning on the window of the car talking kind of low to the driver and he turned his head and said go back in, you don't want to see this. In a little while the car went away and Jimmie came in carrying Billy and Billy was whimpering a little but not much. Jimmie put him in the cupboard under the stairs where he sleeps and closed the door and told me dogs need dark and quiet to get over things. Where'd you get that money I said and he said from the man for Billy and he shoved it down in his back pocket, in case I'd get it I suppose.

Anyway, Jimmie's getting a little pepper and salt now if you know what I mean but the ladies still like him and I don't say a thing. They can have him now and I know they can't help it because he's just Jimmie and I've been there. Jimmie, Jimmie, the man's dead handsome and he'll be handsome dead. Even when his teeth started to go and he had these old-lady lines around his lips and his lips started to fold in. I like that word fold. I used to fold into him some nights. He'd fold away. Skinny, long thin hair, needs the TV on to sleep, nice skanky smell, some guys can get away with that. I've been writing his obituary since the first time we met.

Anyway, I like these misty days. Nothing looks real, just someone's idea of nature or one of God's quieter days. Look at that. It's nearly not there.

A grey cygnet last spring, I remember now. So I've seen more than Billy. One day there was this big white mother swan and she had three little grey ones following her around and then next day there were only two and one of them was lying on a heap of seaweed like it had gone to sleep. Only you can tell the difference, there's maybe more slackness. Anyway, you can tell if something's not going to wake up. The big mother swan and the two little brothers and sisters or whatever, they just walked on past and didn't ask how the other one was. So maybe they don't understand if something's dead. Maybe for them it's always like those dreams when you say oh yeah he's dead and although it's a dead person there's this whole story going on and they just have their part in it and it's not terrible or else you nurse them a little and they open their eyes which is a dream I have about someone I don't know.

Look Out

IAN McNAB

My watch on the tower's nearly done when Milo comes on the radio and asks me how I'm doing. I tell him I'm not great. Petra, my dog, has been torn apart by leopards. She's the fourth pet I've lost that way. I hadn't seen her for a day or so and I had expected the worst, but it's still a bit of a gut punch. Milo asks if I'm going to bury her and I say it's too late, they've already hosed the pavement down and Petra's been guttered. I tell Milo that's another piece of my life turned to shit. He says he's sorry and asks if I want to come out for drinks. When I was a kid back home we never could keep any pets alive, or even my mother, who fell from a fire escape at her bridge club on a poorly supervised Martini Monday.

It's been nice to hear some other thing breathing, even though my apartment's barely big enough for me. But I don't think I can face a fifth pet shop visit. It doesn't pay to get attached to anything these days. The leopards are a scourge, fleet and furious, devourers of anything smaller and furry. The hallways in the tower block all have notices pinned up on the community boards for people to come to a meeting about the leopards, where there's free coffee. The signs have "SOMETHING HAS TO BE DONE!" in big black letters at the top. I'd go, but I think it'll mostly be people sobbing over their kittens and I'm worried I'd be co-opted into a vigilante hit mob out of politeness. I appreciate their sentiment, but I'd rather grieve privately.

There's a thick metal door to the roof of the tower that needs a key card to open. Someone could light a barrel of gunpowder on the other side and it wouldn't fold. So they know when I'm on duty, I sign in and out by swiping my card. A green light blinks when the door opens and a red light when it's locked. I swipe my card to get off the roof. The light comes on orange, with the sound of an electronic cough. I've never seen an orange light before. The door won't open. I try swiping several times, and the door keeps coughing at me, staying shut. I decide there's no shame in panicking and allow myself to lose it for a minute, screaming and yelling into the air. I kick and kick at the door until my adrenalin dissipates and I stop to catch my breath. That was a waste of time and effort but I had to get it out my system. I think of the piece of the world that's mine on the other side of the door, my apartment ten floors down: the crooked number sixty-one, the maroon carpet, Petra's empty dog bed, and the grey wing-back chair I want to buckle into. I try my card one more time, on faith, but the unit's still busted.

I'm high enough to see gulls gliding below me. Thick cloud's coming in, and for a while up here I might vanish in the fog. I retreat to the middle of the roof and unpack my radio. I turn it on and it screeches into life. I put a call out to Milo, but nothing comes back. He'll already be in the bar with Kristina, this stewardess he's seeing. She works, in the loosest sense of the word, on a boat giving little tours of the docks. She wears a white uniform and greets people as they get on. She has incredible cheekbones and a lot of bouncy friends. Kristina thinks Milo's cool because he has scars on his hands. His brother dropped a flowerpot on him when he was nine, but he prefers to tell everyone that a leopard jumped him outside his building and he had to smash its head in with a bin lid. He also says he goes to work in a helicopter. They're quick to believe him because they're the kind of girls who get their high heels stuck in the uneven paving in the Opium district every single weekend and have to be extracted by doormen. Milo will be sipping negronis right now and talking about his gun.

It's evening now and the light is lower. I go to the edge of the roof, lean over the railing and look down. The windows and streets below gleam and blur into each other and I feel dazed and off balance. I back away. On the radio I put a general call out to anyone to come and help me. I say I'm trapped, but I sound too desperate, so I put a call out again and this time I just say the door's fucked. I get some garbled static and then a lot of silence. The battery starts to die, and the radio beeps an incessant warning so I turn it off. I start to think I'll be here until morning.

I look down my rifle scope, which cuts through the gloom and brings everything closer. The one they gave me is supposed to be night vision, but once the sun falls completely, everything is a green mess, so I prefer to use the binoculars. I scan around the end of the dock where the commuter barges moor. A cross-section of labourers, corporate suits, and uniformed service workers are heading home now and the decks get crammed with people. I look a little closer and see that I'd have to radio in several of the commuters if I was still on shift, because a yellow alert's been issued for anyone wearing plaid, and for bald men with holdalls. Central tell us what to look out for at the start of each watch. They call on the radio and all lookouts have to answer with their tower name and number, so I say "Leather 4 receiving" and everyone says theirs and because there are about sixty of us it takes ages, and while everyone's checking in I drink my ephedrine water and try to visualise a cool woodland and a porch seat where I can sit and sip beer. I read that if a person takes the time to imagine himself happy, then the reality often follows. Not all towers are manned at once, but they rota it so that there's always a spread of lookouts covering each part of the docks.

I sit down and scrape the residue of dripped smoothie from the knee of my jeans. My sleeping tablets are inconsistent. They either have me awake at odd hours with night terrors and I have to lie fetal and listen to white noise through headphones, or they put me coma deep and I wake up late and have to take breakfast from the vending machine on the sixteenth floor. In the hallways there's always techno, and K-pop in the lifts. Sometimes advertising jingles play over the top and tell me to try ham water. I'll take a smoothie for most meals, but I hate the pre-packaged ones from the machines, because they only have a few flavours like Haggis and Oat, or Egg Bonanza. They taste powdery and the texture's thick gloop. This morning, Herbs and Whey or Toasted

Cappuccino were all that was left in the machine. I opted for Herbs and Whey, but when I retrieved it from the trough it turned out to be Aubergine and Meatball, which tastes like burnt shoes. When I'm up on time, I prefer to call in at Fresh Start, which is in Sugar 3, just a short walk from my tower. They do their smoothies to order. You can pick any ingredients you want and they blitz it up for you there and then. They also have a smoothie of the month.

Sugar 3 is considerably better than Leather 4, which used to be pretty nice, but now on grey days the drizzle seeps through the corners of each floor and leaves patches of dark stains and a faint smell like secret sweating bodies. And the walls have started to crumble, leaving lines of dust along the carpets by the lifts. Sugar 3 is Milo's tower and it's mainly for young couples or singles who like to party. Every day Milo invites me to come drinking with him after work. We chat on the radio and he tells me to get a place over there, because the swimming pool's always full of hot girls who sit around on loungers and giggle and the vending machines actually have coffee and twelve different waters, not just shitty smoothies. And there's a doorman who'll take your shirts to be ironed. I keep telling Milo I don't have any shirts, and I don't have the money to afford a place over there, not like when I was with Melani. Then Milo says don't start banging on about her again, and maybe I'd have more money if I wasn't late to start my shift every day because I can't get out of fucking bed in the morning. And I say it's the pills. Milo says I should get a silent alarm like he has at home. When I lived with Melani, she had one of those gadgets. She needed it because she works in finance and if someone's late they make them walk around barefoot all day and, sometimes, shave their head. Each morning, before there was even light in the sky, the silent alarm flooded the room with dark vibrations and the sensation that someone with a large hat was standing over us, watching us curled up together sleeping. No one can doze through that. It was efficient, but it coloured the day with a foreboding that had me scowling long after the morning bulletin was over. Even when Radovan on Tobacco 7 told one of his seaman jokes, I couldn't crack a smile.

With the radio out I feel hungry and bored. I grab the binoculars to see what's happening that might draw my mind away from the rooftop and a sky bloated with rain. I've got a low-lying nausea making me uneasy and it has my fists and jaw clenched tight. I check out the Corsican Footbridge, which runs across the river. It dips low enough that if someone, after a few drinks, was dangled off the base of it by their feet, their head and shoulders would be fully submerged. No one's trying that yet, but the night's young. There's a man fishing, bald-headed, with a collared jumper that he's puffed up around his neck and it looks like he's wearing a knitted tyre. He's got headphones on which makes it difficult to tell if he's seriously fishing or mentally ill, but he seems to know what he's doing, casting his line out and drawing it back in. I've never fished, but he's waving his rod around like a method's at work. His rhythm is broken by an onslaught of screeching gulls who descend to the bridge and start harassing him, swooping overhead, dive-bombing his exposed forehead, and tangling his line. The fisherman's quickly flustered, flapping and lashing his rod at the birds like a whip. It's a malicious attack, a mafia of screaming feathers. There's nowhere in the city where gulls can't be heard. And they always sound angry. It's easier, I think, to avoid incident, if a person doesn't try to accomplish anything. This fisherman casting his line, flicking his rod, he's just asking for it. Eventually a kind of miniature hell always descends.

Before the city, at home, I used to work in a pub, which was about as stagnant and inactive as it was possible to be while conscious. That's where I met Melani, when she came to the bar to lunch on fish salad. She was an exciting blizzard of action, for which the world paid her back with a terrible chaos she navigated at terminal velocity. She was funny, and chatted me up, asking who I'd pull out and who I'd let sink, if they were stranded in quicksand. She made me kiss her out the back where I stacked the empty metal barrels and later we had sex next to a skip while an overweight cat watched.

Down on the bridge, the gulls versus fisherman drama is becoming more complex. A younger man in office dress joins the fisherman trying to repel the gulls, swinging his briefcase like a speedball bat. There's something inspiring about their partnership and I find myself rooting for them. I don't think Melani ever felt that way about anyone. She had an obsessive kind of self-belief. We

157

came to the city together because she hated her job, offering loans at outrageous rates of interest to those who had fallen on hard times, like families whose homes had half plunged off hillsides in particularly vindictive acts of God.

The duo on the bridge finally claim the upper hand and there's only one insistent gull still pecking at the fisherman's scalp. I'm tempted to grab my rifle and fire a shot in that direction to end it, but I feel I'd be robbing the men of a victory, and those are harder and harder to come by. I watch them both hammering at the air above them, and the businessman scores a hit and a look of absolute elation lifts his face for a moment. The gull flies off, shrieking madly. The two men look at each other and smile, standing doubled over, catching breath. They nod, shake hands and the business guy continues his walk across the bridge. The fisherman sits down without his rod and starts to cry. He actually doesn't really look like a fisherman. Maybe the jumper edges him in that direction, but he's not hairy enough, unlike the white-bearded version on packets of fish sticks, where the ingredients are only printed in braille.

It's getting darker and harder to make things out clearly. I'm starting to get cold so I go to pull a jacket out of my bag and I find a flare I forgot I had. I twist the end and pull the top hard and the flare erupts into flame. It's so bright I wish I'd looked away when I lit it. A flash of red is etched on my retina. I wander around the roof and wave the flare about a bit, trying to cover all possible angles, in case someone is glancing up here for a moment, or if there's a helicopter. I don't know why there would be. Anyway, if I was piloting a helicopter I don't think I'd land it on a roof just because a guy with a gun was waving a flare. The smoke from the flare seems endless and it smells of overheating electrical wire. It gets in my throat and makes me cough slightly and choke on my own saliva. I balance the flare in one of the gun rests on the guard rail and stand on the opposite side of the roof.

I put my jacket on. Below I can see the flashing orange lights of a bodycart, which means someone's dead somewhere, probably a leaper, so I pick up the binoculars again and track the bodycart to a piazza west of me. I have to blink a few times to focus and then I see the body, looking like a dropped bin bag. People jump from the towers, out of windows and off balconies. I'd hate to be a bodycart driver, because those corpses end up pulverised like a barrowload of mixed mince. It happens so often now, that I really only look to see what they're wearing, and wonder if they chose that grey-and-cerise jumpsuit specifically to die in.

I keep watching as the bodycart guys take some photos, wrap the remains in white plastic, tag it, and hang it off one of the pegs on their cart's rack, alongside the three that are already there. There'll be someone to hose down the pavement later. I think about wanting to die. Everyone wants something. Some people want to jump off buildings. Melani wanted to make money. That's popular too. I don't have that kind of ambition. I just wanted to be with her. A lot of the time she looked at me like she wanted to pull me apart into separate little pieces and scrutinise them in turn, but then she'd smirk at me with a weird sort of desire, like a rat might have for a damp cardboard box.

The Opium quarter has the highest buildings in the city, and they attract a lot of leapers. Melani got us an apartment over there, not crazy high, because we didn't have a lot of money, but from our apartment you could look out through the glass and still see the barges bringing people home from work. I like the boats. A year or so after Mum passed, my dad bought a boat. A little motor cruiser. It was hard to tell where the rust ended and paint began, but Dad worked on it most weekends and, every so often, when he decided she was seaworthy, he cajoled me into going with him. Each time we were only out for five minutes before we sprung a leak and had to be rescued by the lifeboat. Still, Dad persisted, I think mainly because Mum would never have signed off on something like that.

My first lookout post was on Opium 14, Melani's tower. She couldn't care less what I did, she just wanted to be taken out in the city and stroll around in the dark. I saw a recruitment advert on TV, where the lookouts had masks and capes and shone these huge searchlights down from the rooftops and illuminated hooded men hiding Semtex in a school playground, or stabbing the sleeping crew of a coffee barge. When the searchlights hit the bad guys, their faces were revealed and they were all dripping with slime. They'd wince at the camera then run and disappear in a cloud of dust. It was very operatic and had an uplifting techno score that came in at the end. I was kind of disappointed when I didn't get a mask or a cape on my first day.

I can't remember which company Melani works for, but they have a logo with a man carrying a burning sword on a hill, or maybe it was a man running with a spear at the sun, or a man doing star jumps in front of the Earth with a wolf's head. They all look very similar and you can tell how well anyone who works there is doing by which floor they're on. Melani was on thirty-eight, which was in the upper quarter, and she told everyone we met about it. She sold bits of the river to small transportation companies for a lot of money, and then convinced them later to sell the bits of the river back to her at a much lower price. There'd normally be something in it for the transportation companies, like they wouldn't get sued. Melani was very persuasive, so the job suited her well.

She was never home before me. Even now, if I look over at any of the financial towers I can see all the office lights on. For a long time, we only exchanged snippets of our days over coffee, looking out into morning fog. Melani telling me they closed the office for half an hour the day before because someone in accounts slit their wrists with an ornamental oyster knife. Me telling Melani that she shouldn't wear a shawl or anything in animal print, since we'd been told to report that if we saw it. I'd ask her if work was good and she'd say yeah. She would never ask me, but she did arrange my swipe card and binoculars neatly on the table before work.

One night I woke up and heard Melani in the kitchen. She was chopping fruit. She looked up as I came in and said it was time she had a baby. It took me by surprise since most of the time I went to bed alone. She wanted to go out for dinner and talk about it.

Tree is one of the nicest restaurants in the city, since they have heated balconies, and high-end smoothies with foie gras or caviar and liqueurs frozen into sorbet or ice cream. It's very expensive and people always say how it's overpriced and not worth it and what they mean is they desperately want to go there. Milo says he's been there several times with various women, but I don't think he's been there once because he didn't mention the food and kept talking about how square the walls were. When I went with Melani, we raised a glass to ourselves and I said cheers. We'd been together in the city for over a year by then. I used to tally the weeks on the wall in chalk while I was out on the roof. It felt like we were succeeding every time I put another mark up there.

Melani said that yeah, she thought she should have a baby, and had put in a request with her company for their Baby Time scheme, which was a very oversubscribed initiative. The company would buy her a baby, and she'd work for them at least until the baby was paid off. In this deal, Melani would be tied into the company for fifteen years. They let the employee customise the kid in various categories, choosing eye colour, hair, height, disposition. The average waiting time was six months. Melani showed me the form and I wondered out loud whether it wouldn't be easier just to get a baby our own way, if, maybe, we could have some sex. There was a weird pause. Somehow I'd drooled beef-and-ale ice cream down my shirt. Melani looked at me like I'd gutted a small mammal right there on the table in front of her. She did these long loud sighs that made me want to break things, and she eventually said she couldn't see the up side of my suggestion, when she'd already put so much time and effort into fast-tracking this. I told her the Baby Time scheme seemed complicated, and a little cold. She said maybe I was too complicated and actually she was bored and she'd like to leave now. She turned from the table and went to stand up and I remember her face lit from the spotlights above the bar. She didn't look at me when the waiter brought the bill.

Outside we walked from the restaurant and the streets were quiet, like something had drifted away from us, and we were just watching it float off silently into the distance. We crossed the bridge and Melani walked ahead, back to the apartment. She went to sleep while I stayed up, looking out over the river and hearing gulls in the shriek of the wind.

It's got late and I'm tired. I'd be sleepier if the breeze hadn't gained a little lick of rain. I can feel it on my lips. I stand at the guard rail, leaning my stomach against the metal and letting my head bend over the edge. This is the kind of height that makes me think about what the fall would be like, whether I'd have enough time to construct a thought, to wonder about death, to worry if it hurts. This thought has me woozy, and I relax my grip on the rail. Down below, those who have been out are heading home. I watch the sky and it looks like there's a plane, and I think I ought to have saved the flare. It used to be special to be this high, until it became ordinary. Everything becomes ordinary. Stuck out here, dreaming of my bed, food, an open door, I'm a concentrated version of myself, and the rooftops are concentrated too, and suddenly it matters to be up here above everything and it feels strange to be scared and alone and perfectly myself at the same time. I think people pour themselves into drama or they pour themselves into routine. Both those currents sweep away the most interesting pieces of us. I think Melani always knew I wouldn't see things her way. I think she counted on it. We didn't love each other, and when I pictured having a child it was in a warm room, golden from afternoon sun, full of easy joy. Melani was always squirming for change and I folded myself into the everyday like a blanket.

I was packing up the last of my things from our apartment, and I saw one of our neighbours, a lawyer, coming home with his date, a brunette, tall, a smile hiding tedium. He said hi and that he was sorry to hear we were moving out. And the brunette made a sad face. Melani had told me straight she couldn't bear to hear one more breath from me and was leaving to bring up the company baby with Toma, a third-degree managing chief, eight or nine floors up from Melani's office. I never met him. The lawyer told the brunette that I was a lookout, and threw me a glance for confirmation. I said yeah sure. The brunette piped up and said hey wow and then said it must be hard. I told her it wasn't really, and she asked, how can you be that high up and not want to jump? I told her she wasn't the first person to ask that, and I walked out with my box of medicine bottles and toothpaste.

When I was younger, my dad took me with him to a building he was working on, just a skeleton really, no outside walls. But they'd put in staircases of bare concrete. I followed my father up, trying to keep the hard hat he'd given me on my small head. At the top there were crosses and arrows marked on the floor, coded out for whatever the building would become. Dad held my hand and we walked near the edge. He told me to look out over the roads and the houses and think about all the people I knew. I thought about the people I'd never know, giving their best efforts at trying to be happy and not dying. I had my eyes closed, and Dad asked if I was OK. I said I was scared if I opened my eyes and looked down,

I might feel like jumping. Dad told me to open my eyes. I did, and I could see the clouds coming in above people's houses, and chains of cars zipping by. Below, I saw some birds perched on the ledges of empty floors, squawking and shitting together. Dad said you're either a person who jumps or you're not, and a person who jumps would have jumped by now. He said looking down doesn't make the slightest difference.

Elisa May

ELEANOR GOW

E lisa May spent most of her childhood wondering if things would have been better had she been a boy. She would cut off the nose of each of her dolls and wish that she had been given a racing car to play with instead. Each time her parents put her in a dress she felt nauseous and naked. And then facial hair started to grow at a time when it was least expected.

She would sit in front of the mirror before school with a pair of tweezers, plucking hairs from her upper lip. It didn't help. Instead she ended up with a moustache of red spots that bled when she clasped her hand to her mouth, which she did often. From what she understood during her school years, boys were not faced with such problems. The few that had actually succeeded in growing facial hair combed their chins with glee.

Boys also didn't seem to get a football bounced at their head each time they crossed the sports field on their way to English class. Apart from Sam Clark, but Sam smelled funny and wore his mother's coat. Boys seemed to fit inside their bodies in a way that she never could.

She spent the hours at school torn between whether to place her hand to her mouth to cover up the spots or follow her mother's advice and release the hand to let them breathe. This obsession was joined a couple of years later by the onset of her periods. Because of the bloated stomach and the acne, the preoccupation with her physical appearance took up most of her time, resulting in dramatic failure in all of her subjects. At sixteen she left education and got a job cleaning the school instead.

She continued to toy with the idea of what her life would have become had she been a boy, until she turned seventeen and met Frankie Albert Smith. It was in meeting him that she found being a girl had some significant perks.

Frankie Albert Smith was born Francesco Albert, for no other reason than his parents thought it sounded fancy, and at that time they still had hope. However, by the age of eleven he hadn't managed to master the pronunciation and so they deleted the "cesco" and put a "kie" on the end.

Never described as the brightest star in the sky, he was a man who knew who he was, and there was something to be said about that. He never got confused. He told things as he saw them and when he was wrong he didn't admit it.

It was the summer after Frankie's sixth birthday that he realised it was going to be his face that would get him places. A Saturday afternoon and he was on the way to the big supermarket with his dad. The town where they lived didn't have much of a high street, just a handful of second-hand shops, a place that sold pretty good trainers and another that sold a mixture of junk nobody wanted. So an expedition to the supermarket was the best out of a bad bunch, unless there was enough money for new shoes, which there wasn't.

Frankie already knew what he wanted to buy and he marched through the sliding doors with his dad in tow. It was a red racing car he had spotted when he was forced to pace the fruit and veg aisle whilst his mum weighed multiple bags of fruit and mumbled about the price of grapes.

"Yippiddee-doo-da! Got it, Dad," he shouted, making the elderly woman beside him growl and drop her tinned tomatoes.

"Ah, good lad. You go pay then and I'll wait outside."

It was only when Frankie joined the checkout queue that he realised the car was £2.50 and not the £2 that he held within the palm of his sweating hand. He tried waving to get his dad's attention but it was pointless. He was already leaning with his back against the shop window and however hard Frankie thought it he couldn't get him to turn around.

"Just the car, is it?" the checkout lady asked him, holding out her hand.

"But, it's two pounds fifty," he responded with a quiver. "I only have two pounds."

And he did that thing he had heard his mum talk about to her friend Sue. ("I reckon all he has to do is flutter those beautiful lashes and he'll get away with murder.")

"Ah, go on then. How could I resist a lovely little face like that."

Frankie skipped and jumped the whole way back to his house, gripping the brilliant-red racing car and feeling how somehow he had won something in that shop that was worth more than the car and a fifty-pence piece, and it was important and he should remember it.

So it was Frankie's face that got him far in life, although not that far; but far enough out of school and into a job at the Jolly Robin.

His parents threw a party for him when he landed the position of Head Barman. He knew they were relieved. The party was held at his parents' house, across the road and three doors down from the pub. On the front door his mother hung a sign that read, "Congratulations", and then below, "You've passed".

"I'm the king of the world," Frankie shouted, standing on the kitchen table.

"We are so proud of you, son," his father said, wiping a tear from his eye as he took Frankie's arm and helped him down.

"Now you just need to find yourself a nice girlfriend to settle down with and you'll be all set."

"Well, there'll be no shortage of birds at the Jolly Robin, hey Dad?"

"Just remember, it's never good to be too picky," his dad said, tousling Frankie's hair. "Now, let's go find your mother."

That night Frankie lay on his back in bed, staring at Pamela Anderson coming out of the sea, and felt that this was just the beginning for him. He would have money in his pocket and a bank account opened in his name. He would be someone of authority and respect. If he announced "Last orders," last orders it would be.

If school had taught Elisa May anything it was the importance of fitting in, and that she did not. She had since spent much of her time trying on different personalities, like clothes, creating so many versions of herself that she was often unsure which one she was supposed to be. She felt she had gotten lost somewhere along the way. And then she was found, or part of her was, by Frankie Albert Smith.

Elisa May met Frankie at the Jolly Robin. She was celebrating her seventeenth birthday. At the time it didn't seem much of a celebration, although it later proved to be the best birthday of her life.

It was just Elisa May and her parents (who had a particular dislike for parties) and her friend Tina, who was more of a necessity than someone she liked. Tina had brought balloons, two red and three yellow as Elisa May had once said that they were her favourite colours. They weren't any more; that had been when she was going through her artistic phase. She didn't actually have a favourite colour, or really a favourite anything, although she was rather attached to the picture of Bruce Springsteen that she kept in a frame under her bed.

The balloons were suspended from the back of her chair in a sad knot. There was also a banner across the front of the table that read, "Happy Birthday". She couldn't say they hadn't tried.

Everyone ordered fish and chips, as they didn't like to venture too far from their comfort zone. Elisa May was currently experimenting with what it would be like to have an eating disorder, so after the meal she went to the toilet and vomited up the food, which she felt slightly bad about, as it was her birthday and she hadn't paid. It was when she was on her way back from the toilet, chewing a piece of sugar-free gum, that she bumped into Frankie.

Now, although Elisa May knew she had many inconsistencies in terms of character, she felt she had managed to flourish into someone rather beautiful. At sixteen she had discovered wax and was able to remove her facial hair on a biweekly basis. She had also got a hold of her periods, managing to avoid the bloating, and had learnt that if she covered her face in TCP before bed the outbreak of spots could be avoided.

She liked to think her face resembled a surprised doll; long blond curls, piercing blue eyes with a raised eyebrow and strawberry-red lips. Her body was not quite so impressive, but overall she couldn't complain about how she had turned out. It had been quite a shock.

She had recently ditched her horse-riding phase. The "outdoorsy girl" she had been masquerading as was getting her nowhere. She wanted to find a man and the only people she ever saw at the stables were middle-aged women who scared her with their attempts at conversation.

"Having a good night? I see it's your birthday," said Frankie, as they stood surrounded by the smell of urinals and lemon-scented bleach.

She wasn't used to being addressed directly by the opposite sex. She got the occasional beep of a car horn when walking down the road, but she didn't tend to go anywhere where boys could address her. So it came as quite a surprise, making her briefly forget who she was supposed to be.

"Yes, I'm seventeen today," she said with almost a neigh, remembering her hair and flicking it.

"And what a lovely seventeen you are," Frankie replied. He leaned in, put his fingers to her cheek and held them there.

Elisa May had never been touched by a boy before, and because of this, or possibly the previous purging, she felt rather dizzy and rested her back against the wall.

"So, what have you got planned, then?"

"Planned? For what?"

"For the rest of your birthday."

"There's just this and that's it really. It's only my birthday today, so tomorrow I'll be back at the school."

"You're at school?"

"Yes, I work there."

"Are you a teacher?"

"Oh no. A cleaner. I clean."

"Ah, I see," Frankie said, fluttering his eyelashes, somewhat relieved.

"I don't usually come here. Well, ever really. I don't ever come here. It's my first time."

"Well, I'm certainly glad you came tonight. I think you have the most beautiful hair I have ever seen. It's as gold as a pound coin."

"Thank you. It's my own," Elisa May stammered as it dawned on her that at last something was actually happening.

"Can I kiss you?" Frankie said.

And with the taste of chewing gum between them they shared their first kiss, the first of many. Ten months later they were married.

They wed in the local church. Frankie attempted to use his full name during the ceremony but after some embarrassing stumbling he gave up. Elisa May was too busy looking into his eyes to care. She had often imagined what it would be like to play the role of a married woman and now she could.

That night they stayed in the bedroom above the Jolly Robin, a perk of Frankie being Head Barman. She stood in the bathroom and sprayed herself with her new perfume, adjusted the padding in her red bra, clasped her hand to her mouth in her usual way and opened the door. Frankie was sprawled out on the bed, his left arm flopped above his head, his lips parted slightly, a dribble of drool making its way slowly down his chin.

She watched him for a while, not knowing what she was supposed to do. She hadn't imagined he would be asleep and she didn't feel brave enough to wake him. It's not that they hadn't had sex before. They had, many times. It was one of the few things they had in common. But tonight was their wedding night and Elisa May knew from all of the magazines she had read, it was extremely important to bless the marriage.

She crept into the space he had unconsciously left her and held her face inches from his. Slowly she put her tongue inside his parted mouth and began to give it a wiggle, but Frankie didn't move. She pushed it harder and he snapped his jaw shut. The pain was extreme as her tongue was thrust out of his mouth.

"Urrrrrgh," she bellowed. "Aaaaaah."

"Who is it?" yelled Frankie, launching himself into a seated position.

"You've just bitten my tongue! Look, it's bleeding."

"Urgh, God, there's blood in my mouth! I was asleep. How could I have bitten it?"

"I was kissing you."

"Some bloody kiss."

And with that Frankie turned over and went back to sleep.

The week after they were married they took a train to Brighton. The first day of the holiday was spent wandering the length of the pier. There was a high wind, which didn't work with Elisa May's hair, so she bought a red headscarf that Frankie said made her look like a beacon.

"The ships will change course once they get a glimpse of that." He laughed, reaching for her hand, and she laughed too but wished she had bought the blue one. They ate sticks of pink rock in chunks, picking the remains out of their teeth until evening.

Their second and last day was limited to the walls of their hotel room. Frankie suffered from stomach cramps and blamed the sea air, spending most of his time inside the bathroom.

"I told you I swallowed some of that seawater, that's what it is. I tell you. A man like me wasn't made to swallow the sea," he groaned as he clambered back into the bed.

"Poor you, would you like me to give you a massage?" She had recently read in one of her magazines that massages were a welcome addition to a marriage and she fancied becoming a woman with healing hands.

"I don't want you touching my stomach. It's sore, you understand? I'm not sitting on the toilet for the view."

"No, a back massage, Frankie. It will help you relax."

"Go on then, if we must."

So Elisa May rubbed Frankie's back as she sat beside him looking out of the window at nothing in particular, faint daydreams appearing as briefly as the sun.

"Stick to baking," Frankie said groggily. "You're good at that."

When they returned home Elisa May dropped the word "husband" in conversation with as many people as possible. Standing at the supermarket checkout she told the shop assistant how *her husband* had a sweet tooth and ate only white bread.

She wandered the men's clothing department and cornered members of staff to ask their opinion on whether the blue or green jumper would be best suited to *her husband*'s complexion, removing the passport-sized photograph of them on their wedding day that she kept in her purse.

"I wore my mother's pearls as my something borrowed, and something old, and then my dress was my something new. I went for a bandeau style as my upper half is really the bit to show off," she said, pulling her coat open so that they could have a better look. "Frankie likes my neck. He says I'm all giraffe on top."

These exchanges were met with a mixed response. If she managed to catch an older employee their interest would be greater, or at least they would smile, somewhat uncertainly, and nod their head at the photograph. The younger staff members would initially engage with her enthusiastically, but, as they watched her unzip her coat and run her hand down her neck, they would begin to adjust some clothes on a nearby rail or look at nothing in the distance and begin to head that way. She realised that those who recognised her started to avoid her completely, but she didn't care.

She practised the word "husband" hundreds of times in the mirror, watching the way the letters appeared in her mouth so she knew what she looked like when she said it.

"I have a husband," she said to herself as she walked the school corridors with bucket and mop. "My husband will be there when I get home," she whispered as she hurried along the road. She considered it her greatest achievement and wrapped the word around herself tightly like a scarf.

She placed Frankie's dinner before him each evening and took her seat across the table with delight.

"You're grinning in that odd way again," he said with a mouth full of food.

She clasped her hand to her mouth, the corners of her upturned lips peeping out from the edge of her fingers.

In the first three years of marriage Elisa May became pregnant twice but they never had children. After their second visit to the hospital Frankie went out and bought a dog (he had always been a dog man), a black Labrador they called Harry.

Elisa May decided that in order to fill the gap she would start volunteering on a Friday afternoon at the local mother-and-baby group. She figured, as she didn't have children of her own, she could befriend people who did. She imagined she would have a natural affinity with babies and wanted to have the opportunity to demonstrate this in a place where it would be appreciated. She had always wanted to be someone who volunteered.

The first couple of Fridays were spent making tea and coffee. By the end of the first month she had started to chat to the mothers a little bit and by the second month was sharing her life story on a regular basis.

"Yes, it's a burden we both have to bear, my husband and I, but we make the most of our time together," she said, to anyone who would listen.

"I'm sure it will happen for you one day," she was told by one of the mothers as she sat balancing the woman's eight-week-old baby in her arms. "You're still so young."

"Yes, one day," Elisa May said, distantly, holding the baby away from her new pink blouse. She had noticed a little patch of drool on the sleeve and was concerned it was going to leave a mark.

"They look funny close up, don't they?" Elisa May said. "Are all babies' heads this size?"

"What do you mean, little Bella has a perfectly lovely head, don't you, sweetheart?"

"She doesn't have any hair, though, does she. Maybe that's it."

"Well, it will grow."

"It's funny how they all seem the same. Looking at her you could never guess whether she was a boy or a girl, could you?"

"Actually I might take her back now if you don't mind. I think she needs a feed."

"She's pulling a very odd face. Is she supposed to do that?"

"Oh dear, poor Bella, I think she might be feeling a bit sick."

Elisa May quickly placed the baby rather indelicately into her mother's arms, feigned a headache and went home early.

She wouldn't be going back. The blouse had been expensive and the babies disappointing. She decided that evening, with Harry in tow, that she would volunteer as a dog walker instead.

She wanted to continue to feel that she was someone who gave something back to society.

They had become familiar with the doctor's waiting room, closed doors, hushed voices, hospital beds. But it was the summer of their fifth year of marriage when Elisa May was called urgently to the emergency room at the hospital.

She was escorted into a room that said, "In Use, Do Not Disturb", and as she clasped her hand to her mouth she was told by a doctor that Frankie Albert Smith was going to die. They had tried operating on him but it was no good. There was a chance he would make it through the night, if he was lucky, which she figured he wasn't, considering.

It had seemed to Frankie to be a pretty typical day. But that was before he plummeted down the cellar stairs at the Jolly Robin carrying a crate of beer.

As he lay in a broken heap at the bottom of the stairs he remembered the first Saturday after he had married Elisa May. He had arrived home from work and walked into the smell of melted butter.

"All for you. I've been practising," she had said, placing him at the table where before him sat an apple pie, a strawberry tart and a tiramisu.

"You'll get me fat, you will."

"That's what my dad always said. Here, try this one first."

There were many mouthfuls and Elisa May watched him eat each one, standing by his side, beaming.

"Ooh, that's the best yet," Frankie had said, scooping up the last of the crumbs with his fingers.

He had felt then that there was something else waiting to be said. And he wished now that he had said it. But before he could find the words he felt his brain, or what there was of it, somehow float away.

There were many things that entered Elisa May's head as she sat in that slightly damp room, holding a screwed-up tissue that had found its way into her hand.

She couldn't remember whether she had turned the oven off and taken out the blackberry pie, which frightened her. Not because of the gas oven, but that the pie would surely burn and ruin, and Frankie would never taste it and that frightened her more.

She thought of the way that Harry would rest his head on Frankie's knee as they sat, husband and wife, side by side on the sofa watching television, how Frankie would pet Harry's ears and how gently he would reach for the blanket and pull it over his wagging tail.

She wondered what a person looked like once they had been broken at the bottom of the stairs and if she would recognise him and if he would know she was there. She wished that she was wearing something pretty and had brushed her hair as she was certain this wasn't how she was supposed to look and she wanted more than anything to get it right.

And then, when thoughts started to fail her, she heard a high-pitched humming. She briefly wondered whether the sound was coming from her, and if so, worried that the doctor could hear it too, but he didn't seem to be listening to anything peculiar, although whether humming in such a situation would be deemed peculiar she couldn't be sure. She clasped her hand to her mouth and settled on the fact that the noise was inside of her, although she couldn't place it.

So when Elisa May was led into the room where Frankie lay, with tubes sticking out of him in the places she used to touch, she couldn't think of much. Instead she sat staring at his face and wished that she had spent the last five years looking harder.

Pieces of glass had wedged themselves inside his body in each and every place imaginable. By the time the ambulance arrived, he had lost bucketfuls of blood. This wasn't helped by the fact that the ambulance had got the name of the pub wrong the first time and had been sent to the Jolly Roger, which was three miles in the wrong direction.

She reflected on how Frankie had spent his short career working in a pub and some of his final hours lying in a pool of beer, but how he had never been much of a drinker. There was an irony there somewhere.

His pulse was dropping and his heart-rate sank. Elisa May

held his left hand, and stroked the band of his wedding ring with her finger. She wanted to say something to him that mattered, but the words were too big for her mouth. So she sat amongst the beeps of the machines and realised how well she knew grief now and maybe that was who she was really meant to be. And from now on she would wear only black.

Comedown Alone

JACK SWANSON

Jordan watches TC feel around his feet for a beer. He doesn't look down, preferring to pat the carpet until he touches aluminium.

Only one of the cans in TC's vicinity contains anything more than dregs. Jordan knows this because TC squeezes his empties in the middle, giving them a skinny waist.

Just as his hand approaches the uncrushed Carlsberg, it goes back on itself. Jordan gets up and gives him the can.

"Do you think this thing, tonight . . . you reckon it's a good idea?"

TC looks up like he doesn't understand the question. He cracks the beer. It hisses and coughs up foam.

Nathan emerges from the bathroom, accompanied by the sound of the cistern groaning from the pressure of a pulled chain. He begins pacing up and down, clearing a path through the beer and takeaway debris.

"Nath, you sure about this?" says Jordan.

"Yeah," says Nathan, not breaking his stride or even turning his head.

He knocks over a beer. It falls on its side and liquid seeps out, forming a frothy puddle. It looks like a passed-out drunk.

"I'm not sure I am," says Jordan.

Nathan ignores him. He just continues moving and muttering.

"I think I might not do it."

"You will," says Nathan.

"I don't have to though."

"Shouldn't of spent all the money if you didn't want to."

Jordan looks to TC. He seems to be staring out to somewhere beyond the bungalow walls.

"We all spent that money," says Jordan. "It was mine anyway."

"Your spazzy mum's more like," says Nathan, under his breath but loud enough for TC to laugh.

Jordan feels his face heat and water pooling in the corner of his eyes. This is not crying, it's just the way his stupid body works. He takes his phone from his pocket for a reason to look down.

Nathan stops his pacing. "Mate, I didn't mean that. I weren't thinking."

Jordan carries on scrolling through messages that aren't there. He can feel Nathan right in front of him, can smell his Lynx and Mayfair aroma.

"It's just I'm trying to come up with a plan you know," says Nathan. "Because I want more nights like this. The three of us. Together. You want that too don't you, mate?"

Jordan swipes to his calendar and checks his mum's medication alarms are set for the next day, even though he knows they are.

"TC wants that, don't you?"

Jordan still doesn't look up but he sees TC's reply out of the corner of his eye. It's the slightest of movements, more a drop of the head than a nod, but it means yes.

"There we go then," says Nathan. He's back in motion. "Now don't worry, it'll be easy."

An industrial bin obscures the only entrance to the garages behind King Do. Jordan slips past it, sodden cardboard underfoot. He walks a little way down the mossy pavement and waits. It's 1 a.m. Which in this part of town means silence. He pulls the neck of his jumper up and rests it on the bridge of his nose so the cold wind bites only the top of his face.

A street lamp blinks, illuminating the surroundings with a momentary amber haze. It makes visible garage doors with peeling paint jobs and weeds sprouting from impossible gaps.

The sound of a boy racer blaring drum and bass flies along a nearby road and Jordan becomes aware of his heartbeat. With a shaking hand he unlocks his phone to check the time.

A silhouetted figure slinks past the bin and from the walk Jordan knows it is Matty. He moves with a languid lack of purpose, approaching in zigzags rather than a straight line. Matty's not threatening and he's never tried to be. Jordan likes that about him. All the dealers he knows through Nathan and TC have swollen knuckles they try their hardest not to hide.

"All right, kid," says Matty. He's dressed in full black tracksuit with the hood up. A pale face and limp Marlboro Light in the darkness.

"All right, Matty."

"Up to much tonight, are you?" asks Matty in his usual deadened drawl.

"Not really. You?"

"Not much, just out and about a bit you know."

"Yeah."

Matty's eyes look as they always do, kind of vacant like a blind man's. They give Jordan the impression he's looking at something behind him, or through him maybe. It probably has something to do with the drugs he takes. He told Jordan once that he only uses weed and opiates, that his mind don't need speeding up.

"How much was it you wanted again, kid?"

"Just a gram."

"Just a gram," Matty repeats, stuffing a hand down the front of his joggers and removing a sandwich bag. He begins rooting through it. "I don't know why you keep putting this shit up your nose, kid. It's fucking disgusting."

"Yeah."

Jordan feels for the money in his pocket. Before he can get it out two figures appear from behind the industrial bin. They are dressed much like Matty, dark clothes with their hoods up. But unlike Matty they have tights over their heads so their faces are squashed and distorted. And they have objects in their hands. Metal bars. Dumbbells with the weights removed.

They get within a metre but neither says a word. They just stand there. Breaths of cold white vapour escape as their shoulders rise and fall.

Jordan tries to think but there's a noise drowning out his thoughts. It's a low hum. King Do's extractor fan. It sounded like silence until he noticed it but now he's noticed it, and it seems to be getting louder and louder, a constant whirring hum.

"Give us the stuff," is the deep muffled instruction that the shorter figure finally gives.

Matty is wearing that same lethargic, semi-conscious expression he always does.

"We ain't got nothing, I'm afraid," he says. Then he takes a last long drag on his cigarette and throws it at his feet.

The two figures look like they're on pause. All that's moving is their metal. Their shaking hands betray them.

Without warning the larger figure lurches towards Jordan and clamps a hand around his throat, pinning him to the garage door. A handle digs jagged into his lower back but he can't cry out his pain because the hand's cut off his breath.

The smaller figure reacts, stabbing frantic hands into Jordan's pockets, digging out his phone and money.

Jordan's head is fixed in such a way that he is forced to look at the faces of his muggers. He thinks they might be trying to smile at him through the tights. It reminds him of his grandad's stroke.

Behind them he sees something. Matty's hand moving towards a glint at the cuff of his sleeve. Jordan widens his eyes and opens his mouth, the only responses available to him.

The muggers seem to read the look because the clamp lets go of his throat, releasing all the noise and breath that was trying to escape. They swivel and raise their metal. But it's too late. Because now Matty has his own metal. His is sharp and steady. And it's pointing right at them.

"Give the kid his stuff back."

The four of them are frozen now, waiting for a move. Jordan looks at his phone in the smaller figure's hand and wonders what would happen if the alarm went off. What would they all do?

And then a move.

A blurry flash in the darkness and a dull thud. A thud like hitting the crossbar. No cries of pain or exertion. But another thud.

The light blinks on. A snapshot of Matty's face. Exactly as it was before, those same blind man's eyes. Apart from blood's leaking from his hood. And now he's coming towards Jordan. Falling towards him, face first. The light blinks off and another thud. This one's more like a rug being beaten. A spittle of liquid sprays Jordan's jeans. Then Matty lies motionless at his feet. What looks like tar seeps from his head and inches towards Jordan's toes.

Back at the bungalow Jordan removes his jeans and puts them in the washing machine. He turns the dial up to sixty degrees. Then he picks underwear off the clothes horse and goes into his mum's room. She is asleep, as usual. He puts knickers in her top drawer and a bra in the middle one.

The living room is freezing so Jordan plugs in the electric heater. If the doors are all kept closed it actually warms up pretty quickly.

He turns on the TV, the twenty-four-hour news. He always likes watching the news. Not because of what they're saying but because of the way they're saying it, like they're talking directly to him. But tonight it's just noise and images. Still, he keeps it on and shuts his eyes.

There's a knock on the front door. Jordan opens it to Nathan and TC, their faces white against the night. TC's huge shoulders are slumped forward and shaking, but his face is expressionless. He gives Jordan a nod then lumbers past him, making his way to the sofa and easing himself down into his seat.

Nathan is twitchy all over. He removes a drawstring bag from his back.

"All we got is four fucking grams and seventy quid," he says, rifling through the bag. "And that's including your forty." He hands Jordan back his money and phone. Then he locks his intense, wobbling stare on him. "We got rid of your weights in the river."

"OK," says Jordan, looking to the floor. He finds it hard to maintain eye contact with anyone, but particularly Nathan. "Nath, should I call an ambulance?"

"No, they could trace it," says Nathan, moving to the sofa. He sits down beside TC and lays the contents of the bag on the coffee table.

As TC leans in to inspect the goods, Jordan notices splattered blood patterning the fold of fat that connects his head to his back.

"You said you weren't going to hurt him."

TC is unmoved but Nathan stands and faces Jordan. "You said he wouldn't have a weapon."

"I didn't think he would. I didn't think he was like –"

"Well he fucking did."

"I'm sorry," says Jordan. "Do you think he'll be all right?"

"How the fuck am I supposed to know?" says Nathan, grabbing the money and four little bags of white from the table. "I'm off," he says, looking at TC. "You coming?"

The sofa begins to creak with TC's impending rise.

"Stay," says Jordan. "We may as well stay together. For a bit, at least. We can talk about something else, take our minds off it."

"I'm tired. I can't really be fucked."

"We could have a line. Just one or two. Just for a bit?"

"I don't know," says Nathan, although he's stopped heading towards the door. "What do you reckon?" he asks TC.

TC remains seated and removes a debit card from his wallet. The decision is made.

He racks up lines on the coffee table whilst Nathan rolls a ten-pound note into a tight cylinder. Three thin, even lines come and go with a burning of the nose, a watering of the eyes and a stinging of the throat. A switch is flicked, the energy comes on. Even if it hasn't hit yet, it's the anticipation, the knowing what is just around the corner.

Nathan starts talking about the Henley brothers, his favourite topic of conversation when fucked. The Henley brothers, Liam and Connell, are a bit of a myth in town. It's rumoured they're not actually brothers, that one or both of them changed their name by deed poll, but no one really knows. It's said they control all the drugs that come in from London.

He's telling a story he's heard about a guy who owed the brothers money, but could only get half of it.

"So they break into his house, right." He looks at Jordan. "Right?"

"Right."

"But there's no fucking money about so they end up taking the Rottweiler." He pauses to feel for residual powder around his nostrils. "So they've got this Rottweiler, yeah?"

"Yeah."

In the end the punchline is that the brothers only returned half the dog.

Jordan wonders if they killed it before they split it. He feels a little sick. But he doesn't show it. He laughs along. Because it's just nice to be talking. Talking about anything.

They have another line. But this will be the last. They'll sell the rest on for a bit of profit. But if it's the last it may as well be a big one. So TC makes them thick. Three white slugs. And the sting is there again but it is good.

TC's nodding to a beat that must be in his head but he looks like he's in a good place and that's fine.

Nathan is talking about his older brothers now and how much he hates them. His face is jerking a bit as he speaks, little spasms. But he looks happy still.

Jordan brings up his mum even though he rarely does. Because he can tonight. Tonight's different. And now he's wondering why he hasn't talked about her more because they care, he can see they care. Nathan says it must be shit. It's nice that he understands that. TC doesn't speak but Jordan can tell he understands too and that's amazing. So another line.

TC throws a pack of fags on the table. They go outside for a smoke.

The night air is fresh and crisp.

The back garden is just a few square metres of fenced-off concrete and three beach chairs but it's nice. They send smoke into the night. Jordan tries to spit and nothing comes out but that doesn't matter.

Inside they have another line and Jordan says he's scared about Matty because tonight he can say that. Nathan says it'll be all right and TC squeezes his shoulder. Jordan thinks that it probably will be all right.

Another line.

They talk about something else. Jordan connects his phone to Nathan's speakers and it is good. Deep bass reverberating. When he looks at TC he seems to be pulsing with the rhythm, almost expanding and contracting.

They have another line but Nathan's nose is blocked. He's straining to snort the white up but it's not moving and he's going red and the tendons in his neck are showing hard against his skin. He gets it up eventually.

Jordan's mum appears in her pyjamas. She's just there, leaning on her stick. She gives Jordan a glass of squash and runs her fingers through his hair. Nathan and TC are looking at her like they're trying not to stare. And even when she's gone Jordan can tell they're thinking about her. He can tell because no one says a word.

Outside for another cigarette but it's light now, much too light. Sky raw blue and sharp against the eyes. The concrete yard has those same resilient weeds as at the garages, sprouting from non-existent gaps. And the cold is piercing, penetrating the skin. The screech of car tyres and people going to work. They share the one remaining cigarette. When it gets to Jordan it is wet with saliva and out of focus.

They go back inside. And they need another line because that was grim and it's got to be a big one because the feeling's fading now and it's getting harder to get it back. Nathan's struggling the powder up his nose. And TC's sitting there in silence, just pulsing, throbbing, constant. With blood still on his neck. Why doesn't he wipe it off? Why doesn't he speak? Another line but it's not coming back. And nobody is speaking, just all looking like they want to speak. Nathan's jaw locking and unlocking. His eyes on Jordan. Mistrusting. Jordan feels them trying to bore through his skull, work out what he's thinking. And what is TC thinking? He must be thinking something so why doesn't he say it? His face is disgusting, his pockmarks too deep. One more line but Nathan's going, he's had enough. Matty's eyes. Jordan asks TC to stay and he doesn't move so he will. But there's nothing left so they lick their fingers and stick them in the bag. Just his face pulsing and throbbing with blood and no expression. And then he's gone too.

Jordan wakes on the sofa. There's a beating in his forehead and his skin feels too tightly wrapped around his skull. He hauls his body to upright. A spiralled tenner lies unfurled on the table, to be ironed out and powdered down before exchange at the corner shop.

The air is hot and thick with stale pizza and spilt booze. He unplugs the electric heater and goes for a piss. In the bathroom he contemplates a shower. But with the boiler broken he decides against it. The thought of cold water against his skin is too unbearable. Instead he brushes his teeth. They are sensitive – it feels like spikes dragging across nerves.

He tries not to think of Matty. He turns the TV on and the volume up. There is little comfort in it. It only serves as a reminder of what he's trying to forget. It's just shouting over someone.

He reaches for the glass of squash on the table and thinks immediately of his mum. Shit. The time on the news is 15.54. Shit. He pats his pockets but there's nothing there. He sees his phone attached to Nathan's speakers and remembers the silence its battery's death brought last night.

Opening his mum's door brings a slice of daylight into an otherwise darkened room. Particles of dust hover within its glow. Jordan momentarily disturbs these as he moves to the bed. The bed is a double, but with her in it, it looks far bigger. He sits on the edge.

"Mum?" He rests a hand on her flimsy arm. "Mum?"

She wakes with a look that suggests she's somewhere between dream and reality. These days she rarely gets much past this look.

"It's medicine time."

She clutches at his waiting hand and he helps her sit up. He always worries her arm will snap when he does this. It reminds him of the KFC boxes in the living room. Chicken on the bone.

"Are your friends still here?"

"No," says Jordan, turning to the pill organiser on her bedside table. Over the years the organiser has got gradually bigger. It started out as seven boxes, now it is twenty-eight. The rule with MS medication seems to be, the less it works the more you get.

He presents her with four pills of different shapes and sizes.

"That's a lot," she says.

"I know," he says, handing her a glass of water.

A couple of years ago, encouraged by the school counsellor, Jordan went on a field trip to Eastbourne. When he came back he realised she hadn't touched anything apart from the Prozac and painkillers. He shouted and she cried.

She works her way from smallest pill to biggest. She holds the final one, a transparent yellow capsule, between her thumb and forefinger. When she finally swallows it she retches and her eyes water.

"Do you want any dinner?" he asks.

"No thank you, darling."

More often than not she refuses, but he goes on asking anyway. Technically it's his job now. He'd never even heard of being a carer until Nathan showed him the form.

She lies back down and turns the TV on. The shopping channel. The Heavy Grip is being advertised, the best training device for improving hand and wrist strength.

"There's food in the fridge for you, isn't there?" she says, not taking her eyes off the unnaturally happy woman encouraging people to pick up the phone.

"Yeah."

"Good."

He takes two codeine tablets from an open packet on the floor. And then he leaves.

He sits back on the sofa and puts his phone on charge. He waits for it to turn on. There are no messages from Nathan or TC.

The codeine helps him find a kind of numbness. Not quite sleep but not the painful awareness of earlier either.

His mind drifts in and out of a comforting blankness.

His phone is making noise. Not an alarm, a call.

"Hello?"

"Jordan?"

"Yeah . . . Who's this?"

"My name's Connell Henley. I'm Matty's cousin."

A wave of nausea hits Jordan.

"Something happened last night. I heard you was there."

"Yeah," Jordan says. "Is Matty all right?"

"He'll pull through," says Connell. His voice is flat. "Are you all right?"

"Yeah, I managed to get away. I would have stayed like but there was two of them and they had weapons and –"

"Don't worry about it. Matty's told me everything. Sounds like you did the right thing."

"Yeah."

"I mean his mouth's a bit of a mess as you can imagine," says Connell. "But he told me." He pauses to make a phlegmy snorting sound. "I want you to know those cunts are going to get sorted. You don't need to worry about that."

"OK."

"I mean proper sorted."

It seems Connell is waiting for a response. So Jordan musters one. "Good."

"Yeah, good," says Connell. "Because if there's one thing I can't stand it's thieving. Taking someone else's shit. Taking their money. Their phone."

Jordan becomes suddenly aware of an object heavy in his hand, cold against his ear. "I . . . They didn't get my –"

"You're going to end up sharing a wheelchair with your mum, Jordan."

A flat-line beep as Connell hangs up.

As Jordan enters the bright of the subway from the darkness of the night his feet crunch on broken glass. He looks down at scattered white crystals, fragments of two shattered WKD bottles. The pavement is littered with these little trinkets. There are ground-down cans of energy drink, a flat Sondico football and a pack of Rizla with its last paper flapping in the wind.

The first time Jordan set foot in this subway was to meet Nathan and TC. He paid them twenty and they gave him ten's worth. It made sense to him then, that this would be the place for a deal like that. You were hidden, out of sight. And yet now, standing inside this solid cube of light, Jordan can't help feel exposed, like there's a spotlight shining right on him.

Nathan and TC approach from the other end.

Nathan hurries towards Jordan, pulling his hood down as he reaches him. "What the fuck did you pick up your phone for?"

"I'm sorry."

TC just stares at them from the entrance, his arms folded and mouth open, like they're a programme he's watching.

"What're we going to do?" asks Jordan.

Nathan takes a couple of deep breaths and then removes a pack of crumpled cigarettes from his pocket. He fishes one out and brings it to his lips. With a shaking hand he lights it and takes a drag.

"I know this is shit, mate," he says with his eyes on the pavement. "But you're just gonna have to face it."

"What?"

"They don't know about me and TC. There's no point us all being fucked."

"What do you mean?"

"We'd do the same in your position."

There is the sound of a lorry clunking overhead. A woman with a tired-looking face and a babyless pram walks through. She pays them no attention.

"They're going to ask me who was in on it," says Jordan.

"And you're not gonna tell them."

"Nath, please. They'll make me."

Nathan brings his eyes in line with Jordan's and holds his gaze for a moment. His irises seem to be vibrating, unable to keep still in the whites of his eyes. Then he sends a glance in TC's direction. "Keep your mouth shut, all right."

The yellow subway lights hum their electric buzz. If insomnia were a place, this would be it.

Nathan offers Jordan a cigarette from his packet. "Sorry, mate."

Jordan refuses.

Nathan turns and he and TC disappear into the darkness, leaving Jordan alone.

He stands there for a while, just staring at the graffiti. Nathan once told him to write the nastiest thing he could think of, about the nicest person he knew. He doesn't know why they bother repainting these walls but he's glad that they do.

After some time a familiar sound fills the subway. The shrill, urgent cry of his phone alarm. He thinks of his mum asleep. And of the pill organiser beside her. He never asked her why she didn't take her medication that time he went away, but he knew the answer. She had wanted to give up. Maybe he'd been wrong to get so angry.

The Travails of
Uncle Vanya

CLAIRE MONTELL

She wasn't wearing a hat. It made her easy to pick out as she hurried through the formal gardens away from the riverbank, past the closed funfair and the dry fountains. At the top of the broad steps by the colonnaded park entrance, she paused to push her dark, wind-tangled hair from her face. She didn't even glance at the kiosk but marched straight to the car park. Why was it that foreigners only ate ice cream in the summer?

She stood by the car, shivering a little, fumbling around in her bag for her keys. No hat and no gloves either, Vanya observed, as he slid into his shiny black Volga. He turned the ignition and waited for her to reverse out, then crawled round the car park behind her, flicking his left indicator on to mirror hers. They both pulled out into the sparse traffic on the ring road for the return journey from the park to her home.

Soon he was parked in his usual spot opposite the sentry box at the gate to the yellow-brick compound. He was peckish. An ice cream would have been nice. She would be inside now, Julia Johnson, waiting for her attaché husband, Toby, to come home. The Russians had offered the Westerners who lived and worked in the city a beautiful behemoth of parquet floors, tinkling chandeliers, and intricate plasterwork. And the Westerners had filled it with fat refrigerators, hand-tied Persian rugs and VCR machines. Doubtless Julia dined on avocados, steak and fresh milk brought in every two days from Finland. And at weekends and evenings, she lounged on a vast velvet sofa, watching decadent Hollywood films. When the summer came, she would join the other Westerners in the walled garden as they kept the neighbourhood from its sleep with their late-night jazz and shrieks of laughter. Westerners! They who only ever emerged from the compound in their sleek foreign cars, flashing their red number plates, and never, not once, on foot. They were pigs in clover, his father had always said.

But Russia was no fool. She had used German prisoners to build this fine post-war building. And in this new unconventional war, it made sense to keep her ideological adversaries together in a place where they felt comfortable enough to talk casually over dinner and could be monitored using the listening devices embedded in their art-hung walls and elegant light fixtures.

Vanya looked up at the windows of Julia's apartment. He had been watching her for three weeks now, her swirl of dark hair reminding him of the young Olga Knipper in the photograph his mother used to keep on the bookshelf. His mother had seen Olga on the stage three times at the Moscow Arts Theatre in the 1930s. That's what a woman should be like, Vanya, she'd told him: expressive, talented, loyal. What a wife our greatest playwright had! What an actress and what a wife! Difficult, yes, she was difficult, but marvellous. Vanya had been married to two women like Olga but it turned out that the difficult, rather than the loyal side of their character had come to the fore.

His experience of his own marriages had taught him that dealing with women at a distance was easier. And now for twenty-five years he had made a career of following the wives of other men as they glided between islands of Western life in the Russian capital, on school runs, shopping trips and visits to other foreign friends. But Julia wasn't like the others. Julia went out to Russian lessons, leaving her car outside Gorky Park and then striding across it to one of the large classical buildings on the other side, where she met her teacher in his tiny first-floor office.

Igor turned over the last few pages of Vanya's report in noisy succession then let out a tired sigh. Vanya waited, rueing the day that Igor had caught a high-profile journalist meeting a dissident under the clock of the Puppet Theatre. The dissident had spent a few hours at the Lubyanka and there had been the classic reprisal for the journalist: slashed tyres on his new Mercedes. It wasn't the first time that a dissident had met a journalist in that spot and, in Vanya's opinion, Igor had just been lucky with the timing. Nonetheless, it had resulted in Igor's promotion and now, every report that Vanya submitted was read by the younger man with palpable ennui.

"So she's having Russian lessons. What of it?" Igor asked, closing the report and picking his teeth with his fingernail.

"Because none of the wives ever does that. They learn a bit of Russian for fun with the teacher who's been assigned to the compound."

"Ivan Nikolaevich, you would be the first person to tell me that a commitment to a language should always be applauded."

How typical of Igor to choose to play down Vanya's insight. It went without saying that Igor could speak only Russian.

"But not when it is going to be used for nefarious purposes." Vanya tried not to sound irked.

Igor wrinkled his forehead. "Those American media people, CBS . . . She lives in the same block as them, doesn't she?"

"Yes, but –"

"How old is she?"

"Thirty-five."

"Still attractive?"

"Attractive?" Vanya felt his cheeks turn pink.

"Americans always want to impress attractive women. So they tell her about Seriozha in his little office near Gorky Park. You know they like to believe they discovered him, that he's better than the 'official' teachers. She's a polite Brit. It would be rude not to take her new friends up on their recommendation. That's all there is to it." Igor wiped his hand on his trousers, cast the report into the tray for filing and pulled another pile of papers across the vast desk towards him.

"I still think it's suspicious behaviour."

"What are you afraid of? That she'll start sharing her lemon cake with the refuseniks?"

Vanya regretted telling Igor that the most exciting thing he'd learnt from the bug transcripts that week was that the wives were planning a coffee morning to raise funds for the Anglo-American school and his new charge had offered to make a lemon cake – if she was able to get hold of any lemons.

"But in all my twenty-five years –"

"Vanya, take it easy. Check with Seriozha, if you like. Find out if she's mastered double imperfective verbs. If she has," Igor chuckled, "then we'll start to worry."

Vanya sat in his car outside the compound, recasting the conversation with Igor in his head. So maybe he was only in the seventh directorate and not yet in the first department, but he had a specialised role. Not just anyone could follow these women for twenty-five years. Anti-Soviet activity from this group may be more subtle. It needed a keen eye. And his command of English was "top notch" as they would say. He didn't have cause to use it much but he had the ability. Shouldn't Igor think about something other than the refuseniks? So what if their gripe about the lack of exit visas got into the foreign press. So what if Igor would be in a spot of bother. Refuseniks were small fry. Before you knew it, Julia might be using her Russian to uncover state secrets then sharing them with the British! Vanya slammed his fist on the steering wheel, which proved to be rather painful. Couldn't Igor see his skill? Couldn't he see that Vanya's commitment to his country was exceptional, just like his father's had been?

Vanya's eyes filled up at the thought of his father. He could see him now, coming in from a long day of polishing official cars for the Committee for State Security, his fingertips raw from being scrubbed clean, his thinning hair combed neatly back. He remembered sitting on his father's lap as a small boy and his father telling him how they were all working together to build a new country. You see, Vanyushka, the people rose up against oppression – and now an equal world is within our sights. And our route to that world is work. Just like in Chekhov's plays, his mother would add. And imagine having our own little worker. Here she would plant a big kiss on Vanya's curly blond locks. Vanya's father had continued to call him "our own little worker" until the day he died, just after Vanya's fiftieth birthday.

Vanya stopped following other wives on the school runs or trips to the foreigners' food store. It would be worth it. Sooner or later, Julia would come out and use her Russian for the nefarious purposes he had predicted. Igor had been lucky. But Vanya was professional. He would make sure he was there. However, Julia did not leave home frequently and Vanya was soon spending more hours sitting waiting outside her apartment block in his shiny black Volga, than he spent in his own small, increasingly untidy apartment.

Then he found out from a colleague who was trailing the German press that Julia had been talking to a West German journalist at a party in the Reuters office on the second floor. Vanya requested the transcripts – never easy to monitor those noisy conversations. However, it appeared to be a conversation about gardening. Nonetheless, Vanya was rather taken by the discovery that Julia could speak German. Curiously enough, Olga Knipper had been able to speak German. No significance, but it was still an interesting parallel.

Apart from her Russian lessons, Julia did make a weekly trip to the British Embassy shop for essentials. Two days after the Reuters party she exited the compound in her silver car on schedule. Vanya was ready. He looked forward to the drive into the centre of town, despite having to follow Julia's rather circuitous route. She spent longer than usual inside but emerged eventually, three carrier bags in her hands and a big pack of pink toilet paper under her arm. A Russian woman, noticing the toilet paper, stopped right in front of her and demanded to know where she had got it. Julia opened her mouth then closed it, gesturing feebly towards the Embassy building behind her. The Russian woman looked at the flag in front of the building and then at the car. Cursing loudly, she brushed past Julia who quickly shoved everything into the boot and drove off, narrowly avoiding a trolleybus as she did so. Vanya, watching from his parking spot on the other side of the road, shook his head. What was the point in learning a language, if you were never going to use it?

The week after that, Julia didn't go on her Embassy trip and even missed one of her lessons. Vanya checked with Seriozha. He was enthusiastic about her progress. That cheered Vanya up a bit. At least she understood the genitive case. On the Thursday, Julia sent a long-overdue letter to her aunt to thank her for her birthday present (a purple handbag Vanya had never seen her use) and had coffee with the German journalist (for which a transcript annoyingly could not be produced due to a failure with the listening device). Two weeks passed. There was a lull in parties after a row with the authorities about a broken chandelier. Even Vanya got bored of reading the transcripts from evenings that Julia and her husband spent reading quietly or watching films. There was regular marital intimacy (relevant to Vanya's surveillance only to show him she was close enough to her husband that he might tell her something of his work). Sometimes there was music: a British song about someone called Oliver who had an army. Vanya was unable to find out who Oliver was. They had friends over for dinner on one occasion and there was some humour about the simplicity of the Soviet way of life and some slightly tactless observations on Russian fashion, woolly hats in particular. Vanya was beginning to dread the possibility that Igor was right and there was nothing much to Julia Johnson.

Then one Tuesday afternoon, Vanya had just opened the sports pages of *Isvestiya*, his feet up on the dashboard, when he caught sight of a figure talking to the sentries in the box at the gate. It was Julia, on foot. One of the sentries pointed to the left. She still wasn't wearing a hat but did have a silk scarf round her neck and fine leather gloves. She scowled at a small map in her hand and set off at a determined pace down a side street. Vanya climbed hastily out of his car and followed her, nodding to the driver in the Volga parked behind his to keep an eye on it. Julia wound her way down smaller thoroughfares, glancing up at the grey housing blocks around her, stopping at corners to read the road names. When she got to Gorky Street she took the underpass. He followed her down into the long white passage under the wide avenue. A man in a nylon sports jacket was leaning against the tiled wall. An empty bottle lay on its side by his booted feet. He pushed himself away from the wall when he saw Julia. She looked hard at the ground and kept on walking. The man soon caught up with her and put a hand on her shoulder, whispering something in her ear. Vanya paused, watching the exchange. Was this it? Who was he? But Julia looked at the man in confusion and he heard her say in Russian, "What?"

The man took hold of her arm, held her back and shouted in her face. "Vi rabotayetye?"

Vanya ran forward, the pompom on his favourite snowflake woolly hat bouncing on his skull. When the man saw him coming, he let go of Julia's arm and backed off, spitting on the ground before he walked on to the exit.

"Are you all right?" Vanya asked her in English.

"Of course I am," she replied, looking up at him. "He was just asking me if I was working. Mistaken identity."

Vanya tried not to laugh but failed. "He thought you were a prostitute."

She didn't flinch. "Thank you for clarifying that." Then she turned and walked away. She was impressively cool in a threatening situation, softly spoken, but firm. He strode quickly after her.

"Can I help you to get somewhere? Where are you going?"

She glanced at him with suspicion. "I'm just going for a walk." There was a challenge in her tone as though she was expecting him to stop her.

"It's not great weather for a walk," he said, measuring his pace against hers as she went up the steps to the street. "In fact, it's raining cats and dogs."

She didn't reply but he saw her mouth curl into a smile. He had her.

"Can I accompany you a little way? To make sure there are no further issues. And it's good for me to practise my English. Why bother learning a language unless you use it, I always say."

She hesitated, clearly looking for a way to say no.

"Or Russian? You can speak a little Russian. Let me talk to you as we walk." He switched to his native language as they came out onto a broad street lined with solid apartment blocks and criss-crossed with tramlines. "Look to your right. Up here is the junction with Sadovoye Kolt'so. 'Garden Ring' in English. Sounds more beautiful than it looks, no?"

She looked at the multiple lanes carving their way round the city and laughed.

"Why don't I show you the Chekhov House?" he suggested.

"It's just five minutes' walk this way. You'd like it."

They paid the sullen attendant at the ticket desk and hung their coats in the cloakroom. He explained the need for them to exchange their shoes for soft leather slippers that swished over the wooden floors. She slid over the parquet, turning like an ice skater and laughing. How charming she was! He watched her as she drifted around the study and stood beside her as she admired the ornate inkstand on the great writer's desk.

"I'm impressed you're learning Russian," he said, his mouth close to her small, milky-white ear.

"You're easily impressed."

"Not at all. It's a difficult language. What made you decide to tackle it?"

"I'm not saying. It's silly." She moved round to read the spines of the books on the bookshelf.

He followed her. "Tell me," he said in Russian. "Please."

She looked at him with her big brown eyes and replied in his native tongue. "Because I love the literature."

What a marvellous woman, he thought.

"He's a masterful short-story writer," she continued.

"His plays are better."

She shook her head. "I disagree."

He looked at her in surprise. "*Uncle Vanya* is a masterpiece. Just think of it. Those people on that decaying estate, believing they are supporting the learned landowner to make the world a better place – but he is a fool and the old order is corrupt. And where do they find their redemption? In work – work to support their country. It is the message for our times. In fact, my parents named me after the lead character."

"Ah, an egocentric love of Chekhov."

"No!" Then he saw the glint in her eye and blushed.

She switched from Russian to English and spoke quietly so the room attendant couldn't hear. "But, Vanya, surely you shouldn't be giving your name away to me?"

"Why would you say that?"

"It's the bobble hat, Vanya. I see it behind me every time I walk through the park."

She was observant – and had the honesty to tell him she knew who he was. He could do business with this articulate, intelligent, open-minded woman.

He pointed to a photograph on the wall. "This is Chekhov's wife, Olga Knipper. I think you look rather like her. Especially with your hair like you have it today. Wouldn't you agree?"

She looked at the image of the bespectacled writer with a younger woman, dressed in white, her dark hair swirled around her head into a topknot.

She grimaced. "Hardly."

"She was an actress. A remarkable actress. German by birth but chose Russian citizenship."

"Really? How times change!" Julia looked at him as though she was waiting for him to laugh.

Vanya didn't see anything to laugh about and tried a different tack. "In *Vanya* she was the most marvellous Yeliena you could think of. All languor one minute and fire the next, according to my mother. She saw her three times at the Moscow Arts Theatre in the 1930s."

"Seriously?" She put a long-fingered white hand on his coat sleeve as she spoke.

"Next time there's a production of the play, I'll get some tickets for you and your husband. Your alter ego won't be in it, of course, but it's still worth seeing."

Julia smiled. She was grateful – charmed by him, he could see it. Soon, with his experience, he would be able to extract all sorts of information from her. Igor's achievements were about to be dwarfed by his.

To Vanya's delight, a production of the play had just opened at the Arts Theatre. To his frustration, Igor gave him extra evening shifts to do. A hullaballoo about the West German press running a piece on ethnic German refuseniks was threatening to blow up into a diplomatic row. Igor stormed round the office, shouting about how there was a chain of contacts in Moscow who had been feeding information to the West German press.

When Vanya was finally released from his extra workload, he made sure he sent Julia two tickets for a night when her husband was away in Tbilisi with a trade delegation. He spent the afternoon at the special access store for government employees, looking for a new shirt that didn't strain too much over his tummy. Then he called into his barber for a shave and a trim.

"Be generous with the cologne," he instructed.

"We're out of cologne," his barber told him.

Vanya left a note with the sentry at the compound to say he had heard about the Georgian trip and he could change the tickets or he would be happy to escort Julia and a friend to the theatre himself. He knew she would come alone. How could she possibly explain to another English woman that she was friends with a Russian? And at six thirty that evening, there she was, by herself, waiting for him by the sentry box, hair in a topknot, heels on, a delicate smudge of pink lipstick. He offered her his arm and led her, through the first wet snowfall of winter, to his newly polished Volga.

"It's marvellous, Vanya," she said to him as she sipped the champagne he had ordered. "I've been longing to get out of the compound, away from the Western bubble. And, although going to a play with a man who spends his life following me around might not be entirely what I had in mind, I'm grateful."

He patted her hand and then clinked his glass with hers.

"Here's to the USSR," he replied, offering her blini and caviar. "Now, let's take our seats."

They walked slowly into the auditorium, so that Julia had time to express her delight at the fine plasterwork, the Art Nouveau frieze and the dark walnut panels on the balconies Vanya pointed out.

And as Vanya sank into his seat, feeling the warmth of Julia's arm next to his, he allowed himself to entertain the notion that this bond between them might not just be about the enjoyment of language and literature, nor even about him extracting little bits of information, but that she might, actually, be the perfect person to work for his country. He stole a glance at her watching the play, watching the characters walk and talk and weep their way through the crumbling estate, as their lives and loves turned out to be not what they seemed in the corrupt old order. All the years he had worked, all the hours waiting in his car would culminate in a glorious outcome and all his efforts with this expressive, loyal, talented woman would be vindicated.

As the play drew to a close and Uncle Vanya, Sonya and Astrov settled down to the only solace they could find, working for a better society, Vanya felt tears prick his eyes. When the curtain fell, he leapt to his feet to applaud his namesake on the stage. "Bravo, bravo!" Julia got to her feet, too, clapping vigorously and calling out with him.

"So?" he said to Julia, after the applause died down. "You see how that old way of living in this country was judged to be a failure by our greatest playwright?"

"My dear friend," she replied, "what I saw was only the disappointment of a man called Vanya who had spent his life working hard for something that didn't deserve his devotion."

His cramped flat with its broken oven, his father's years on the waiting list for a Lada he never got, his mother's steadfast belief in her son's better future, all flashed through his mind. He thought of the vast velvet sofas and VCR machines in the yellow-brick building. He looked at the young woman with her entrancing brown eyes fixed on him, her lipstick washed away by the champagne. He thought of the ethnic Germans who wanted to get out of the USSR, and of Julia, speaking to the journalist, of her lengthy visit to the Embassy, of the few words she exchanged with the man in the underpass before he was within earshot, and of her quip about citizenship in the Chekhov House. There was no way she was part of that chain, was there? And her comment about the play? She didn't mean that. No, no. She was just being difficult. He smiled, took her arm and led her out into the foyer. Then he thought of his shiny black Volga and hoped it was out of harm's way in the backstreet where he had left it.

All the Words
He Ever Spoke

KIT DE WAAL

Every so often I would find myself talking with my father. Through a gap in his indifference and inattention, he would turn a yellow eye on me and speak.

He would start with a question, something I could never answer about the meaning of life or loss, sometimes a riddle or a joke, but the conversation was always lumpy, uneven, difficult to hold. And it would slip away from both of us, often at the same time.

But by infinitesimal degrees, I learned everything about him, or so I thought. I watched his mouth move as he massaged the heel of his palm with the pad of his thumb and I believed everything he told me, his easy beliefs, his elaborate justifications, until, over the years, from the clues and fragments, I constructed a résumé for him that read like the epitaph for a great ship – forged in fire, strong, unsinkable – and I used it as a charm against loving him or expecting, ever, for him to love me.

I thought a big man would make a lot of ash but it blew away in seconds, all the words he ever spoke and all the words I couldn't hear.

What Hamdiyya Vowed
NADIA WASSEF

" I, Hamdiyya Mohamed Ahmed Al-Qahry, offer you myself
in marriage and in accordance with the instructions of the
Holy Koran and the Holy Prophet, peace and blessing be upon
Him. I pledge, in honesty and with sincerity, to be for you an
obedient and faithful wife."

"I pledge, in honesty and sincerity, to be your husband."

Mohamed Ahmed Al-Qahry stood up and clasped the meaty
hand of his new son-in-law, cementing their alliance. Hagg Fakhri
was an excellent catch by any measure. If Hamdiyya's mother had
lived to see this day she would have approved, Hamdiyya's father
felt sure. She wouldn't have minded too much that the groom was
closer in age to Hamdiyya's father than to Hamdiyya herself, for
age is wisdom. Nor would it have bothered her unduly that his
children were older than Hamdiyya, for that would mean they
would embrace her as a younger sister. Or that his left eye looked
outwards, leaving you unsure where his gaze rested, for that meant
he was a man of wider vision. Nor that he dyed his white hair with
henna, rendering it the colour of her favourite fruit, tangerines. No,
this was meant to be. And most importantly, his wealth matched
Hamdiyya's own lofty aspirations – animal husbandry was an
extremely lucrative business and Hagg Fakhri was one of the
biggest suppliers of sheep in Egypt. He only hoped his new son-in-
law wouldn't mind that his bride had gone to an international – of

course an all girls – school, learnt languages, and read books. As he had assured him on their first meeting, all this was done under her mother's watchful eye, because – may God have mercy on her soul – she was a mathematics teacher at the school, so how could she not take advantage of such an opportunity?

He would miss having Hamdiyya around the house. She knew to leave him alone until he'd had his first glass of tea, in which he took four spoonfuls of sugar. Then after he had performed his ablutions, along with his morning prayers, he would return to the breakfast table and satisfy himself with his favourite dish of fuul, which Hamdiyya had pressed into a paste, seasoned with cumin, lemon, and salt before covering it with a shiny film of olive oil. She made the tastiest fuul, even better than her mother's, though he'd never admit it, not wanting to tarnish her memory in that way. And she knew exactly how long to heat the bread for: so that it was hot enough to be crisp, without breaking into annoying bits once he curved it into the shape of a cat's ear to scoop up the fuul. Unlike her mother, she never tried to put less sugar in his second helping of tea. She understood that we are on this earth for as long as God deems fit, and nothing we mortals attempt will alter the course He has chosen for us. Hamdiyya's mother often lectured him about his diabetes, but it was she who was destined to leave them first. Hamdiyya took after him, she was a bright girl. She knew that it was more important to let him be.

Only after his morning ritual was complete would she begin to talk to him about news of her four brothers, their wives and children, and, of course, the neighbours. He enjoyed hearing the saga of Abdou the mechanic who was forbidden from returning home by his wife until he had curtailed his hasheesh habit; and Morcos the pharmacist whose daughter had resorted to practitioners of white magic because she was unable to breed. What would they be saying about Mohamed Ahmed Al-Qahry today? That he had found a crown in which to place his most prized bort. Hagg Fakhri had assured him that she would be allowed to visit often, but he did not want to take away from the attention she should be lavishing on her husband. After all, he was her world now. And to ensure her own happiness, she must ensure her husband's. But then Mohamed Ahmed Al-Qahry needn't worry. Hamdiyya was a bright girl, she took after him.

"Sign here, here, and then here again," instructed the cleric, tapping the long, perfectly filed nail of his pinkie at the space inside the leather-bound register, already crammed with the alliances of so many families. Hagg Fakhri watched his new father-in-law bend over the register and impart his name to the page before presenting the pen to him. He waved it away much like he would a fly. Hagg Fakhri thrust his arm forward out of the loose sleeve of his freshly pressed galabiya, his prayer beads slapping the desk. He then drove his thumb into the square pad of purple ink, smearing his print next to his father-in-law's careful letters.

Hagg Fakhri observed his new bride as she respectfully embraced her father and stooped to kiss his hand, which he quickly withdrew. He enveloped her in the most paternal of embraces and kissed her forehead, while his eyes filled with tears. Hagg Fakhri turned away hastily and made his way to the door, dividing his impressive weight between his feet. He was aware of Hamdiyya following him, but did not see her shoulders pressed back and her head held high. Nor did he see Mohamed Ahmed Al-Qahry release that tear under the weight of his departed wife's critical eye.

Hagg Fakhri descended the steps of the dilapidated Ministry of Justice building with Hamdiyya still a few paces behind. Nageh, his short and eager driver, opened the back door of the silver Mercedes. Hagg Fakhri impatiently scolded him, pointing to the front passenger seat with his worn cane. Nageh frantically opened it, head slightly bowed, leaving the back door open for Hamdiyya. They settled in silence.

Hagg Fakhri muttered his thanks to God for the day having passed as he expected thus far and quietly relished the anticipation of what was to come. He studied Hamdiyya in the rear-view mirror. Her profile reminded him of his grandmother: a proud but kind woman. Hamdiyya's eyebrows had been threaded into shape. She wore enough make-up to accentuate her full lips and big brown eyes but not to excess like the silly tarts of nowadays. He guessed that her hair was long and honey-coloured beneath her flowery headscarf. He prided himself on his ability to gauge what lay under the surface of things. After all, this was his line of work and one of the reasons why he was an expert with livestock. He could tell that beneath that skirt and blouse was a body that would please him. Her breasts suggested a fresh firmness that he appreciated, just as her rump looked like something he would enjoy holding on to. Once they got to his villa in the elegant district of Giza, he would allow her time to bathe and prepare herself. He had explained to his father-in-law what he expected of a wife. Tonight he would not rely on the blue pills his apprentices supplied him with, but would go easy on her. Then with time he would break her in. If she was anything like the last one, he might even offer her a puff of his hasheesh cigarette. But the important thing was to ensure that she didn't become too demanding. He would manage that. He was a master at managing God's creatures. The deep warmth in his crotch bloomed into throbbing. He longed to release the pleasing tension. There would be plenty of time.

Nageh admired Hagg Fakhri's resilience, and his broad taste in women. He didn't remember the characteristics of each one in great detail, but he did recall that Hagg always slipped him a little something to celebrate the start of a new union. Nageh was curious as to how long this one would last. He catalogued her predecessors: the first was the mother of Hagg's three sons – apparently she had been the best of them. Alas, she was no more, but Hagg often said that one day he would join her, and she would make him as comfortable in the heavens as she had on this miserable earth. The faces of the other five paraded past his eye. There was the one who stole from Hagg, the one who hated his sons, the one Hagg caught flirting with the milkman – thanks to Nageh's inquisitive nature – and the one with the beautiful long hair that went down to the crack of her ass, an ass Nageh was sure was as round and perfect as the moon. And the one with the generous breasts. Nageh imagined his own face buried between those warm breasts, lapping away at their tender white flesh. He wondered how this one would be remembered.

Nageh wasn't judging his master. After all, who was he, a lowly chauffeur, to criticise Hagg Fakhri? Besides, what was a man in Hagg's position to do? Allah had forbidden prostitutes, and pornography was not for a man of his age or means. Fornication was a sacred act and had to be performed under God's ordinance.

On second thoughts, he did envy his master, but God would not punish him because the envy in his heart was not of a malicious nature; and he was a loyal servant.

"They will be sending the meat as usual this morning."

"Yes, Hagg."

"Distribute it to my children and then divide the remainder for the coming week."

"Yes, Hagg."

"Don't let the maid do it unsupervised."

"Of course not, Hagg."

"I will be back early today. I need to rest this afternoon." His good eye confirmed what his lips didn't say.

"I will refill your prescription and, with your permission, visit my father," she replied dutifully, while holding the abaya open for him to slip into. He nodded. Hamdiyya placed her husband's cane into his open palm and wished him a prosperous day.

Between managing Hagg's household and visiting her father, the days had slipped by. Her father still urged her not to visit so often because she must give all her energy to her husband. But she knew how to manage more than one man. Her father was always grateful to receive the large dish of fuul, more than the meat she often brought with her. Once he'd enquired after Hagg's health, he would spend most of their time together regaling her with stories of the neighbours, peppering her life with their news as she used to pepper his.

Hamdiyya made her way through the streets of her former life, nodding to all the faces of her childhood and exchanging greetings with the shopkeepers. She stopped to buy Hagg Fakhri's medicine from Morcos the pharmacist, who always needed the business.

"Sitt Hamdiyya, we miss you. Your father misses you. But his loss is our gain. We spend more time with him in the coffee shop, but you really should ask him to lay off the sheesha."

She thanked him and expressed the hope that next year he would have a grandchild sitting on his knee.

"From your lips to the doors of heaven."

Hamdiyya emerged onto the heaving street to search for an empty taxi to transport her out of her old dusty and crowded world to her new lavish abode. Had she turned abruptly, she might have glimpsed the quivering figure of Nageh pretending to wander from shop to shop in search of an item that eluded him. The afternoon prayers reminded her that she had just enough time to return and prepare Hagg Fakhri's meal; and herself.

Hamdiyya let herself into Hagg Fakhri's home, where the cold of the marble floors did little to add warmth to her surroundings. She heard her husband's voice booming angrily at one of his sons from one of the rooms downstairs.

"What news of the factory in Qena? I need you to travel there tomorrow since you have so much free time to wonder about what doesn't concern you."

She knew the pattern well: after the crescendo of insults Hagg would storm out of the sitting room and head upstairs in her direction. She needed to be ready to soothe him.

"I didn't spend my entire life toiling away to leave my business to a limp-dicked son of a whore. Now go and prove your worth to me."

Hamdiyya smiled, knowing that Hagg wouldn't wait for his son's response, as none would be forthcoming.

Upstairs, as she undressed and put her clothes away, Hamdiyya filled her bedroom with the songs her mother used to hum. Hagg Fakhri abhorred untidiness. She checked her underarms in the bathroom mirror and tweezed out two stray hairs, the rest of her body still hairless from the last time. She showered, dried herself, and appeased her flesh with rose water. She applied blue kohl to the contours of her eyes, brushed her hair repeatedly, and finally slid into the pink chiffon nightdress Hagg Fakhri had left on the bed the day before. She placed his tablets on the side table, and filled a glass of water next to them. She was now ready to receive him, to assuage his anguish, and make herself indispensable to him as only she knew how.

Hagg Fakhri's buttocks were numb. The air-conditioning unit in his office was no match for the hot fumes seeping out of the cars on the grid-locked streets below, or the relentless sun that had just made its comeback. He had been seated for too long listening to the idiotic ramblings of the messenger of one of his distributors. Worse than the state of his buttocks was the restlessness of his mind. When he praised her cooking skills, she smiled and thanked him politely. When he reprimanded her that his galabiyas were not properly ironed, she apologised and spent two afternoons improving her ironing skills with the maid. When he commanded his sons to treat her well, she extolled his kindness. When they ordered her around, she complied willingly. When he positioned her on top of him, she knew to look sideways. When he straddled her from behind, she didn't look back. Not one misstep. Perfection unsettled Hagg Fakhri. What if he died in his sleep? He wasn't a horn-thrusting ram any more. She would inherit some of his hard-earned money – a small fraction, but she didn't deserve it. Was that her game? Or what if she planned to slowly make him lose his head so he would be a doting fool under her control? Whatever she was plotting still escaped him, but he would foil it, somehow. How can a man look into his wife's face and see nothing? How does her mood never change even during that time of the month when all wives were more unstable than usual?

He shifted his torso forward to relieve his ailing buttocks. His palms came down hard on the glass table.

"I don't take it up the ass. I give it. Or have you forgotten who Hagg Fakhri is? Now go and tell your little pimp of a master that these are my final prices. And if he cancels his order, well let's just say it's going to have to take a lot more than that to stir one of the hairs on my dimpled ass!"

With that he dismissed the flustered messenger, retrieved his prayer beads, which had ricocheted across the table, and pulled his stocky self up.

Hagg Fakhri's agitation had increased with the heat of the summer day. If only he had a trusted soul in whose ear he could deposit his concerns. His sons would take his desire to talk about his worries as a sign of age, or worse still, weakness. He thought of going to visit his grateful father-in-law, but couldn't imagine the conversation. For all he knew, he was a co-conspirator, living from Hagg Fakhri's siphoned-off wealth. No, he would have to take action. A man who didn't take action was a corpse and he was still brimming with vitality. No slip of a girl was going to get the better of him. Who would admire him, fetch his water and coffee and tea, and administer his medicines? Who would he thrust into?

Who would put food on his plate? She was replaceable. She was an enigma to him. Not that he cared, but did she actually like him? Hagg Fakhri was the man. He had to be in control of his wife, like he was in control of everything else in his life. If he couldn't understand her game, he would end her turn.

Nageh rang the doorbell and asked the maid if he could speak to the lady of the house. She was not a Hagga after all, and he couldn't address her as Madam Hamdiyya. It wouldn't be right to utter her name. A daft smile accompanied his nervous laugh as Hamdiyya appeared before him dressed in a floor-length galabiya, her hair loosely covered with a scarf.

"My master has sent me to tell you to pack your bag. I will drive you to your father's house. Hagg will arrange for you to receive your divorce papers when he has the time."

Nageh felt frustrated. Each morning, as he stood outside the house waiting for his master to emerge, holding the car door open, he had anticipated, even longed for, the moment he might glimpse Hagg's current wife in her nightgown with her hair uncovered, and now it would never happen. Instead, she would leave him with the memory of her inscrutable perfection.

Hamdiyya saw the words hanging in the air around her but it was as if she were encased in impenetrable ice – air, sound, human touch were all denied entrance. She nodded her understanding. The chipped paint on her bedroom walls, her father's dish of fuul and the endless stories about the neighbours' lives imposed themselves in turn on her mind's eye.

"Daughter! I knew today you would come and visit. What a wonderful surprise. I have news for you. But why are you standing in the doorway like that? Come in and close the door behind you. What's in this suitcase? Hagg Fakhri's generosity is greater than I could have imagined! What a gracious soul. Allah will not forget his deeds when He remembers him."

The father waited for his daughter's mouth to do something. Then it occurred to him. "Maybe she doesn't take after me as much as I thought."

Penalty Clause Six

DAVID KNIGHT-CROFT

I work for GlaxoKraftDisney. We're one of the biggest, and the oldest. If you've got your pension tied up in a Death deal – and who doesn't these days? – then you want it to be with us. We've got the widest range of franchises, the biggest ships, the most departure dates. Yeah, *sure*, if you want to go and be an Ewok for the next few centuries then choose ToyotaLucas. But who'd want to be one of those furballs?

I was largely responsible for my parents' Deaths. Back when they were starting to look at their options I was still getting by on copywriting. But what had begun as a cool way of being paid for writing had become a slow-moving self-lobotomy. What was the advertorial story tree for selling his & his engraved whisky glasses? What line would catch the attention of ninety-something NewDawns® to make them want to buy a candy G-string? The usual shit. Anyway, I'd known a guy who was with GKD – I'd done some work for them on the To Infinity And (For Our Premium Customers Only) Beyond! campaign. He said he'd give me commission if I signed my parents with the GKD Death package. I did, and that's how I got into the business. It was my big break. My parents snagged a great discount on their Deaths, too.

As their D-Day approached, I began to get nervous. Coming with it, of course, was the final instalment of my commission. If they missed their ship's launch date, they'd be hit by penalty clauses in the Death package, and then the overpopulation tax, which would slash the inheritance due to me and my sisters. Exponential increases every year in the overpopulation tax mean that only the richest can afford to stay on Earth after their 150th birthday, and then only for a handful of years. Instead, the old say goodbye to their worldly lives, host their own funerals, and then blast off to spread humanity to the stars. Sure, my time's a long way off, but when it comes I'll go gladly – my own Death package is top-of-the-line, featuring me as a certain very special animated cowboy. Reach for the sky!

This policy ensures we all have space to roam in our youth, clean air to breathe, food to eat, and mercifully no more than four generations to cook for at Christmas (not that I subscribe to the social tyranny of spending the holiday season with family). The tax enforces funerals on all, no matter what their circumstances. It's a wonderfully elegant streamlining of taxes and death, fuelling the entire Death and Interstellar Entertainment industry.

It's taken millennia of human evolution to reach the perfect balance of contractual obligations with mortality, family, and franchise.

But my father thought he could cheat Death.

You can't, of course: they've got the best contracts people.

"Da, it's me. Ma sent me."

The flooring of his studio used to be tatami, but he'd replaced it with a polished concrete, hard underfoot. The front door let me in, remembering me from when I'd lived there. I'd forgotten how cavernous the studio was, its ceiling two storeys high. The place was stuffed with canvasses of different sizes, leaning against each other, against the wall, against all reasonable expectation of how many unfinished paintings one man could own. It seemed to me like a gratuitous amount of space for one person. I thought that I'd probably persuade my sisters to sell it when Da had checked out.

"Da?"

"Marco."

I saw him as he spoke, high up in the room, on top of an elevated platform. He was painting. What I had taken for wall was a vast canvas, blank except for the upper-right quarter, where my father had painted the night sky, white stars bruising an inky nothingness. As I stood and watched he began to paint a crescent moon.

"I was thinking of painting two," he said, after a while.

I waited for him to say something more, but he didn't.

"Maybe Oreo 5 has two moons," I said. Then, when he didn't answer: "That's where your ship's going, right? Oreo 5?"

"Haven't looked."

"It is where it's going. I've looked. There was a piece about it in the brochure. They make quite a big deal of it. Because, you know, it's where you're going to live."

"When I get there."

"Yes, when you get there."

"In four hundred years."

"Well, it's three hundred and ninety-four years, but yes, about four centuries."

"I'm a century and a half old."

"I know, Da."

We were silent for a while. I took off my shoes and felt the cool concrete beneath my feet. Then, because there wasn't really much else going on, I started moving some of the canvasses. Made some space so I could line my shoes up, heels to the wall. My shoes were a dark blue, near real leather. They looked good against the grey. I sat down next to them, on the floor, and stretched my legs out.

"My canvasses always annoyed you," said Da, from up on his platform.

"Not particularly," I said.

"Yes they did."

"I didn't like the way they took over the place."

"I suppose you didn't have that at your mother's."

"No, I didn't." I picked up my left shoe, began examining it. One of the laces was fraying at the end, and I'd scuffed the toe. Those really were fabulous shoes, though. I still think about them now.

"Annabelle and Char-Char came to see me," said Da. "One at a time. Not together. Can't remember the last time I saw them together."

"They don't get on particularly these days."

"Aha," said my da, in that way he has.

"So why'd you go for concrete?" I asked.

"You try keeping tatami clean."

"I did."

"I'm not going to live on a planet that's named after a biscuit, you know," he said, referring – in a tone I considered to be inappropriately dismissive – to his future home and his part in the programme that would take humanity to the stars.

"It's not just any biscuit, Da. It's The World's Favourite Cookie."

"I don't even know what that means."

"The hi-res imagery in the brochure makes it look really nice. It has trees. Well, they think they're trees."

"I hate trees."

"Da, now you're being childish. You're going to have a mega-awesome time on your way there. You can inhabit any of GKD's franchises. Do you know how special that is? How lucky you are? You want to be Spock aboard the Starship Enterprise? You can *be* Spock. Want to chase bad guys as Batman? You *can* chase bad guys. Want to –"

"Save the pitch, Marco."

"Well, what *do* you want, Da?"

"I want to be an Ewok."

"Well you can't. You can't be an Ewok, Da, you know that. *Star Trek*, yes, Batman, yes, Mickey Mouse, *Mission Impossible*, *Pride and Prejudice*, Winston Churchill – all yes. *Star Wars*, no."

He took a step back on the platform to get a better look at his half-finished moon, tapping his paintbrush on the rail.

"You can paint moons just as well somewhere else, Da."

"I know," he said. "Anyway, I don't really want to be an Ewok."

"Good. That's good, Da. You know, I think you'll really enjoy your time en route to your Earth sequel. An opportunity to try new things. Meet new people. The LiveCasts we get back from those already on their way mean that we're constantly improving things. I mean, the people seem happy. On the ships."

"Is it like a cruise?"

"Yes, I suppose it is."

"For four hundred years?"

"Well obviously it's a lot more sophisticated than a cruise across the North Pole, I mean –"

"It sounds like hell."

"It is absolutely *not* like hell. We don't own the rights."

He leaned in to apply a few more brush strokes. "I don't see why I can't stay here."

I guess that's when I lost it with him. Said some things I probably shouldn't have, at a volume I'm ashamed to have reached when addressing my ageing father. I mean, he was 150, at death's door. It wasn't the touching reunion I had envisaged.

When I'd finished, he stopped painting and looked down at me, half smiling. "You sound like your mother," he said.

But I thought he must have forgotten what my mother sounded like. He was probably senile.

Leaving Da's studio, I walked along Street 54. Back in the day, his business had revolved mainly around all those chichi eateries that used to line the street. They liked to compete for the most outrageous expression of their food ethic with a different piece of advertorial art every day. Later on, when things were beginning to get out of hand, they used everything from old-school neon lights to hallucinogenic olfactories to bring in the punters. It was about that time I moved in with my mother.

These days Street 54 is just office space. There's a plaque, though, marking the Asparagus Riots of '73. I paused to read it as I walked to the Tube. Remembered playing on empty streets as a child while Da did his stuff before the tourists arrived, dawn just breaking over the city like God had razored a slit in the celluloid sky. That's pretty much how I like to remember my childhood: as if viewing it through a vintage filter. Who knows what the people in the film are really thinking?

It was then that I stopped and thought to myself, You know what? I am not going to let my stubborn da take away our happy ending. I thought about Annabelle and Char-Char. About the time when we were kids and they LiveCast me having one of my tantrums, with the tag, "My little bro has a shitfit and pisses himself. LOL." Of the montage someone made of me denying that

I'd pissed myself: clips of me repeating my denial, again and again, sometimes angry, sometimes quiet, sometimes just sad. Of living with them later, with my ma, and how it had been good between us. And of how we all fell out again. I thought of Da rinsing his savings only to stay on Earth a few years longer. Of the money we could get from his studio. How it would make us all happy again.

Isn't that what parents should do? Stand aside for their kids? No, I was not going to let my da negatively adjust the narrative arc of this family. Did Tony Stark lie down and take it at the end of *Iron Man 136*? Did Bruce Wayne let the zombie Joker have his way at the denouement of *The Dark Knight Returns, Again, For The Eleventh Time*? No, he did not. Endings should right wrongs, not make them worse. They should draw a line, allow people to move on.

So I went back to the studio. And on the way, I called in Mickey.

The snatch team were outside when I arrived. There were only two of them: Mickey, looking a bit sheepish, fiddling with one of his ears, and Pluto, who was gently bobbing up and down in what I took to be anticipation. It used to be that we had professionals on the snatch team, ex-military types with all the training. People used to shit themselves when Mickey Mouse burst through their skylight in night goggles. But they were super expensive, and it turned out that actually most people would come quietly when faced with members of the Disney pantheon in full combat costume. So now we just rotate the folks that work in the parks – one week you'd be handing balloons out to toddlers, the next you'd be bundling obstinate old-timers into trucks. They're mostly students. Obviously they wear different costumes in the field than in the parks – more Kevlar, fewer smiles. Pluto looks positively rabid. It's important to have a strong brand. Otherwise people might think they were being kidnapped.

"OK," I said. "Thanks for getting here so quickly. Like I told the dispatch operator, this guy's stubborn but old. He might fight a bit, but he's pretty decrepit. His family, who are co-signatories to the contract, are simply looking out for what's best for him. So let's make this quick, let's make this professional. And remember: we're taking humanity to the stars, one person at a time. This is for the good of the race, and this guy's going to have a wicked awesome time in one of the best franchises in the universe."

I generally give a pep talk to the troops before we go in. I like to think that it helps give them some pride in their work, and that this might bleed over into other parts of their lives. Some people call it corporate social responsibility. I just call it being human.

"All right, boss man, we get you," said Mickey.

"Let's do it, let's do it, let's do it," said Pluto, bouncing up and down. I thought he might be on drugs. I hoped that they were Glaxo-approved.

"Give me a yeah," I said.

"Yeah," said Mickey.

"YEAH!" said Pluto.

"Mickey, you're on point. Pluto, you cover me."

The door opened to my touch and in went Mickey. No "Hello Da" this time. I followed and Pluto took the rear. Mickey was in the hall with his back flat against the wall, peering round the doorway into the studio space. He seemed to do a double-take at the size of the room, then turned back to face me, twitched his mouse nose, and ponderously winked one of his creepy giant eyes – the sign that he'd acquired the target.

"Hit it," I whispered.

Mickey pressed a button on his suit and the first bars of *The Circle of Life* from *The Lion King* started to throb out of his oversized mouse ears. As they did so, he rushed into the room and I followed behind, raising a hand to hold Pluto back.

Da was standing facing away from us, flicking through canvasses as one might when idly browsing an art gallery bargain bin. He turned at the sound of the music and the clomp of Mickey's combat boots on the concrete, his face a rare picture of shock that I won't forget in a hurry.

"Hakuna matata, motherfucker!" shouted Mickey, as he charged towards my da, lowering his head and diving for the tackle. But he must have slipped or something because his tackle quickly became a headlong dive into the canvasses, which sort of both exploded and crumpled at the same time as he went through them ears first and hit the ground hard. *The Circle of Life* continued to play, muffled, from amongst the artwork, and Mickey thrashed about but didn't seem to be getting up anytime soon, so I gave the signal and Pluto plunged past me into the room.

"Let'sDoItLet'sDoItLet'sDoIt," he said, the words tumbling out of his lolling, canine-concealing, dopey great mouth as he sped past me. And – what was that? This shit really used to get to me back then – an unauthorised activation of his own sound system, to play *A Whole New World* from *Aladdin*. The two songs clashed horribly and I think it's *so* unprofessional to play divergent sound sources during a brand event, but I had to let it slide because Pluto was going for the target.

Da had turned to face him straight on and I thought he was stooped with age, his back bent and his legs not able to extend properly. But this must have been a diversionary tactic because before Pluto was upon him, my da lunged – I mean he actually *jumped* at Pluto – catching the big, stupid dogman at an oblique angle so the two of them went down, my da on top. He was pummelling Pluto and Pluto was making this sort of "Wah wah wah!" baby sound, and holding his paws up in a futile attempt to protect his face. I mean, really, it was pathetic, getting beaten up by an old man who, as I kept telling everyone, *was at death's door*. I don't know where he got the energy – I didn't even know he had so much movement in his limbs, which surely must have been arthritic. Meanwhile, Mickey seemed to be rolling around in the canvasses, unable to get the two that were stuck around his neck off his head because his ears kept getting in the way. Needless to say, if our Brand Manager had been there, he would have been shaking his head.

"I. Am. Not. Going," said Da, as he sat astride Pluto, still pummelling the now limp figure, punctuating his words with punches.

That got me really mad, and I thought to myself: Let's give the old bastard what he wants. So I strode over there, on my way picking up off the ground a tin of paint that my da had left out in his infuriatingly untidy manner, and I swung it hard at the back of his head. It connected with a glonk! sound and off the lid hurtled, spewing Sumptuous Plum over both of us as my father fell forwards onto Pluto, and then rolled off, groaning.

I grabbed him by the arm and dragged him towards the

elevated platform – to be honest, I was expecting to be able to just hoist him over my shoulder, on account of how old he was and probably being mostly skin and bones, but he was surprisingly heavy. So I got him to the platform, opened up the little safety gate, bundled him on and then stepped on myself, closing the gate behind me. By this point he was still woozy but struggling to get up a bit, so I put one foot on his chest to keep him down – old people can be surprisingly strong, no wonder doctors sometimes have to sedate them – and reached over to activate the platform.

We began to rise towards the studio's ceiling, so that soon we were up there, amongst the stars, the crescent moon beaming out at me, as big as my torso.

"Marco –" gasped my da. "Marco, I only wanted –"

"I'm afraid I'm going to have to interrupt you there, old man," I said, stepping on his chest a little more heavily. "As Chief Contracts Manager for Region 584, under the authority of GlaxoKraftDisney, and representing the wishes of the co-signatories to your Death contract – which is to say, your family, which is to say, myself – I hereby find you to be in breach of contract and thus subject to Penalty Clause Six."

"But I only wanted to make art, Marco," he said, croakily.

"I know, Da," I said, recognising that this was the moment of the touching reunion and mutual emotional reconciliation across the gulf of our relationship, "but that's the problem. You *only* wanted to make art. And we – I – needed you to want more, more of the time."

The platform stopped within reach of the ceiling. I bent over and put my hands beneath his arms, pulling him up from his armpits like one might a child, first to a sitting position, and then to standing. He was unsteady on his feet, like a toddler. I touched his cheek – how vulnerable we become in our old age. As I looked into his face I saw that we had the same eyes.

Then I heaved him over the edge of the platform and he whumped onto the concrete floor below, his blood transforming the Sumptuous Plum into a Volcanic Red.

Sure, the whole sorry episode with my da could have gone better. But making it in this industry takes blood, sweat and, yes, maybe even a few tears. Happy endings: there's a price attached.

The Tea Dress
CHRIS LILLY

"I wander by the sea-side; and the eternal ocean
and lasting despair and her face are before me."
Liber Amoris, or, the New Pygmalion by William Hazlitt

O nce upon a time there was a woman – a girl – a woman, and
her name was Antoinette. She always insisted on the full
"Antoinette"; not Toni, not Tonya, not Anto, never Toinette, and
certainly not Netty. Antoinette, the whole thing, always, every
time. Kevin thought this was a little bit extra, a little bit over the
top, but then Kevin had been called Kev for as long as he could
remember, a cross he bore with equanimity, and Kevin wasn't even
that hard to say. Not like Antoinette, which had a slushy second
syllable that got lost so that if you weren't careful you wound up
shouting "Net" which wasn't cool at all.

Apart from the name thing – and even there he agreed with her
about Netty, Netty was bad – apart from that, she was practically
perfect. She radiated. Whatever she was feeling, everyone for miles
around knew about it, and most of the time they felt that way too.
When she was happy, he was happy; when she was sad, he was
sad – and also very concerned to find ways of making her not sad.
He thought she was awesome always, and he wanted her to know
that, to know she was appreciated. Cared for. Loved. By him. By
lots of people. Was that a bad thing, wanting that? Was it wrong?
He didn't think so. Really, he didn't think so. Though maybe; now,
he wasn't sure. There was the whole dress fiasco. Fuck. Let's put
that on the shelf for a moment.

*

Once upon a time there was a girl. There was a girl and there was a show, and there were many people who laboured hard on the show, but the girl laboured hardest, building sets, sourcing props, sewing costumes. A sort of competitive-suffering culture developed, in which working for twelve straight hours with a twenty-minute break was really lightweight. Antoinette worked side by side with whoever put in the longest shift, then did another couple of hours mopping floors and emptying bins, getting the venue ready for the next day, the next big push, the next assault on every health and safety directive ever promulgated. Did they have a health and safety officer? Oh yes; Antoinette was the health and safety officer. Also the production manager, the caretaker, the one who kept the accounts. And day by day, the light in her eyes dimmed, and her smile was a bit less dazzling, and her warmth, her astonishing warmth, diminished. When people got ill, they went away for a while, and then came back when they were nearly better. She got ill and carried on working. Just to show that she really didn't have any limits, she took a couple of weeks off to play Mercutio in an all-women *Romeo and Juliet*, helping out a friend. Kevin went to see it. She was really good. Power was seated on her brow, passion emanated from her breast as from a shrine, as Hazlitt might have said had he seen her. He wouldn't want to argue with Hazlitt. Hazlitt knew a thing or two about acting. And about passion, come to that.

So there it was. She was awesome and inspirational and lovely, and really, it would have required a heart of plasterboard to deny her anything she wanted. What she wanted was a dress. She put a post on her Facebook page, a little bit needy, a little bit wishful thinking. Here's a dress; would anyone like to get it for me? There was a link. It was a tea dress, '50s style, black with huge red roses and a flared skirt that really needed a big petticoat, a low bodice, a lower back, a dress for the confident and the beautiful. A dress for her.

It wasn't his idea, buying it. That needs to be said straightaway. He didn't think of it or have anything to do with it, initially. He approved of the idea, he thought it was nice, he thought she deserved to have the dress, he just didn't do any of the planning. That was the Lithuanian lad who organised the volunteer rotas, and lived in the prop store, as far as Kevin could tell. "Let's shall we get Antoinette that dress!! It will make her so happy!!!" he had messaged. Kevin had pictured her in the dress and got a really vivid image of Monroe. That's a reach isn't it? Monroe? Yes, it's a reach, but it isn't stupid. Bear with me. Monroe had a body to die for, yes, but she did that little-girl, simper thing; grown-up body, little-girl face. He didn't like that. Antoinette had a face and an attitude that she had grown into, that she had earned. It was . . . better. Also – and this is a very important consideration – Anto was both alive and adjacent, in a way that Monroe had probably never been and certainly wasn't now. In his head he called her Anto. He'd known a really nice woman called Anto, and they'd been friends, so thought-calling her Anto made him happy. He didn't think she could hear what he called her in his head. In his head, he could see her in that dress, and she looked wonderful. He texted back to say he was in; he would like to be part of that gift-giving consortium. It would tell her she was appreciated, her efforts were acknowledged, she was recognised, she was loved. All of them together, letting her know she was special. The wheels fell off that particular scheme, though, because no one had any money. Volunteers working all hours, six or seven days a week, because the sets were like small houses, and the props had to look right and also work, and then there was painting and cleaning and polishing and sanding, so where were they going to find time to earn money? Of course they were skint. Besides, most of them had been in school ten minutes ago, or college or uni or stage school or some establishment where no one paid you and you came out owing the government a million quid. He, on the other hand, had a redundancy package in the bank and an occupational pension, and positive net worth due to thirty-some years in paid employment. He'd spent two whole mornings talking to someone at the bank about an ISA, for God's sake. He didn't really know what an ISA was, but it was a thing you didn't think about unless you were quite solvent. So he'd fronted up. Let's get her the dress, and you can all pay me later. Yeah, right. Later. Was that it? Was that the problem? He thought that might be the problem.

The Lithuanian boy had made the presentation with a peculiar blend of charmlessness and care, and possibly a bit of resentment because of the single-source funding, unless Kevin was imagining that as well and he was just a rude Lithuanian boy, and Anto had been happy. She'd worn the dress, she'd looked fabulous. Of course she had: she looked fabulous in sawn-off combats and a dust mask. In a flattering dress that showed just enough of her to tell the world that it was indeed a nice frock, but it was only a scrap of fabric, the main attraction was the woman inside it, she lit up the room. That was the good bit. She had given him lots of hugs, splendid hugs. She looked great, he was happy with the gesture, it had all been good. Happy and glad and just the right amount of grateful. And no lust. He wanted to put that on the record. No lust. Did he fancy her? Well, yes, a bit. She was lovely, and he might be old but he wasn't dead. Really, though – she was thirty – slightly older than his daughter. No one thought fancying your daughter's mates was all right. His daughter would have disapproved, and so would his wife. He would too. Rich fucks with arm candy thirty years their junior were despicable and grotesque. They used fat wallets because they had no soul. That wasn't him, really it wasn't. Really. Fuck.

The next day he'd come in to work the show like he'd always done, like he always would. He'd signed up for it, so while there was a show, he'd be there working it, that was what he did. He was checking his bit of set, the rigging, the cables, the stuff for which he was responsible, and he turned to see her doing her own pre-set checks, like she always did, like proper stage managers. Usually there would be a few words exchanged, a bit of conversation, busy people but closer than polite acquaintances. That was the usual way of things. This time there was the merest touch of frost between them, an ambient temperature of about two degrees Kelvin. Two degrees Kevin. She used to be affectionate, playful, offering slightly tentative high fives and pats on the arm, encouragement, contact. Now she glanced at him and the glance slid rapidly across and settled on something else, anything else. Anything that wasn't him. What had he done? What had changed? It was bad, whatever it was; it was awful, it might be terminal. All that show he thought about it. He tracked back through their interactions, everything he'd said, every gesture. What the hell had he done? Something he'd said, something he'd done, something he hadn't done? What? They hadn't said anything much. A couple of months building stuff, a few more doing shows, and they'd barely had a conversation that he could remember. She'd been too busy to sit still, let alone natter. That hadn't struck him before. How can you work with someone for the best part of a year and not have a conversation? He had thought there was a connection, but maybe there wasn't, maybe they just worked together. The thought arrived new and fresh and horrible in his head, that there had never been anything between them. He had thought, God help him, he had thought that they were friends, but they weren't, really they weren't, they hadn't been, ever. He had friends, he had good friends, he was a good friend. If your delayed flight got into Stansted at four in the morning, he was someone you could call to rescue you. If your teenage son got hurt and hospitalised, he would sort stuff out. Lost luggage found, warm beds, warm baths, bus fare home. He did that stuff, he did it a lot, he could be depended on. He didn't make a big deal about it, that was who he was. He was reliable. He was diamond. Not predatory, not an ageing perv trying to buy her favours with a frock, no, no, no. Was that what she saw? That might be what she saw. That might be it. That was it. Fuck. Fuck, fuck, fuck.

From then on it was just hard. Hard, and cold, and a bit joyless. They worked together, did the shows, were civil; professional even, but always a hundred miles apart. He still found her – what? Impressive? Wonderful? Awesome? Those didn't seem right any more. She was those things, but they were warm things and there wasn't any warmth. Maybe there'd never been any warmth. This felt like being out-of-love, but without the in-love bit. Maybe that hurt worse, being in love and then not? It was difficult to miss something you hadn't known you'd had. Perhaps this was actually easier? It was so hard to describe, so amorphous. The amount of time he spent thinking about it was frankly ridiculous. It was a very good thing she didn't have any idea how much time. If a misinterpreted present caused so much froideur, what would hours of obsessive and misplaced reflection do? She had access to tools with points, drills, saws, crowbars. It didn't bear thinking about. He thought about it a lot. Fuck. He was enthralled. Enraptured. Ensorcelled. Significantly bewitched, constantly bothered, and however hard he tried to rein in the paranoia and the self-loathing, to place the whole thing in a reasonable, manageable context that bore some relation to his proper life, his real life, he remained bewildered. One day he posted a comment on her Facebook page, then went back an hour later to find she'd blocked him, he couldn't read the thread. Cut off. Cyber-snubbed. No lines of communication, just what was needed for the work. There were another dozen shows, and they worked them and then they finished; they did the get-out, then it was over. There was a party after the get-out but he didn't go.

He did see her again, once, and she was wearing the tea dress. He'd gone to a weird piece of theatre in the vaults behind Waterloo Station, which had been no fun from the outset, and then there was a sort of tribal thing, with a bunch of hipsters in exotic make-up threatening some women. Antoinette was one of the women. She was in her dress, looking stunning, being scared, and then a numpty with a plastic machete grabbed her and ripped the top off the dress, smothered her with make-up, and pretended to slice bits off her. Kevin didn't enjoy it half as much as the numpty seemed to, and her expression was unreadable, so he had no idea what she thought about it. It occurred to him that he'd never known what she thought about anything. Though he knew now what she thought about the dress. We want you in a dress we can rip up, they'd have said. I've got just the thing, she'd replied. Probably. That was interesting. After the performance, he waited in the bar to say hello, and she came in with the other performers. He could see shreds of black fabric in her shoulder bag, bits of ripped rose, bits of a long time ago.

"Hi, Antoinette. How are you?"

"Oh, hi, good thanks, look, I've just got to see someone . . ." and she moved away to the other side of the room. It is salutary to discover that someone you hold in the highest regard has no regard for you whatsoever. If what art or culture or drama or literature, any of those things, gives you is a sense of connectedness, she showed him such total, brilliant lack of connection it represented a completely new form. Anti-art. Anto-art. Strong and cold and distant and –

"Indomitable!" he shouted. It felt right – the word he had been searching for. Whatever she was, she was that.

"What?"

"You are indom . . ."

But she was gone.

"She is dead to me; but what she once was to me,
can never die!"
Liber Amoris, or, the New Pygmalion by William Hazlitt

Rooting in the Dead
LENYA SAMANIS

I t happens the moment you step onto the main drag of Ome Kaido. You're considering the two-hour train journey ahead and wondering what you and Matthew will find to talk about for so long, when the shoulder of a salaryman slams into you, spins you around; you see the suit fold himself into the crowd without even looking back. You've told people back in England that, because this happens so frequently, you're always ready for it, but the truth is the sheer physicality of another, male body punching itself into you still takes you by surprise. Your shoulder hurts, but there's no time for this: Matthew's metres ahead, probably sunk in fantasies of the rocks he'll find in Chichibu's rivers, and you quicken your pace to catch up. You wonder how much more aggression it'll take for you to start shouting at strangers in the street, then why you're spending your one day off travelling deep into the Japanese countryside to search out rocks that look like mini landscapes. You have nothing against microcosms, you think, but why travel so far out of town to find one? Matthew.

He was cagey from the start, even about inviting you back to his place. As though it meant something. It took a few weeks and, when you did finally go, there they were: six rocks, lined up against the far wall, each in a discreet base, on top of a wooden box painted with kanji. Your first encounter with what he called his hobby. When you asked him what they were for, he called them art, pointed out his favourite, and how it looked like a mountain range. You tried to find something appealing in this and failed, but his skin against your shoulder was warm and you could feel his blood pulsing under the ink. You made appreciative noises. Nobody could accuse you of not trying.

A fortnight later, you're still trying. The Yamanote line is rammed and you stand inches apart, clutching the rail, and rocking with the train. You will him to kiss you. He raises his face to the ceiling of the carriage. The salaryman behind you repositions his shoulder in the groove of your back and the city's crush pushes in on all sides, indifferent-mean and spiked with elbows, umbrellas, the corners of briefcases. It's a relief when you can stop fighting it at Ikebukuro and let the tide of bodies pull you out of the carriage.

The line to Chichibu is mostly empty and you sit with the sun on your back, trying not to stare at the woman opposite you, who is reading a newspaper in English. The headline on the front page says that mobile phones are killing all our ghosts and you wonder if you're more likely to see a ghost in a country full of people who believe in them. You look at Matthew, engrossed in his map, and mull over the bonsai exhibitions he's taken you to, the flea markets, the suiseki viewings; how you've put your roots in dead things and hoped they'd take. He looks up – sandboy happy – and tells you there's a river not far from the station. The fact that his idea of happiness looks like nothing you've ever wished for makes you feel more like a tourist than ever. The city's fringes blur beyond the train window like a shuddering Rothko and you, you wait for the landscape to sharpen into something you can believe in. You have been waiting for almost six months now. Keep going. Keep going.

In Chichibu, with the high-rises turned to forest and the pound and shuttle of the city shrunk to birdsong, you feel weirdly exposed. The river is long and Matthew is always metres ahead of you, squinting into the water. You spend an hour like this, watching the strip of his neck turn pink. Finally, you see him stepping carefully back to where you crouch, his eyes bright and wide, a rock in one hand. He shows you his find. He explains exactly how it will sit in the base he'll have made. His pupils never dilate when he looks at you, and because his eyes are so blue, it's hard not to notice. It's not just this, you think, as he tucks the stone carefully into his bag and wades away: he has an unhealthy interest in the zodiac, a cracked, ten-year-old pair of Dr Martens he refuses to trade in, and he never capitalises the kisses at the end of his missives. And there it is – the tight-hearted pinch at his core. Your mind naturally edits out details like the cringe of his laugh, how fragile his jaw feels beneath your palms, the way he rubs up against you like a dog in the dark, but you can't quiet the siren of those feeble kisses. Remember: lead with your head – you've held too many magnets against your heart for its north to stay true. Hear through the voice you've constructed out of his texts, his emails, the notes he leaves by the bed. His real voice hit a dead-end brick wall in you. You'd imagined it would be deeper. You'd wanted it to be deeper. Stack it up. Keep going. Remember: all you need is a functioning eye with the right blind spots. It doesn't really matter what colour it is, but the darker the better. Remember: everyone is searching out the best possible reflection of themselves. This is just how it goes.

The river is sometimes narrow, bordered by forest and surfaced by the black rocks so prized by collectors. At other points, it runs into wide, shallow flats where the sky yawns, expansive, and the water flows more calmly over smooth cream bedrock. Here, where you are no longer fighting the slip and pull of the river, you squat on your heels and watch Matthew forage, elbow deep, entirely immersed. You gaze down into the river, through the looking glass, remotely bemused. Beyond the rings of light the sun has burned onto your retinas, a red stone catches your eye. The currents have cut deep, narrow grooves all over its surface so that it resembles a piece of meat wrapped tightly with string. You know Matthew would throw it back, but it's impressive waterwork and it feels good in your hands. You put it in your bag, take out your mobile to check the time and see last night's text from Matthew, finished off with a trademark tiny "x". It follows a full stop, which means, you think, that he went to the trouble of overriding the automatic, predictive punctuation. You look at him, bent over the river, his neck now red. You've never known whether his holding back is a matter of shy or sly, and this is the problem: his lukewarm in the heat wave of your 20s. His kisses have a short shelf life; are deliberately weak. When you press them for more, they buckle, and you go back to gnawing on your fingers.

A deep rumble bounces across the clouds, like an oil drum down a slope, culminating in a loud crack. The sky darkens. You see him pause; glance up. It starts to rain, and it's like nothing you've ever known. It pummels; punches. You scramble to shelter under an old bridge you passed half an hour before and, by the time you get there, you're drenched. To-the-skin-and-bone soaked. You press one arm against your chest to squeeze the rain from the padding in your bra, and flash him a smile. "Ah crap," he says, pulling his phone out of a pocket and shaking it, pointlessly. "It's not working." And suddenly there's a shape descending through the long grass of the riverbank: an old woman, incomprehensibly bent at the waist. She calls down. When you glance at Matthew, he's looking up at her, his head jerking between a nod and a bow. He tells you she's invited you both to shelter in her house. "I like it here," you say, but he's already clambering up the slope, his bag of rocks slung low over his back.

So you find yourself crouching in the square metre of sunken space inside the entrance, trying not to drip onto the tatami. The old woman brings two cups of green tea, and seaweed-wrapped fish-shaped crackers. Through an open screen door, you can see an old man sitting in a chair, televisual light flickering on his waxen face. Occasionally, he turns to stare at you. The ache in your legs is interminable. The rain, too, goes on and on. Matthew pulls his findings from his bag and points in the direction of the river. You see the old woman recoil. She starts to babble. You look to Matthew to translate, but he's frowning in concentration. She disappears and, before he can formulate a response, she's back, with a book, which they pore over. You wait. You're getting bored. You wait. This happens a lot. His Japanese is sketchy but he can stumble through the basics. He's an unsteady rope bridge, a starry-eyed buffer. He interrupts your thoughts to tell you there was a battle here, in which three hundred samurai were slain. The old woman is saying their spirits went into the rocks. This is why people don't take them, he explains: they're cursed. He grins; keeps a protective hand on his bag. It's so humid, you feel as though you're trying to breathe underwater. The rain is still pounding on the door. The old woman runs out of snacks. Matthew runs out of Japanese. In the end, you leave mid-downpour, and the umbrellas she insists you take are as useful as paper hats in the wet violence outside.

The sky is black all the way back to Shinjuku. The rock in your bag is a souvenir of a day of distance, and it feels weighty. Tell yourself things are still new. It will make no difference. You're far from home and you think you know he's not the thing you were hoping for. And yet, you could find a different place to stand. You could remember how he says your name, as though it tastes good, or that he's developed a whole mythology around your belly button. Keep going: his hand on your neck, stroking it clear of hair in one upward sweep; his fingers hooking hold of your hip bones from behind; the bend and squirm of his toes against yours at the end of the bed. On the train home from Ikebukuro, back in the familiar Tokyo crush, he puts a hand lightly on your neck and the bodies pushing in lose their communal menace. You stare out of the window, rocking with the push-and-pull, push-and-pull, push-and-pull.

Walking back to your apartment from Shinjuku station, Matthew's talking inanimate objects and you're letting his voice fade into the whoosh and growl of the traffic, when you spot a salaryman a few metres ahead. The blank determination on his face says he's already written you off. Just in time, you pull your arm inward, cage your chest. Your bag, previously held back by your arm, swings forward and, weighted by the rock, slams squarely into him. You feel the impact, see him fold at the edge of your vision. "I'm telling you," Matthew says, "small countries have been bought with suiseki stones." You look back, but the suit's been swallowed up by an indifferent collective.

When Matthew gets up early for his nine o'clock shift the following morning, you play dead. He showers with the door open, singing quietly to himself. The first time he did it, a surge of happiness filled you up as you lay there listening to the pitter-patter behind his voice and watching the fat slice of bathroom light at the door. You relive it, in miniature. You've lost the yen, but you could get it back. You lie there with your eyes closed and wonder if you should.

He plants a tiny kiss on your shoulder as he leaves and you feel it there, trying to stick. You remember a day, mere weeks ago, when you sat alone on the futon with the shower running just so you could blow smoke rings at the ceiling and pretend he was there, in another room. Enough with all the halfway houses. These are the words you say to yourself. *Enough with all the halfway houses.* You take a deep breath, get up; pull the curtains and whitewash the room with sunshine. And there's the city outside, her skyscrapers rising like prayer sticks in a cemetery – an eyeful of glistening glass and mysterious detail that will keep your heart glad irrespective of whether he is there to sing in your shower for the foreseeable future. You reach for your bag, root around looking for your wallet: a notebook, a crinkled sushi wrapper . . . Your hand closes around the rock. You remember that punch it gave out – that speak up, that fight back – and relax your grip. Pile your things on top of it. You have the morning free. Take the notes from the kitchen drawer and turn his tiny kisses into paper aeroplanes. Head out into the city. Follow the U-turns of your gut. Get lost in her streets. She will do what it takes to win you over. Let her daytime razzamatazz make mincemeat of his shallow voice and those pinprick-steady pupils. Let her swallow you whole. Occupy her. Fuck it, if you need to, go to war. You have the soul of a dead samurai in your bag.

Notes on Contributors

Jay Barnett grew up in Macclesfield, Cheshire. He now lives in London and has completed the first year of his Creative Writing MA at Birkbeck. For a decade he has worked in the post room of an investment bank. His work has appeared on BBC Radio 4, in Hamish Hamilton's *Five Dials* magazine and in *Jawbreakers*, the first National Flash-Fiction Day anthology.

Daniel Bourke lives in North London and works for the *Daily Mirror*. He is currently writing *Overland*, his first novel. His short story "Wood Green" appeared in *Nutshell Magazine*, and "Seaweed" and "Margaret Thatcher's Tits" were published in previous issues of *The Mechanics' Institute Review*. His people are from Farnham, Surrey, and Co. Mayo. He is trying to learn Welsh to understand his many daughters.

Kit de Waal was born in Birmingham to an Irish mother and Kittian father. She worked for fifteen years in criminal and family law and writes about the urban underbelly, forgotten and overlooked places where the best stories are found. She has an MA in creative writing from Oxford Brookes University and is a founder member of Leather Lane Writers and Oxford Narrative Writers. Her debut novel, *My Name is Leon*, was published by Viking in June 2016.

Edwin Dixon taught English language and literature to Dartford's willing teenagers for four years. He has recently taken up a position at an international school in Phuket, Thailand. Having already lived and worked in Seoul, he is open to more destinations to get the creative juices flowing. Edwin graduated from the Birkbeck Creative Writing MA in 2016. His work has previously appeared in *Ambit* magazine.

Damien Doorley's writing has appeared in the *Dublin Review*, *The Stinging Fly* and *The Moth*, as well as in *The Mechanics' Institute Review*, Issue 8. In 2010–12 he followed a Creative Writing MA at Birkbeck, receiving a distinction. He is a Jungian analyst in private practice in London, and working on a collection of short stories. He is interested in likenesses between the short-story form and the analytic hour, and between writing and listening.

John Forde was born in New Zealand, and completed degrees in law and English literature at the University of Otago. He was a runner-up in *North & South* magazine's Short, Short Story Competition in 2014. He lives in London, and is a student on the Creative Writing MA at Birkbeck. In 2016, he was the recipient of the inaugural Picador Bursary.

Elizabeth Fremantle is the author of *Queen's Gambit*, *Sisters of Treason*, *Watch the Lady* and, most recently, *The Girl in the Glass Tower*, all published by Penguin. She holds a BA in English and an MA in creative writing from Birkbeck, and has contributed to various publications, including *Vogue*, *Vanity Fair*, the *Financial Times* and the *Sunday Times*; she also reviews fiction for the *Sunday Express*.

Eleanor Gow studied English and creative writing at the University of Portsmouth, then moved to London to work in the advertising and publishing industry, taking the occasional career break to travel the world! She completed the Writing a Novel online course with Faber Academy before starting her MA in creative writing at Birkbeck. In 2011 Eleanor relocated with her husband to Cambridge, where they live with their two children.

Sally Hinchcliffe is a writer and editor living in South-West Scotland. Her first novel, *Out of a Clear Sky*, was published by Pan Macmillan in 2008 and was Radio 4's Book at Bedtime and Radio 5 Live's Book of the Month. She was one of the very first graduates from the Birkbeck Creative Writing MA, and helped to edit (and name) the first issue of *The Mechanics' Institute Review*.

Melanie Jones graduated from the Creative Writing MA at Birkbeck in 2015. From September 2016 she will be returning to the college to carry out a PhD on time management and spoilers in short stories. She was shortlisted for the 2014 Poetic Republic Short Story Competition and her submission "Silence" is published in their anthology *Kissing Him Goodbye and Other Stories*. Her work can also be found in *The Mechanics' Institute Review*, Issue 11. Melanie is currently working on her first novel, alongside a collection of short stories, and is the Managing Editor of MIROnline, Birkbeck's creative writing website. In her spare time she sings, draws and takes photos. Follow Melanie on Twitter @jonesmonster.

Aliyah Kim Keshani is a London-based writer and musician. She studied English literature at UCL, and is currently undertaking an MA in creative writing at Birkbeck.

Stella Klein was born in Sydney, Australia. Since the age of seven she has lived in London, and its streets and people are her biggest source of inspiration. She is married with two grown-up children and is a very sloppy housewife. When she is not writing short stories, Stella is a writing coach and dyslexia tutor in higher education. She loves cinema, walking, and swimming at her local lido in all weathers, and sings in a soul and gospel choir.

David Knight-Croft leads a glamorous life working as a civil servant and living in South-East London. He studied English literature at Leeds University and the University of Guelph, Ontario, Canada, and is currently studying for the Creative Writing MA at Birkbeck. In 2014 he took a career break, travelled for a year, and hasn't quite been the same since. He has been longlisted for the Fish Short Story Prize and published on fivestopstory.com, and is working on his first short-story collection. David writes about travel at www.elsewhereunderwritten.com.

Chris Lilly was born in 1953 in Dartford, home of Mick Jagger and the Vox amp. He left Hull University in 1976. He taught in Tower Hamlets until February 2011, lives on the Isle of Dogs, and has been busier since retirement than ever before. Chris studied Shakespeare and contemporary performance at Birkbeck, and received a Certificate in creative writing from Birkbeck in 2009. He currently drives a horsebox for Vauxhall City Farm. He was a stage manager for immersive theatre group You Me Bum Bum Train throughout their last two shows.

Toby Litt's most recent book, *Mutants* (Seagull, 2016), is a collection of essays, "a manifesto of sorts, for a weirder, wilder, more wilful fiction". He writes short stories, novels, non-fiction, comics, opera libretti and songs. He teaches creative writing at Birkbeck.

Ian McNab lives with his family in London, where he teaches media studies. He graduated from the MA in creative writing at Birkbeck in 2015. Ian writes short stories and is currently working on a novel. You can follow him on Twitter, where he tweets about music and other cultural obsessions @Ian_McNab.

Lauren Miller is currently studying part time on the Creative Writing MA at Birkbeck. She has participated in salon readings in London and New York, and performed at the Literary Kitchen Festival in 2015. She has a BA in fine art from Central Saint Martins, lives in East London and works as a teacher for children with special educational needs.

Claire Montell grew up in Leeds, studied Russian at university in Scotland and lived in Spain and Northern Ireland before settling in London. She works as a freelance writer and editor, and has just completed her first year of the Creative Writing MA at Birkbeck.

Tom Norton is a London-based writer born in Aldershot, Hants. He was shortlisted for the To Hull and Back short-story competition in 2014 and has had stories and poetry published in a number of anthologies. Alongside his career in higher education policy and planning, Tom completed the MA Creative Writing at Birkbeck in 2016, has a growing collection of short stories and poetry, and is working on his first novel.

Melody Razak is currently studying for Birkbeck's Creative Writing MA and has completed her first year. She lives in Brighton and owns a café/cake shop called treacle&co. She is working on a volume of short stories about people who fall in love with inanimate objects. She believes that everything is possible.

Nadim Safdar completed an MA in creative writing at Birkbeck in 2012. In that year his short story "Roar" featured in Issue 9 of *The Mechanics' Institute Review*. His debut novel, *Akram's War*, was published by Atlantic in 2016. He is married with three children and lives in London.

Lenya Samanis lives in London and writes.

Jack Swanson graduated from the University of Liverpool with a degree in philosophy in 2013. He has just completed his MA in creative writing at Birkbeck and is working as a teaching assistant in a primary school. He was born and brought up in Welwyn Garden City, a place that inspires much of his writing.

Nadia Wassef co-founded Diwan, then a small bookstore in Cairo, with her sister in 2002. It has since grown into Egypt's leading chain, currently with ten branches, and Nadia has been on *Forbes Magazine*'s list of "The 200 Most Powerful Women in the Middle East" for two years running. She holds two MA degrees – one in social anthropology from the School of Oriental and African Studies, University of London and another in English and comparative literature from the American University in Cairo – and is currently working on a third, in creative writing, at Birkbeck.